BLIND ALLEY

By
Pippa Wood

(The story behind The Racer)

2012

BLIND ALLEY
(The story behind The Racer)

This is a work of fiction. Names, characters, places and incidents are either
the product of the author's imagination or, if real, are used fictitiously.

Published by Pippa Wood @ Self Perception.

Copyright © 2012 Pippa Wood

First Published in Great Britain in 2012

The right of Pippa Wood to be identified as the Author
of this work has been asserted by her in accordance with the
Copyright, Designs and Patents Act 1988.

ISBN 978-0-9574282-0-1

Printed and bound in Great Britain by
Taylor Thorne Print Ltd, Somerset

Pippa Wood was born in Somerset, she still resides in the county and her love of the West Country, in particular the levels and surrounding hills is reflected in her work. This book has been a long time in the making, having originally been penned in the early '90s. Its production over the last year has been a painstaking, yet enjoyably retrospective journey and it is hoped that you the reader will find some amusement and entertainment in its story.

Thank you for your time.

Pippa Wood

DEDICATION

To the beautiful man within,
I send these things.

Many thanks for sharing time,
And love and luck to help him shine.

Precious dreams to treasure deep,
Wrapped up with hugs for peaceful sleep.

Original Manuscript 1992

Re-typed 2012
By
Pippa Wood

Author: Pippa Wood

CHAPTER 1

Looking through the lens of her camera across a crowded paddock, Martha saw him. Not for the first time, but this time, she knew he saw her. Twenty feet or so separated them but the intensity of his first stare remained as strong today as ever.

The date was October 23rd 1983. The weather was dank and dark under threatening grey skies, and he was cold. She knew he was always cold. He wore a padded, logo coat that produced a stature larger than reality and his shoulders were hunched forward, shortening his neck, as he warmed a pair of gloves on the exhaust manifold of a recently run engine. Simultaneously, the pair turned away and resumed their lives.

Martha was a bank secretary, back in the days when banking still held a modicum of respect. She had been married to her carpenter husband, Robert for a year and two months. Her work was mundane and she was not particularly suited to its nature, but it paid well, with benefits and her husband was a good, enterprising man, who allowed free expression and for this she was deeply grateful. Most acquaintances discouraged her wistful ambitions long before they even took off and labelled her foolish, but not this one. Perhaps he knew her too well.

Together they carved a comfortable life, one which in many ways was different from that of their friends; they were not extravagant, and had no desire to possess the latest gadgets. They kept their borrowing to a minimum and worked hard to accomplish a ten year plan to pay off the debt on their home, a two bedroom cottage, which also commanded much of their attention in terms of maintenance and restoration. They strove each day to reach their ultimate goal, a chance to escape with dreams of their own, both jointly and severally. Although very much a couple, each respected the other's need to be an

1

individual. So much so that they could spend hours, even days, together attending to whatever satisfied, without the need for irrelevant conversation. Time would pass, blissfully uninterrupted, yet in the secure knowledge that each was there for the other.

A few years passed and their plan was on course, a course from which they were never tempted to stray. Both improved their earning capabilities and benefits, but the possession of grandiose real estate or exotic vehicles never impressed either of them, although they could easily have lived with both. They were more than happy with what they had.

Every now and then, possibly in boredom and especially when work was slack, Martha would study the picture she had taken on that Finals Sunday in October. There was something curious about it. Strangely, she could see herself in the scene captured by the viewfinder. Its grey light held a quality of transient intimacy, the molecular structure of which seemed to arrange itself in the form of a single silhouette, projected against a back-drop of white canvas and mechanical engineering. She felt like a third party, highly privileged to have been allowed to witness such a private moment between two apparent strangers. The photograph inspired a magic that only Martha could see but one she did not fully understand. Secretly, she treasured it and its silence often crossed her mind.

The young man in the frame had grown strong, vibrant, and aggressive on occasions and singularly determined to succeed in his chosen profession. Increasingly, Martha found herself following the course of his somewhat turbulent career, through brief, noncommittal media interviews and television footage which were, in the main, technically precise and business like. He drove on pure adrenalin and possessed a knack for upsetting the establishment.

During his early days on the circuit, he had quickly acquired the nickname of "Iceman". The inappropriateness of such a handle tickled Martha every time she read it. Oddly, however, nothing he did greatly surprised her, although his achievements were quite remarkable, as record books may reflect. Martha simply knew and accepted that he was the best at what he did and, no matter how he faltered personally, no one would ever be able to deny him this fact; it was a point which never failed to fuel his enigmatic commitment.

Each morning, on her way to work, Martha collected her newspaper from the corner shop at the bottom of Park Hill. She would by-pass her office, ignoring the gestured referrals to a large clock overlooking a corridor which led to the vaults, as she was rarely late barring the odd speeding ticket or breakdown, and head straight for the kitchen where she made a cup of tea and smoked a cigarette, whilst flicking through the sports pages and reading her star sign for the day. It was impossible to even begin to contemplate the pile of work stacked in the corner of her office, until this ritual had been completed.

By the end of 1988, his career had rocketed to the highest mantle attainable and on reading the triumphant headlines through a blue haze, Martha felt a burning pride in her lower abdomen that made her wriggle with delight. His following season, however, was controversially traumatic and as she examined the fortnightly reports, she began to notice an interaction with her own feelings.

He was bitterly disappointed by the season's performance, on and off the track, but undeterred, returned twice more to reclaim his crown.

On seeing him this time, Martha became concerned. Behind the joyous elation he appeared drawn, exhausted, and his red-veined eyes showed no light. She remembered those fleeting moments from eight years past, the dishevelled dark curly hair, the tautness of his small frame and his attempts to combat the cold, English, autumnal air. His image prompted the recall of a dream Martha had had, in the September of this year, 1991. It had disturbed her greatly at the time but she tried to dismiss it along with others. Now it was fresh in her mind.

There had been an accident and a car was precariously balanced, upside down, with its back end resting on the narrow parapet of a bridge. The driver was desperately trying to release himself from the safety harness which restrained him; he was hanging in limbo and could not, despite valiant efforts, undo its buckles. Emergency service crews arrived in seconds, an exaggerated commotion broke out, but their approach was blocked by some sort of invisible force-field. Martha was merely a spectator in the foreground but it was she who heard his agonised pleading, she who experienced the pain as his breathing became more and more rapid and she who sensed his body tiring in its struggle for freedom.

Severely shaken, with droplets of cold sweat dripping between her breasts, Martha had gone downstairs for a glass of water and a cigarette before being able and even only then apprehensively, to return to her bed. By sunrise, his vivid portrayal of fear had forged a valley inside her so deep, that she was totally incapable of coping with the trivia of monetary facts and figures at work, or the banter of her colleagues as they recounted every last detail of their weekend shopping expeditions, sexual encounters and what they had or had not eaten. Her senses roused, other such visions came to light. These episodes had been occurring with increasing frequency over the course of the last couple of years. The stranger on the shore, the white sand that slipped too easily through his fine fingers, the way he tried to save the grains, the worn chinos, the way his pale blue shirt, minus buttons, billowed softly around his body; his chest – his gorgeous chest – and the fact that he didn't wear shoes. He had woken her and Martha reached out in her sleep. She could remember crying in despair at the immense, physical distance between them and she could feel her eyes prickling again now.

CHAPTER 2

Our Ref; AS'S/POW
Date: 21.10.1991

Dear Sir,
I am writing to advise you that your current account is
overdrawn by £......

Martha sorted the pink and yellow, flimsy copy paper into neat
piles according to size, placed her headphones in her ears, and
adjusted the volume on her audio machine, as another letter
began in a similar fashion to a thousand other letters she had
typed. She was dreaming from her office window. The view was
not spectacular, in fact a brick wall obscured 90 per cent of it,
but by raising her sights she could see a patch of sky
approximately six feet square. That was enough. There was a
whole world out there and she wanted to be part of it...

Martha sighed. Glancing down at her hands poised over a
keyboard she gently twisted the band of gold which still adorned
her finger. She had never contemplated a life without Robert
and due to this sudden change in circumstances; she had not
been out much lately and had been suppressing an inner desire
to return to the location of her secret picture. Finally, and with
much deliberation, she gave in and telephoned the Track
Information Office at Thruxton race circuit. One event
remained on the calendar.

Thruxton, the nearest major circuit to Martha's home, is set
amidst the exposed, gently rolling hills of Salisbury Plain. At the
far end, looking past the old aircraft hangers, the tower of the
village church can be seen, its concealed bells used to bring a
halt to all noisy activities in progress on the Sabbath, at around
midday and again at 6 o'clock. Martha couldn't remember ever

having attended a meeting here with Robert, when the weather had been anything other than cold. She wrapped up well with scarf and gloves and even popped her wellies into the boot of Morris just in case.

As she wandered amongst the diverse assortment of vehicles which tightly packed the paddock area, on that late October weekend Martha thought of her young man from years gone by, eagerly fussing with wing mirrors, diffusers, tyre pressures and the like, making certain, personally, that every last important detail of his machine was properly attended to in the correct fashion. He had been anxious to begin the race and Martha, not wishing to cause disruption to his routine, had forfeited the opportunity for an autograph. In a passing moment of fancy she had felt curiously attracted to the slight Latino figure. He was cute back then. He still was now. As she stood alone in the watery sunlight, slightly bemused by the technical activities surrounding her, she sensed a warmth within and saw again his instant smile of sheer delight as, decked in laurels, he had raised a fist in victory.

Martha strolled on. Whilst dodging to avoid the large bonnet of a meandering pick-up truck, she heard a gruff shout like that of a fairground roustabout's efforts to drum up trade.

"Hey – babe, wanna ride?"

"That's original," she thought, hearing the colloquial vibes again.

"Hi, I'm Jim."

"Really? Good for you." She was walking away.

"Do you wanna meet a real racing driver?"

Martha spun round on her heels. Jim was standing on the running board, leaning over a highly polished black cab. He wore a red peaked cap, slightly twisted to one side, and a broad grin.

"Yes – as a matter of fact, I do." Martha grinned back at him and as she approached, Jim swung himself onto the driver's seat, leaned across the gearbox and opened the passenger door.

It transpired that Jim was a mechanic with the Sabre Race Team who competed in the special saloon car championship. He drove Martha to a cramped corner of the paddock where the rest of the gang were brewing up.

"Want a cuppa, me love?"

"Yes – please." She was feeling chilly and a hot drink seemed just the ticket.

"That's Pete, he's our driver – he drinks tea till it comes out of his ears, very specific as to how it's brewed too – prefers an emulsion!" Jim was hollering from the other side of a makeshift tent. He pointed to a dumpy girl, slumped untidily on a pile of tyres. Strands of lank, brown hair curtained her face and she made a noise of sorts but Martha wasn't sure it was a welcome. Jenny looked bored to tears.

"There has to be something else," Martha quoted, as she took a long hard look at Jenny, which convinced her beyond doubt, that her theory of change being a vital element of survival was correct.

Martha sat down on an old car seat next to Jenny and tried to make conversation. It was not easy. She could sense the girl's thoughts. Martha did not need to be told that she wasn't the first one Jim had used his pit-lane banter on. She was far from innocent and certainly not about to drop everything, for some cheeky grease monkey. Her sole objective was to enjoy the day as it unfolded.

The fourth and final member of the band was David, Pete's younger brother. He was sixteen; shy, spotty and his rangy body seemed to take on a rigidity like that of a flag-pole in close proximity to Jenny.

The lads were fussing around the car, fixing this adjusting that and generally yelling and blaming each other when things went wrong. The "team" were due to compete in the first race of the day and although the equipment was slightly worn, having been recycled several times, Pete appeared to possess the confidence and ability to steer it in the right direction.

A loudspeaker, close to Martha's head, hailed the drivers and vehicles to the start line.

"Coming with us?" asked Jim.

"Sure am!" replied Martha, eagerly jumping to her feet – Jenny didn't budge. "Oh well, I'm going," thought Martha. "I've got a valid interest in the race now and I want to see the boys in action."

It was as hectic as ever in the pit lane, even for such an inauspicious event. People were running here, there and everywhere, wearing headphones and caps, clutching clip boards with precious information attached, and all clad in their appropriately named jackets. Martha felt somewhat out of place until Jim tossed her his coat, complete with famous name embossed across the shoulders. He also hastily, to her dismay, shoved a board in her hands.

"What's this for?"

"Lap information!" came the hurried response.

Martha was, to say the least, a little perturbed. "What am I supposed to write on it?" Her gloved hands fumbled with the board. But Jim had vanished.

David, who was standing close by, quietly took the board and said that she could watch him and he would explain things.

By this time Pete had taken up his position on the grid. He was seventh and Martha jested with David that this was a lucky number. The young man smiled accommodatingly but kept his eyes fixed sharply on the lap data board.

Jim returned from the grid, having helped Pete with some last minute mechanical adjustment and was climbing over the pit wall, when he shouted.

"Hey! Um –" He stopped, mid-sentence, realising he didn't know her name.

"Mart...," she replied, just as 16 highly tuned engines revved into action.

He smiled awkwardly, embarrassed by his initial lack of knowledge, but after a wink from Martha, this soon returned to that charming grin which lit up his entire face, especially his eyes.

"That's a boy's name isn't it?" he yelled back.

Martha frowned, she wondered what the hell he was talking about, but the race was about to begin. David nervously tapped the clip board with a black marker pen, and all three perched themselves on the pit wall, eagerly anticipating the start. Martha felt a lump in her throat. The man on pole position led the racers in an orderly fashion for the parade lap. They disappeared from view, consumed by the undulating green surface of the infield and Martha waited with baited breath for Pete to re-appear at the final chicane, before resuming his place in line astern.

"Wish him luck!" Jim shouted as the lights went red, held for a split second, and then turned to green.

The engines roared with all their might, tyres screamed throwing up clouds of blue smoke which hung heavy in the air, as it mixed with the vegetable based fumes of burning Duckhams oil; long after the cars had vanished. Pete got a flyer.

The 10 lap race took no time at all. They were soon at half distance and after a few bumps and spins involving the leaders, Pete found himself sitting in third position.

He was in the slip-stream of the car ahead and used this advantage to edge past on the straight.

Just managing to hold the race line for the final bend, tyres screeching and with rubber visibly torn, he took an extremely well contested second place right on the line! Right in front of their faces!

The small time crew leapt from the pit wall in ecstatic disbelief. Jim kissed Martha full on the lips.

"This is our best placing yet!" he yelled.

Martha felt a little sad, however, as this race had brought the season to its conclusion.

Although only a few hours had passed, Martha was already beginning to find Jim's boisterous company pleasantly enjoyable. Sure he was brash and cavalier on the surface, but she sensed he had a heart and an aptitude for making people laugh in situations that otherwise could have been uncomfortable. He wasn't exactly what you'd call handsome: about six two, straight shortish, sandy hair. Nothing special really – apart from his eyes, bright blue and surrounded by exceptionally long lashes which gave them a blurred appearance. His nose had been broken at some stage and when he smiled the laughter lines were plentiful, emphasised by the high form of his cheek bones.

The three of them rushed off to find Pete taking his place on the podium. He looked pleased to say the least and was searching the crowd for his mates. But Martha detected a certain degree of disappointment. Jenny was not present to share his moment of glory. Pete was handed a bottle of champagne which he proceeded to shower over them – laurel wreath around his neck.

Back at base camp, Jenny was already packing the cooking gear into a rather rusty blue van, and as the excitement subsided, Martha felt it an opportune time to say farewell. Jim offered to walk her to the spectators' car park but she declined.

"I still think Marti's a boy's name." Jim was searching for more time.

"My name's Martha." She pointed out with a bit of a giggle.

"Oh – so where can I find you?"

"The City Line Bank, Southton-on-Sea."

That evening Martha returned home to the small village of Roebuck, close to the foot of the Mendip Hills in Somerset – The land of perpetual summer, magic, myths and legends. Avalon 'rendezvous of the dead', is also here.

It was during the drive home, across the Plain, past the austere, grey shadowy stones of an ancient temple of worship, through the sheltered market towns and finally negotiating the endless, twists and turns as the road descended a steep gorge that Martha realised Monday was fast approaching. A strike rate of one in seven was not good enough and for a while she toyed with the notion of simply keeping her old Morris Minor rolling west.

CHAPTER 3

The winter months passed, Christmas came and went but despite depressing moans from others about the lengthy evenings, Martha was inspired. She was so preoccupied with her latest venture; the thought of darkness hours had not even entered her head. All her available spare time had been spent in writing. What had begun life in the spring of '91 as a means of venting her own frustrations and commenting on the injustice of the changing dynamics in her professional world of commerce, which quite frankly was a disgrace, had now expanded into a full-blown manuscript. She thoroughly enjoyed the experience and was amazed at the ease with which the story had been created. It was like watching a film projected through her subconscious. All Martha had to do was to record the details.

However, there were some difficulties. Despite having worked as a secretary for many years, Martha's spelling was atrocious and her impatient nature often exploded, as she searched the pages of her well thumbed dictionary for the umpteenth time, invariably for the same word. When tired, she wondered if her inability to recall the proper arrangement of letters could be attributed to the modern label of dyslexia, but if she was honest with herself it was just a fancy excuse for being lazy or stupid. Whichever it was, she was quietly confident that the subject matter would invite attention.

Only one point bothered her. Martha had reservations about a paragraph on page 114. A friend had suggested erasure but Martha feared her tale would not then be complete. Having written the words down, she could not simply abandon them or ignore their significance.

Quite out of the blue, in mid-February, whilst Martha carried out her menial office duties in her usual state of apathy, she received a telephone call.

"Hi Marti! – Remember me – the mechanic?" How could she forget? Jim's speech was rapid: he wanted to meet up for a drink.

"I've got some fantastic news!" he shrieked.

Martha found his excitement strangely infectious but they had only met briefly and that was some while ago. Surely he had a more substantial friendship in which to confide. Jim detected the vagueness in her voice, adjusting the tone of his demands. He had not stopped to think that she might be otherwise involved. He could feel the heat of his embarrassment and was about to hang up when she agreed to see him.

"Brilliant!" he blurted. "I'll pick you up from work on Friday."

Grinning, Martha replaced the receiver. She glanced at the large holiday planning calendar on the wall opposite her desk. It was only Wednesday and she already questioned her ability to cope with the suspense.

Martha spent much of the last working day of the week wondering if Jim would turn up. But as she signed out, she could see him by the main entrance, jumping up and down his breath visible against the night sky. He clocked every colleague that left before her; and when Martha finally emerged from the building Jim rushed her with open arms, pulling her into a fierce embrace which lifted her clean off her feet.

"Marti, it's good to see you," he whispered directly into her right ear.

Martha was so overwhelmed by such a passionate greeting that words failed her, she even let the fact that he insisted on calling her Marti drop. Once Jim had calmed down, stopped babbling and the warming rush of adrenaline had drained, she suggested that as he had so much to talk about, they should go to a quiet country pub. Jim, not familiar with his surroundings, amiably agreed.

"Fine then, I know just the place. Where are you parked?" Marti breezed.

There followed an awkward silence and Jim, coughing through his hand mumbled. "Urm – well, um."

To relieve the stress Marti quickly blurted "We'll take mine."

It was already dark as they walked to her car. The clocks hadn't yet changed to British Summer Time. A biting, blustery wind chilled their faces. It was starting to spit with sleet and the bare trees in the park offered little protection. Jim gave a disdainful smirk as they approached her vehicle. "What's wrong with you?" Marti enquired. Jim squirmed: the car was old and judging by his reaction, shouldn't even be on the road. The heavens opened as Marti unlocked the doors.

"You can walk if you like," she said spitefully as she turned the key in the ignition. Jim was visibly impressed by the ease with which Morris's engine fired, though he made no comment. Marti leaned towards him, "It's what's inside that counts."

Taking a well trodden scenic route with chassis skimming bumps and deviations and wipers battling to combat the elements, Marti sensed Jim's numerous jolts and swallowed gasps as she sped forth, maybe a little sadistically, enjoying his momentary discomfort.

"Here we are" she announced as she cranked the brake lever, banged it into second and killed the engine.

"Yeah, but where?" exclaimed Jim, catching his breath.

The Crown, situated in a tiny hamlet amidst the Somerset wetlands, appears to be in the middle of nowhere, but in reality it is only a few miles from what some perceive to be the safety of civilization.

"Come on." Marti beckoned Jim toward the door. Inside, the low-ceilinged lounge was packed with 'those in the know,' and the welcoming warmth of a huge, inglenook fire at the far end of the bar encouraged a sense of ease and well-being. Jim cast a gaze over the bowed heads.

"We'll never get a seat," he muttered anxiously.

"Yes we will," Marti assured him, "and the range of food and drinks is exceptionally good."

Originating from an inner-city environment, Jim's scepticism of her statement was evidenced by a deep scowl but Marti's arrival had already been acknowledged. Joe, the barman complete with bushy beard, gave her a thumbs up and was already pouring her preferred tipple, long before she'd got anywhere near the bar.

"Ello me lover, not seen you for a while – what's your friend drinking?" he said whilst placing a large gin and tonic that fizzed with ice and a slice on the counter.

Jim half looked up. "A pint please, and can we see the menu?"

"Is he going to try our local zider?" Joseph was as ever playfully inquisitive.

"Whatever – and a menu," Jim repeated "Not that we can sit down."

Marti struck a glancing kick on Jim's shin, making Joe snigger with delight. His organisational skills were second to none and Marti and Jim were soon comfortably accommodated in a cosy fireside settle.

Jim examined the delights on offer. His stomach was clearly declaring its emptiness and Marti recommended a hearty steak and kidney pie as a filling remedy. Not to cause confusion, she decided on the same and Jim went to place their order. On his return Marti was impatient to hear his news.

"Come on then, spill the beans, why are we here?" she said removing her gloves.

Jim fixed his eyes seriously on her, he had not spotted a wedding ring before, and his discovery was tinged with anger.

"Are you married?" he exclaimed.

Marti was stunned, touched the band of gold and with slight hesitation answered. "Yes and No." She had naively gone into this meeting with no thoughts of it becoming a relationship. She and Robert had been together since their early teens, nobody else had ever seriously entered her head but, she could understand Jim's sense of deceit. "It's not an existing bond." Martha couldn't believe she had said those words – 'existing bond' – "Does this make a difference to you telling me why you are here?"

Apparently it didn't, Jim eased back and began his story.

Initially, Marti thought it all too good to be true and felt Jim was more than anything else seeking moral support. He had been offered a job by an acquaintance, in itself good news bearing in mind the current economic climate, working for a motor racing magazine.

It was a marvellous opportunity involving world-wide travel

and the chance to meet his professional mentors. Jim obviously wanted to accept but was unsure as to the reasons for his selection. He had no experience in this field. He could fix cars, but writing about them was another matter and this cast doubts as to whether the offer was genuine.

The couple had finished their meal. Joe shuffled over to place more logs on the fire and clear their plates.

"Would you like that topped up?" he asked.

Jim was staring vacantly into an empty glass. Marti accepted Joe's offer and nudged Jim encouragingly to go for the interview.

"What have you got to lose?"

"Not a lot," Jim mumbled dejectedly.

Jim had lost his job as a tyre fitter, which meant the truck had gone, been evicted from his flat for non-payment of rent and for the last six weeks had been living with Pete and Jenny. Unfortunately, their domestic circumstances had become extremely unbalanced and Jim felt he was making matters worse, so he left. And here he was? It also came to light in the course of conversation that Jim had no family. For whatever reason, he never elaborated on this topic.

Marti could tell, despite Jim's bravado, that he was at a loss to know which way to turn and offered assistance. If he wanted to go for the interview, she vowed to do all that she could to assist him in his preparations. Placing a compassionate hand on his knee and giving it a gentle squeeze, she advised that this was a chance he really could not afford to pass on. Jim nodded in quiet agreement.

It was getting late and as Marti and Jim came out of the pub they were engulfed by a thick damp mist, common to these parts. The journey home was slow but held no cause for alarm. Marti and Morris knew the narrow lanes well and although Jim insisted on sticking his head out of the passenger window on several occasions, to check road references and issue distance warnings, the soft peat verges held little fear.

They weren't speeding, so if they should happen to over-step a corner, no harm would be done. Both Marti and Morris had been pulled from a ditch by the local farmer on more than one occasion and neither was the worse for the experience. A bit smelly for a while, maybe, but not damaged.

Jim had made no mention of any pre-arranged digs and Marti accepted, quite naturally that he would be frequenting her cottage for the night. He did make a half-hearted suggestion that she dropped him off at a nearby motorway lodge but that was beyond her address and she really couldn't be bothered with the pretence.

As Marti drew up next to her house, Jim grinned wickedly.

"How many bedrooms?"

"Don't get any ideas."

Marti was firm, and Jim, not in a position to argue, apparently felt it unwise to abuse the generosity she had shown him thus-far. He was rambling, trying to exonerate himself from any doubts she might have had as to his integrity. Right now Jim evidently didn't want to be left out in the cold. He was becoming far too morbid for Marti's liking so she interrupted.

"With a body like that you'd do alright on the streets so I don't know what you're worried about." Jim clearly revelled in her remarks.

Once inside it took Jim about two minutes flat to explore the entire property including the contents of her fridge. On returning to the lounge he expressed his approval, unfortunately marrying this comment with questions on how much it had set her back. Marti considered this point irrelevant and certainly none of his business. It had been a long day and both were sleepy and slightly under the influence so they retired to their allotted rooms.

Marti sat at her dresser and began to remove her earrings and other bits of jewellery. Again she touched the ring; it had been two years since Robert's fateful accident on a construction site in the northeast. Gently she slipped it over her knuckle; it was a little tight and a white band was left behind, encircling her finger. Carefully she placed it in a small box and put it in the top left-hand drawer. Scanning her bedroom, a stack of black sacks containing clothing stood ominously in the corner.

Marti lay in her bed, its space was emancipating, and although her eyes wished desperately to close, it was impossible to knock her brain out of gear. The endless spiral of whys and wherefores had begun, each one leading to another equally hypothetical notion.

"What if Jim was making it all up?" She wanted to trust him but if the job was so good, how come this so-called friend wasn't after it? Did it exist? Oh God! – The possibilities were endless. She kept looking at the clock, the hands of which never seemed to move. She wanted to sleep.

Keeping perfectly still, holding her breath, she listened intently to the darkness. Not a murmur could she detect. Marti had hoped to hear a similar restlessness coming from Jim's room as he tossed and turned, but no. She was slightly annoyed but on thinking again, decided that if he wasn't worried, why should she be? This idea seemed to have the desired effect and soon body and mind came to rest.

Both parties woke early the next morning, which was surprising. Marti didn't usually get up early on a Saturday, no matter what sort of night she'd had. They sat down to breakfast in a small dining-room at the back of the house which had originally been designed as a utility space. It was then she saw that Jim noticed the missing ring, although he made no mention. A wide window almost the length of the outer wall overlooked the garden, not expansive but beyond its perimeters, a protective moat formed by a rhyne, lay the open fields of farmland, giving an impression of greater light and space. At the far end of a lush green lawn, stood a dominant crack withy – Marti's 'Thinking Tree'. She would often laze for hours on its low limbs day-dreaming or simply trying to put her life into perspective. The only intruders were a few wild rabbits, the occasional badger and a heron who had misguidedly not noticed her presence.

Marti treasured her privacy and was, notably, regarded as a bit of a loner for wishing to preserve this state. Although perfectly able to interact with colleagues and friends, pub lunches, fancy dress and gala parties always excited her. She had no real need to be close to any one in particular. It wasn't that she didn't like people – simply that by the end of the week she had had enough. Saturdays and, in particular, Sundays were set aside for her own enjoyment. She was quite secure in her own company.

Marti and Jim spent the best part of two hours discussing the pros and cons of his newly proposed employment offer, until finally, after Marti had offered to provide travel arrangements, Jim made a firm commitment to go for it.

The interview at Power Play, a recently established forum magazine, was to be held at their London offices that coming Thursday and after some persuasive advances on Jim's part, Marti agreed to take the day off work in order to accompany him. He was in truth, nervous at the prospect of being alone in the Big City, particularly if the deal disintegrated.

The next problem was Jim's attire. The only clothes he possessed were the ones he stood up in and slept in. Marti raised one eyebrow.

"How long is it since you left Pete and Jenny's place?"

Jim pulled his t-shirt up to his nose and the onus again fell on Marti to come up with a solution. Upstairs, gathering dust, those sacks of clothes were cluttering her bedroom and probably her life. There was great discomfort in her acknowledgement of their availability, but still, she granted Jim the right to take what he wanted if there was anything of use. He threw his arms around her neck, bringing her head close to his.

"I promise to repay every penny if I get the job." he whispered before scarpering up to her room. Jim soon returned dressed in a clean, red and black, lumberjack style shirt. He had the bags with him. He stuffed his own kit in the washing machine, added the liquid and set the programme. Marti was impressed.

"Give me the car keys!" Jim demanded. "The rest of this is going now."

Marti offered no resistance, even in this fraught, emotional situation, seeing Jim in one of Robert's shirts was an odd concept to say the least, but she decided, "What the hell, what purpose could these items serve?" It was kind of nice to let someone else take control and as there was little else happening in her life right now, a diversion of this type might give her some incentive, bearing in mind that she would never put in more than she was prepared to lose.

Whilst Jim was out, Marti cleared the decks and washed up. On his return they headed for the shopping mall to sort out some formal attire for the impending interview. Jim was slightly uncooperative, finding the whole episode boring; and the fact that he was totally unsure of the image he wished to project didn't really help matters. They must have visited every man's outfitters on the high street. Designer, cheap chic – every suit available but, still Jim kept wandering in the direction of the jeans and sweat-shirt department.

He managed to find some petty fault with everything and the atmosphere between the two was becoming fraught. Eventually, in exasperation, Marti made the decision for him. She convinced the would-be model that he looked good, which was no word of a lie. The cut of the jacket was trendy but still sufficiently businesslike to command attention and his broad shoulders filled the garment to perfection. The trousers hung neat on the hips yet still revealed the cuteness of his rear view. Marti matched shirt, tie and shoes to complete the outfit. Carefully, she examined the end result. Jim's appearance had been completely transformed and this alone should ensure a favourable, initial response from any employer. Eyeing him up and down Marti sensed a wicked smirk tracing the corners of her mouth. Jim caught her looking at him in the finger smudged dressing room mirror.

"What's wrong?" he demanded.

"I just thought..."

"What!" Jim snapped back again.

"I just thought – how professional you look"

"And?"

"So long as you keep your mouth shut the possibility of a job might just be on the cards!"

Marti could feel the outrage burning her coat collar.

"Can we go now?"

Jim snatched the curtain, its metal rings chinking on the rail and began to undress. Needless to say Marti picked up the tab and whilst she was still queuing for the pleasure, she could see Jim pacing up and down on the pavement.

During the drive home, he again made the solemn promise to repay Marti everything as soon as it was possible to do so. She assured him it wasn't necessary, but he insisted, so she agreed and let the matter drop. Marti wasn't a fool, and if she had wanted repayment it would have been highly unlikely that she would have bought into the deal in the first place.

"Look at it as an investment," she told him. But Jim was uneasy with this notion. He'd never had anything for nothing and was unaccustomed to such a show of generosity.

"Are you hungry?" Marti asked.

"Sure am – I'm always hungry," – his eye contact was hard to grasp.

Back home, Marti told him to try on his new gear once more whilst she prepared dinner. Of course he was not enthusiastic about her idea; having felt harassed enough in the shops. It's strange, thought Marti, how so many of the male species rebuffs the delight of enhancement, yet when they view the end result, strut like peacocks! Although the thought of cooking wasn't enthralling her, once she had begun with a large casserole on the hot plate the creative juices began to flow, anything that was in the fridge was going in the pot with loads of herbs and spices designed to tantalise the taste buds.

Jim reluctantly stomped upstairs, clutching the many carrier bags in his fists and muttering. He was up there for ages. Dinner was almost ready and Marti had to go and find him. Creeping quietly up the stairs, making sure to miss the squeaky treads, she stopped on the small landing next to the spare room. Peeking around the door she caught Jim checking his newly acquired image in the full length mirror. She watched him mischievously for a while as he posed, front, back, sideways and all the way round again. Pretending to hold a microphone to his lips, Jim mimicked the delivery of some once heard commentary.

"Dinner's ready!" Marti's shout startled the man. She was laughing which caused him to blush from a certain degree of rage. Jim squeezed his knuckles and moved quickly to the far corner of the small single room.

Marti was surprised by his reaction and apologised for making him jump.

"All right – looking good!" She reassured him. Jim took another glance in the mirror which was framed by sun parched reclaimed timber. She could see that Jim quite fancied his new look.

"Should pull a few?"

"Yeah." Marti agreed, nodding approval.

"But I think the trousers are a tad short."

He enquired as to the imminence of dinner but Marti was already on her knees at his feet. Jim began undressing as she stripped the stitches to adjust the hems. Her eyes were automatically attracted upwards as he towered over her. He loosened his tie and unbuttoned the crisp white shirt. Marti wanted desperately to touch – his broad smooth chest and shoulders made her feel weak and vulnerable. Turning away quickly from his sight Marti made the excuse that their meal would be ruined if they didn't get on and eat soon.

She jumped up, almost upsetting her pin box, and scurried back to the kitchen where pots were bubbling.

Jim passed the evening working on his interview technique, whilst Marti curled up on the snug terracotta sofa to read a book. After persistent interruptions however, she finally gave up her task to offer Jim her full attention. Sunday was a typically lazy day, it rained as usual and Jim and Marti spent the afternoon watching rugby on TV. Jimbo was impressed, Marti being a girl and all that chauvinistic crap, to find that she actually wanted to watch the game.

And, that her knowledge of the teams and rules was on a par, maybe even greater than his. Lunch was prepared to coincide with kick off.

Monday morning arrived and Marti surveyed the array of tailored suits, which hung in her wardrobe, each with complimentary bag and heels. She had to arrange for the day off on Thursday. Such requests invariably provoked inane grievances which Marti found laboriously time-consuming. A simple Yes or No was sufficient and she wasn't relishing the prospect of seeking the requisite permission. Marti chose the navy one, with a peplum jacket; this gave shape to her slightly straight boyish figure, and teamed it with a red blouse, shoes, and bag.

Having submitted her holiday form, Marti sat at her desk mulling over the potential of the impending interview. She still couldn't fully understand how or why she had become so involved in the whole escapade. OK, Jim didn't have any money, that was one reason, but he had been fairly honest about this point. However, he was a stranger, and Marti couldn't help wondering if there was another side to his character, although she hoped this would not turn out to be the case.

"Oh God!" – Martha put a hand to her lips.

Jim was in her house, alone with all her worldly possessions! Swiftly she picked up her office phone and dialled the number – it rang and rang. "Come on please." She thought "He's gone!"

Just as she was about to hang up, simultaneously grabbing for her handbag and keys, she heard a tentative reply. Marti let out an audible sigh of sheer relief.

"I didn't want to answer it." Jim said. "You know in case – we'll you know in case somebody wondered....?" Jim stumbled over the sentence.

"It's OK." Marti said "I'll see you later – about six."

Marti kept her suspicions as to Jim's integrity closely guarded from there on, if only to prevent her from becoming romantically entangled with some hobo. She wasn't ready for that. As she contemplated this subject in more depth, the possibility of an affair seemed more and more remote, somehow. Although she admittedly found Jim physically attractive, the thought of them as a couple made her burst into hysterics, much to the amusement of her un-be-knowing colleagues.

Martha's mind was definitely not on work today and it showed in the amount of rejected letters she found in her post tray at the end of the day. She re-shuffled the multicoloured copy paper again and again. Her boss kept asking if she was ill. This in itself was unusual, as most of the time he was generally too wrapped up in his own health problems to notice others' and if he did, it was only to take great delight in explaining how awful it was when he had suffered likewise.

Her old typewriter was clicking frenetically and Martha's mind drifted out the window. As it did, a bright idea came to her for their journey to London.

"A train!" she squealed, prompting more wailing laughter from her work mates.

It would be simple – she thought – no traffic or parking worries. From the start, she hadn't fancied the idea of Morris in the big city jams and carnage, so when lunch time arrived she legged it down to the local train station and booked two return tickets.

They would have to leave early on the day as Jim's appointment was for 10.30 a.m. The most suitable departure time was 0644, peak travel time – arriving at Paddington at

0855, allowing an hour to locate the address and sort themselves out. Marti visualised Jimbo as she had left him that morning, snoring his head off.

The next three days seemed like an eternity, but eventually Thursday morning dawned. Expectations were high. Marti was startled to be woken by Jim, already washed, clean shaven and ready for the off.

"Gosh! I hardly recognised you," she said, rubbing sleep from her mascara smudged eyes. "I thought some dashing prince had come to whisk me off to paradise." Is there such a place?

Jim was raring to go and finding it impossible to keep still for a second. In playful exuberance he whipped the duvet cover off Marti, who screamed, "I'm naked!" – Which made Jim run away like a scalded cat. Talking of which Gato the cat, who had been dozing peacefully on the end of Marti's bed, was now clinging to the curtains for dear life, snarling and spitting venomously.

Marti crawled out of bed. Early morning was not her best time. She stumbled down the open back wooden staircase, to find breakfast already on the table and Jim sitting there in the window grinning from ear to ear, barely able to contain his excitement. Marti squinted at the kitchen clock – five past five was the unearthly reading she established from its hands. On entering the dining-room, now able to stand upright, Jim made an announcement.

"To new beginnings," he declared, raising a mug of tea to toast his philosophy.

"This is going to be the first day of the rest of my life." Jim was determined not to let things slip away this time. "I can feel it in my bones," he said, rubbing his hands together before devouring a full English breakfast.

"I can feel something in mine too," Marti thought. "But I hope it's not the rest of my life." The words 'I and my' struck a nerve somehow. And she wondered from where, the ingredients for breakfast had materialised. It was years since her fridge had contained such products.

Jim, understandably, was particularly lively and Marti, not wishing to quash his confidence, jollied him along. In the back of her mind however, her own destiny by the end of the day gave cause for concern. If Jim got the job it would be the end of their relationship, platonic or otherwise, and if he didn't – God forbid – she could imagine herself lumbered with a mental cripple. "Don't think of such things!" she told herself sharply. "A positive attitude is needed now if ever it was. Besides, you make him sound like some kind of parasite."

In all honesty, Marti feared for her own emotional state. She didn't want to be dumped but, more importantly, she didn't want to be dumped on. She had taken care, in the past, not to expect anything from anyone – that way she couldn't be let down. It was a self-preservation mechanism which, until now, she had been perfecting. These thoughts continued to clog her cerebral passages throughout the train journey. 'And how many times do they need to announce forthcoming destinations, are we all idiots?' Tongue in cheek Marti pondered her last internal question. Her quietness prompted Jim on several occasions, to ask whether she was alright – perhaps he thought she might have been suffering from travel sickness or something. Marti hid her worries under a brave face. After all, it was Jim's day and it meant the world to him.

They arrived at Paddington and disembarked. The platform was awash with commuters rushing in various directions toting cases and sporting bowler hats. Marti and Jim were carried along with the wave, unable to tell where they would end up. They could hardly see the sign-posts overhead, let alone have time to decipher them. Neither had a clue where they were but, as the bodies around them gradually dispersed they found themselves next to an exit.

"This is horrendous!" Jim gasped.

"I think we should get a taxi," Marti suggested.

They dashed to a waiting rank, and scrambled into the back of the first black cab in line, much to the aggravation of a gentleman in a navy blue pin striped suit, furiously waving a rolled umbrella.

"Oops!" Marti glanced across at Jim.

"Quick! Give the driver the address and let's get out of here." Bundled onto the back seat with Jim in close proximity, Marti felt enthused by his dominance but, why did he assume that she had the address?

The city traffic was chaotic, horns were blasting and arms were waving, indicating rude gestures. As they drew up outside the magazine offices, which in truth, they could have reached on foot – Jim attempted to exit the vehicle from the right-hand side.

"Hey!" yelled the panic-stricken cabbie as he grabbed the door, slamming it shut.

"What you trying to do, get yourself killed!?"

"Not particularly," muttered Jim in a state of shocked anger whilst clambering across the seat to the 'relative safety' of the pavement.

Together they sussed out the whereabouts of the offices. "Power Play" was smartly engraved, in capitals on a large brass plaque next to a tall glazed and pillared entrance porch. Opposite there was an inviting cafe/wine bar and as the time was only just approaching 9.15 a.m. they decided to go for coffee – although both could have consumed a stronger beverage, neither admitted to the sin. Jim wanted to eat as well.

"How can you be hungry at a time like this?" Marti asked as she lit up.

Jim glared accusingly at the cigarette. "I eat when I'm nervous – you do that!"

Marti was not in the mood for this but, realising she was on slippery ground, kept quiet whilst Jim ordered a Continental Breakfast, although he wasn't sure what he was actually going to get. On its arrival he grimaced at the equally continental waitress "Is that it?" The young lady ignored him with a shrug of her tiny shoulders. "How much do they want for this?" Jim's question was directed at Marti who stirred her coffee. "It's a rip off, whatever it is." The many people present turned to look at him.

"Don't worry about it," Marti whispered, glancing through the logo painted window. "Just eat."

The minutes passed like hours and Marti was convinced the clock on the wall was broken. Jim must have thought so too, as he kept asking the gentleman on the next table what the time was. If he asked once, he asked a dozen times. Finally, somewhat annoyed with Jim's persistence, the man pointed severely at the clock. His action drew Marti's eyes once again to the dial. It was 10.20 a.m.

"I think you'd better be going." She urged Jim to leave, wishing him luck.

Marti watched him from the cafe window, as far as she could without craning her neck to cause attention. Jim straightened his tie and adjusted his undergarments once more. She noticed that her fingers were crossed.

Ordering another coffee, she lit a cigarette. Through the blue haze, she imagined far off continents, rich and famous people. She wanted to be there. "Stop it!" She cursed herself, inhaled deeply and took a large swig through the froth, from a thick-rimmed cup.

An hour passed. Marti had drunk so much coffee she was almost floating on the ceiling. It wasn't her usual beverage.

Suddenly in rushed Jimbo. "Pretend you're a photographer!" he screeched, "I think I'm in, but they're asking about photographs – I told them it was no problem. I know a pro." His voice was getting higher. "Come on!" Jim was lifting Marti out of her seat.

"Hang on a minute, you told them what?" She was astounded by the nerve of the man.

"You can do it, you've got a camera – I've seen it!"

"When?" she snapped, horrified by the idea that he'd been snooping around her cottage.

"Quick!"

Marti had no time to digest the information further; her feet were hardly touching ground as Jim dragged her out of the cafe, still insisting that she could carry the show, "Wing it," he kept saying, "you can do it, it'll be great fun!"

"More like a nightmare," Marti thought, just managing to pull herself together as they reached the Editor's office. Her heart was pounding against the wall of her chest, like a bass drum; she was sure it could be heard by all present.

Half an hour later they emerged, shell-shocked and barely able to remember much of what was said, but the job was *theirs!*

The Editor, Derek Bennett, had asked them to return the following morning to go over some finer details in preparation for their first assignment. The Grand Prix season was due to start shortly and little time could be wasted.

Jim and Marti were so excited and overwhelmed that neither

could think straight. "Let's celebrate!" Jim's initial thoughts were of beer, perhaps to calm the system. Marti willingly agreed, suggesting with a cheeky smirk, that it was his round.

The couple walked straight into the first pub they came across. Being lunch-time, it was packed to capacity with designer suits and striped shirts. Jim exuded confidence, proposing that she get used to this situation as this was going to be their style from now on but Marti wasn't so sure. Every bloke looked exactly the same, like clones resembling the models you see in catalogues. Jim tried to squeeze his way to the bar with Marti almost tucked into his back pocket. Their route wasn't made any easier by the crowd's unwillingness to move any more than was strictly necessary.

"Excuse me," Jim said politely, again and again, but the reaction was muted. Finally he reached the polished mahogany counter. "What do you want?"

"A gin and tonic," Marti replied. "Make it a double!" She was in need of it and doubted their chances of making a second trip. The atmosphere was weird and Marti frowned as someone stood on her foot, she could just imagine the damage to her brand new black suede courts!

Jim's next task was to attract the attention of the barman, who seemed to be deliberately avoiding him, fussing with and wiping anything in sight in an attempt to look otherwise occupied. Jim was becoming annoyed with the bloke's rudeness.

"Hoi!" he shouted, temper fraying. His tone was threatening and brought the desired response. He was approached, though none too pleasantly, by a guy in a strappy t-shirt wearing one diamond-like earring and a nose ring. His jet-black hair sported a streak of fuchsia pink which stuck straight up from his forehead. Customer service was obviously not foremost on this employee's C.V. However the last straw broke when the effeminate barman, rather acidly informed Jim, "We don't serve pints." About to blow a fuse, Jim noticed that the room had filled with a deadly hush.

Marti glanced up at him.

"Let's get out of here," she said in a mousey squeak. But Jim was not one to be beaten, he ordered two halves instead, loud and clear. The man banged their drinks on the bar and they side-stepped the counter gracefully.

Marti felt strangely uncomfortable, "You know something?" She turned to Jim, who was pressed against a post.

"Yeah – they don't drink pints in the city!" he snarled.

"No – Apart from that?"

Jim puzzled, surveyed the collective audience. "F— You're the only female!" His eyes narrowed.

"Oh shit! You don't suppose..."

"Hush!" Marti put one figure to his lips.

Jim downed his second half in record time, grabbed hold of her arm and they made a hasty exit.

Marti jokingly suggested that one or two of them fancied Jim, but he wasn't amused and became viciously enraged by her insinuations. "Don't say that, don't ever say that again!"

"OK," Marti said submissively. She was only pulling his leg but had obviously touched a nerve. "Come on, calm down," she said, slipping her arm into the crook of his elbow. Jim's hands were firmly wedged in his pockets, which made him easy to hang onto.

Changing the subject, Marti suggested lunch and gestured to a small bistro across the street. The waitress ushered them to a vacant table and took their order. As they were eating, Jim brought up the subject of over-night accommodation, a point which had been nagging at Marti from the moment Mr. Bennett had requested their return.

"So what are we going to do – the cash-flow's not unlimited – is it?" Jim was looking down at a fast emptying plate.

Marti sighed, "We could have one room, two beds."

Jim was physically knocked back by her offer. "You trust me?" he gasped.

"Call me stupid if you like, but it does make the most sense."

The waitress brought the bill and Jim asked her if she could recommend any, well – cheaper hotels in the vicinity. She obliged by jotting a few names onto a napkin and Marti and Jim set off in search. They hailed another cab and again gave the written information to the driver, asking him to start at the nearest address.

Marti waited in the car whilst Jimbo nipped inside to enquire if there were any vacancies. While he was gone she chatted to the cabbie, asking anxiously if he thought the place was any good. They were in Sussex Gardens, close to Paddington. He nodded in approval. "They're all about the same luv."

Jim returned, sporting a satisfied grin.

"You're gonna love this place," he said pushing open a large heavily painted half glazed door. "It's got a TV, phone, coffee-making facilities the lot, even a view." He impatiently hurried Marti up the stairs, telling her that the lift was out of order, and jubilantly flung open the bedroom door. Directly opposite, there was a window with the unbroken view of a brick wall. "Lovely isn't it?" he chuckled. "I chose it especially – Oh – they want a cash payment."

There then ensued a hike and a hunt for the nearest cash-point machine under the instructions of the hotel receptionist, whose command of the English language was slightly dubious.

Marti's feet were killing her! But with the tariff settled she finally kicked off her shoes and slumped onto the nearest bed. Jim made a big issue of the fact that there were two. They decided to spend the evening in, so Jim popped around the corner to a nearby newsagent for a paper. Together they scanned the TV guide and agreed on a film.

There was a small hand basin in the corner of the room. Marti decided to freshen up while Jim, the perfect gentleman, buried his head in the newspaper. Marti turned on the taps and the water pipes rattled and rumbled around the entire building – so much so that she quickly turned them off again. She leant on the sink, laughing to herself. "One day I'm going to stay in the best hotel in town!"

As she examined her skin in the mirror, she could see Jim watching her closely. He blushed, realising he'd been caught and quickly ducked behind the sports pages.

He was definitely a cad, but quite loveable in his own inimitable fashion. Most of what he said and did was for show, a front he liked to hide behind. He was a survivor though, albeit a lone survivor, but Marti sensed his heart was in the right place and she was certainly more secure with him around. For the time being they needed each other.

"The film will be on in a minute." Marti heard the voice, but it was distant. She was dreaming again. She was far away on sunny shores, with a very special man in mind. He'd been there for a long time and occasionally she let him out. On being disturbed, however, she collected her images and neatly tucked them away in a safe place for another day.

"Burr..!" Marti shuddered, "it's a bit cold in here."

"Come and sit on the bed with me, we can keep each other warm – I promise..."

Marti stopped him. "Don't make promises you may not be able to keep." She winked; Jim frowned – resting his arm across the pillow. "You've got goose bumps, come and have a cuddle – the film's started."

Marti nestled beside him. He was warm and solid. Jim let his arm relax, dropping it loosely around her shoulders. It had been some time since Marti had been physically this close to a man but she felt quite safe in his embrace.

The film was a second-rate sci-fi movie and Marti, already sleepy, was soon having difficulty in keeping her eyelids propped open. She could sense herself helplessly drifting closer and closer to Jim until she laid her head on his chest. She could feel his heartbeat and the security of its rhythm made her more listless. She closed her eyes and re-opened her secret images. It was whilst in this warm sanctuary that she decided, for sure, that if she was careful and took her time, she could coax the boy in her dreams to come out.

The new job would provide the vehicle and she was confident in her ability to steer it to the crossroads. Unfortunately, there is always a price to pay and it would be at this junction that the fee would be levied.

The couple woke early, still in each others' arms and under cover. Marti couldn't recall actually getting into bed. Jim was still in a caring mood, kissing her gently. He could see she was a little disturbed by their close proximity. "Don't worry. I didn't take advantage of you."

"Oh – um, that's good, I think." Her voice wavered slightly as she pondered the correctness of his behaviour.

Jim raised himself slowly from the squishy mattress, stretched himself to full height with arms raised above his head and stumbled to the sink.

"Wow check' cotton boxers!" Marti blurted – followed by an immediate apology.

Thoughtfully, Jim rinsed his face with cold water; it seemed he had never before considered the attractiveness, or indeed, the non-attractiveness of a blokes underclothes?

They both washed dressed and headed down an old dark stained staircase to the basement breakfast room. The food was reasonable, there was plenty of it and they ate everything, not being sure where the next meal would come from. Afterwards they collected their few belongings and returned their room key to the desk. As they walked the city streets to Power Play's Head Office, Jim proclaimed that this was the last time they would have to do things on a shoe-string. Marti again warned him of the pit-falls of making such statements.

"A girl could back you into a corner if you persist."

"How do you know?" Jim retorted sharply then immediately remarked. "There's a lot of traffic."

"That's because it's a city." Marti was patronising, not a nice personality trait – a view Jim obviously shared as he gave her the sort of scowl that says 'Smart Ass.'

Marti and Jim were greeted by the Power Play staff and given an in-depth tour of operations. Introductions were made to those who would be providing back-up for their assignments and everybody made them feel extremely welcome. The editor was now ready to see them and they were shown into his office, a glazed-off corner of an otherwise open-plan suite.

Pre-season reports had already been compiled before the sudden demise of the previous crew, although it might have been useful for the newcomers to have been involved in their production. Some contact with teams and individuals would have been helpful. Being novices and strangers, both Marti and Jim felt it may be difficult to become involved and accepted by the F1 fraternity. However, as time did not permit such a luxury, they would have to wait and see what transpired in the competitive arena before crossing that bridge.

Plenty of information was provided as well as examples of the type of photography expected. A request for Marti's portfolio of previous work was made and she mumbled something about putting it in the post as soon as possible. They also met Andy who would be their co-ordinator at base and he provided his personal phone, fax and contact details which he assured them they could use at any time of the day or night. This was an important factor for on occasions, the time differences between countries would be great. Flight information and travel agendas would be posted to them during the week, prior to practice sessions which would normally begin on Thursday. Everything was made quite clear and it was really down to the pair of them to do the rest, initially by reading all the available data in an effort to gain as much knowledge as possible before they took off.

It was the travelling that inspired the pair most. Both relished the prospect of jetting around the world and imaginations could get carried away. Marti and Jim had to focus on the reality that they were expected to do a job and at the end of the day had to produce the goods. This daunting task intimidated them slightly and they were given a three race probationary period. If things didn't work out, at least they could say they had tried and no doubt this experience would prove invaluable.

On the train journey home, neither Marti nor Jim had much to say. It was all rather exotic and would take a while to sink in. Marti gazed at the landscape rushing past the window, which became more familiar as the engine progressed. The rhythm of the steel wheels in motion rocked the carriage gently. She imagined the Technicolor movie epics of the 1950s and could hear the pulsating twang of steel guitars, plucked in time with a back beat you couldn't lose.

The train soon slowed in its approach to their station and the drive home took a further twenty minutes. Marti kicked off her shoes, closing the back door with her heel; it was difficult to believe that in less than two weeks they would be flying off on their first official assignment. The destination was Mexico City and Marti immediately rushed to the porch for her atlas to make perfectly sure where she was going. In her mind, all her journeys had to be directly linked to home.

There was only one problem left to solve: work. Marti would have to resign and officially she was required to give one month's notice.

Marti couldn't rest all weekend. There would be questions

fired at her as soon as she walked through the door, due to the fact that she had taken Friday off without asking, so the ground was already rough. She felt guilty too, which astounded Jim: "I thought you hated the place!"

"Yes, but that's not the point."

Jim suggested that if she wasn't there they would soon get the message. His morals were abysmal at times and Marti shook her head disapprovingly, although her concerns went deeper. Jim was unashamedly capable of packing his bags and leaving at the drop of a hat and she wondered if this Romany streak was the reason for his lack of acquaintances. Not for the first time, Marti began to question Jim's reliability and felt it would be unwise to place too much faith in him.

The weekend dragged but when Monday arrived Marti was fully prepared for her confrontation with Mr. H., whom she regarded as a reasonable man despite his gruff exterior and mumbled words of derision.

In her anxiety to get things over with, Marti was prepared to leave home far too early and this would never do – she usually dashed in at a minute to nine. She scanned the living-room in search of something to occupy her spare time. In a corner, behind a small chair which Marti was in the throes of re-upholstering, she spied the old red Fender, it was dusty through neglect. Picking it up lovingly, she ran her fingers over the rusty strings. The sound was awful and made her cringe, even though it wasn't plugged in. Marti tuned it as best she could in its sorry state and began to play the few chords and changes which were the extent of her repertoire. Tearfully, she recalled hearing Robert play it so loudly that the horse brasses hanging over their beamed fireplace used to vibrate violently, sometimes even crashing to the floor. She wanted to give it a quick blast right now but, Jim was still sleeping. "Later," she promised herself, "later."

Marti glanced at the digital clock on the video. It was almost 08.30. She scribbled a note to Jim, in case he should stir and left the house. It was only a short trip into town but inevitably it was impossible to find a parking space anywhere other than at the top of the Park. It often occurred to her that if she'd had to walk up the hill to get to work, she would have packed it in long ago. She reached the main doors at five to nine, and rattled them vigorously to annoy the messenger, Mike.

The assembled members of staff had settled in their allotted positions and were busy making preparations for the day ahead. Mr. H. presided over operations from The Podium.

"Good morning," Marti said cheerfully.

The response to which was a grunt, emitted through a ginger moustache. Marti stared him right in the eye and he elaborated on his statement, "Where were you Friday?" His dialogue still lacked clarity but odd words could be recognised and some sense made.

Marti handed him an envelope but before he could open it, she blabbed "I'm leaving – today!"

Mr. H. took this to be a joke. "OK, 'bye then." He smiled quite endearingly as a ray of sunlight glinted off of a small balding patch at the back of his head.

"I mean it." Marti repeated herself with some sadness.

The general office was hushed, the silence only being broken when somebody shouted "Are you pregnant?"

Marti smiled wryly, "Highly unlikely," she thought.

As Marti continued to explain her circumstances, it became clear, even to Mr. H. that no amount of persuasion was going to change her mind. He knew she wasn't happy in her work as a secretary and she was only marginally good at it anyway. Finally he accepted her resignation, offering a slightly envious, congratulatory handshake whilst lifting his phone to set about the necessary calls to Human Resources in the city. Meanwhile, Marti leapt up stairs two at a time, to tell the girls her fantastic news.

As the day drew to a close, Marti began clearing her desk of all personal possessions. The clutter of the past was unbelievable. She took a sheet of pink copy paper, wrote a brief note and placed it in a white envelope. She sealed it, placed this envelope inside another and left it in the days post tray.

She had quite a spring in her step as she walked back to the car that evening, clutching a card containing gift vouchers which had been hurriedly organised by her department head. The steep incline proved no sweat. Two grey squirrels scurried across the path in front of her and she suddenly realised this would be her last hike through the park. Marti had no reservations about her decision; she now had the freedom she had promised herself for years. She did, however, experience some feelings of sorrow and would miss the girls, Alien's mammoth hugs and maybe a couple of others from time to time. Marti gave her shoulders a hefty shrug; it was as if a great burden had been lifted from them. She had struggled with her conscience every morning for the past two years, for she had had an abhorrent dislike of the new business techniques which had recently been introduced into the world of finance and commerce. She had also felt sadly disappointed at the way in which competitive bonus schemes, employed to increase productivity, had adversely affected the judgement of many of her colleagues. Marti had witnessed one too many cheap tricks to which a blind eye had been turned and had fallen victim to the system on occasions, when she felt it her duty to question the ethics of sales jargon and conduct. "It's policy" or "I've got kids to think about." Were favoured excuses, which although sounding plausibly admirable, didn't convince Marti of any virtue; she wondered if we should sacrifice our lives for our children or indeed, if our children were our lives?

Marti returned home just in time to see Jimbo staggering down her open-backed wooden stairs. "Hi!" she said in an up-tempo manner.

Jim rocked, still in a daze. "Oh – hello." His greeting was muffled by a wide yawn, followed after a pause with "How did it go? – you did pack it in, didn't you?"

Marti tormented him for a while by skirting around the subject. His jaw dropped open.

"Yeah of course I did. Mr. H. took it well. I'm out – free at last after thirteen years' service!"

Jim grinned gleefully, "Brilliant, just what I need – a loose woman!" He made a lunge for her, lifting her by the waist and one arm over his shoulder, fireman style. Marti screamed. "I can't breathe!" She was giggling and pounding his back to make him release her, which he did gracefully.

"Phew! – That's better," she gasped tidying her suit.

"Good – I'm hungry." Together they searched the fridge and whilst Marti prepared tea from the leftover chicken and some cheese and veg. that were tucked away on the bottom shelf. Jim reminded her that they were in the big time – in control of their own destinies. He put his arms around her again but Marti pulled away.

"Let's get some food in you – we've got loads to do before next week."

CHAPTER 4

Sure enough, one week later, their flight tickets and accommodation details dropped onto the door mat. Jim, whose behaviour on the whole had been very subdued since their return from London, now had the tickets in his hands and his enthusiasm increased dramatically. All of a sudden, it was Jim scrutinising the maps and Jim asking the questions. "What's the time difference in Mexico, Marti?"

How Marti was supposed to know this off the top of her head was beyond her. "Look in the front of the phone book – it'll tell you the time anywhere in the world."

"Umm..." Jim was impressed with this knowledge. There was a difference of six hours. "That means..." Jim concentrated on his battered stainless steel wrist watch. "Right now," he announced "it's 8.30 in the morning over there."

During the past week they had been dashing around the shops, collecting appropriate equipment. Jim had bought a portable tape recorder to assist with interviews. (It's easy these days, although somewhat impersonal. Just shove it in someone's face and the machine does the work.)

Marti was sitting in the lounge examining the contents of the large brown envelope from Power Play. Everything was there, including Press passes hung on red corded tape allowing admission to the Inner Sanctum. Marti held one to her chest in admiration. "Yes!" she said to herself with satisfaction. It was like winning a holiday and both were finding it difficult to keep hold of the fact that they were supposed to be working. Then the phone rang; Jim answered it. It was Andy asking for Marti's portfolio. Confidently he assured Andy that it was in the mail. "I took it to the post office myself!"

Marti flinched at his blatant fib, but Jim just hung up and laughed loudly.

Their departure at seven forty-five on Tuesday evening was from London Heathrow but it was an indirect route, stopping in New York for three hours and twenty minutes. In total, the time spent in the air was thirteen hours and in all honesty Marti and Jim found the flight a little tedious: even though films were shown, it was impossible to sleep in the cramped seats and the break in New York only prolonged the agony. There was insufficient time for sightseeing, so they had to remain in the departure lounge – one can only digest a certain amount of duty free.

Back on the plane, it was hard to relax – Jim asked Marti if she had the passports for the eighth time in succession, so to put his mind at rest once and for all, she took their flight bag from the overhead locker and physically placed the documents in his hands:

"You look after them!"

Jim declined her offer on the grounds of his irresponsible nature.

At last the pilot's laboured American voice came over the radio announcing their expected arrival time. There were only another fifteen minutes of the journey remaining and this news came as a great relief.

The approach to Mexico Airport was quite breathtaking. Beautiful mountains, sculpted and moulded by thousands of years of changing ethereal powers, loomed on either side of the aeroplane as it descended. The pilot's landing of the craft, however, left less to be desired. He simply dropped it and its cargo on the runway and slammed on the brakes. All the passengers lurched forward in their seats, straining on their safety belts and glaring at each other in silent disapproval.

The first thing that hit everyone on disembarkation was the atmosphere – dry and choking. It soon became apparent why this city is said to have the poorest air quality in the world. Surely though this had not always been the case questioned Marti, as she and Jim squeezed past the front seat of a two-door cab to suffer the short trip to their hotel, which was an adventure in itself.

Mexico City, built on Aztec rubble, has its roots buried deep in the heart of an ancient metropolis, situated at the centre of a once great lake. Unfortunately, only a few canals and tributaries now remain but they are awash with brightly painted boats, busying themselves for pleasure and gain. Historically the land of advanced civilizations such as the Toltec's and others, it has in the 20th century been invaded by the V.W. Beetle which, apparently is still produced here. Millions of the grubby, battered bugs scurry around the dusty streets, providing transportation day and night.

En route, they passed the Aristos Hotel, of late a grand establishment and one still popular amongst the Formula One fraternity with its heavily employed helipad, conveniently placed on the roof top.

Marti's eyes were becoming sore from the strain of trying to absorb every piece of information available. Mexico is a colourful city, to say the least, and as their lime green mechanical beetle paused momentarily at traffic lights, she spotted a dubious notice, crookedly fixed to the front entrance of a modern hotel. The sign boasted of the structure's singular ability to withstand earthquakes. Marti chuckled, "Useful in this part of the world," she thought as the taxi lunged forward, continuing its battle for command of the road, "but unnerving if one was not a resident of such a sturdy edifice."

The local sense of humour was akin to hers but, by the time they reached their allotted accommodation, Marti felt less jovial. In fact, she was decidedly hot and bothered – not to mention grimy from the effects of the all-engulfing fumes.

The rooms were reasonably equipped and had adjoining showers. Marti checked out these facilities by turning on the taps. "Peaceful," she thought deciding that this was where she wanted to be and very soon! While she was unpacking her minimal luggage, she noticed a leaflet on the bedside cabinet. Flopping across the bed on her back, Marti began to read the Do's and Don'ts. The low-down on the water condition was not impressive. She contemplated her planned ablutions but, doubting her ability to endure five days of this intense heat without a shower, went ahead with her original strategy – "Hang the consequences!"

It was mid-afternoon and Marti was relaxing, feeling she would need to conserve her energy, she suggested Jim do the same. But Jim had recreational therapies of his own in mind. The couple agreed to meet for dinner at seven thirty.

Jim sauntered along the street – from every bar, music could be heard echoing forth, as guitars of every size and description were strummed with a vigorous passion. 'Feeling lucky', Jim was sure of some 'Tidy Trim'. Basing his theory on intuition and the assumption that there was bound to be an element of fortune seekers in close proximity to any available or willing Formula One notables, it came as no surprise when he stumbled across a group of native girls in a nearby cafe.

Jim ordered a drink – some kind of bottled beer appeared before him, at the sight of which he recoiled. The beverage was however chilled to perfection. Jim pulled up a stool and positioned himself in a predatory fashion at the end of the bar. He watched and waited, cunningly ensuring that the possibility of competition was limited. Once satisfied, he proceeded to carry out his operation.

"Hi, mind if I join you? I'm from England." Jim could be utterly charming and his choice from a wide repertoire of one-liners was carefully considered.

"You know..." He began with a well rehearsed patter of how he was the luckiest bloke in Mexico. Some of the females giggled hysterically, and Jim clinically erased at least one from his mental list. Not that he was opposed to a 'bird of little brain', but he could not handle one that constantly giggled and cooed.

"So what makes you think you're so lucky?" This response came from a dusky beauty in a low-necked white T-shirt. Her voice was deep with a smoky quality evoking attention, Jim moved around the table, making room for himself close to her youthful body.

"I'm sitting here with you, aren't I?"

The girl gave him a lingering examination. "What are you doing here exactly – have you come for the race?"

"Funny you should mention that." Jim was curious. Her English was good, almost too good – he paused before continuing his sentence. "I'm actually a reporter."

Without shame Jim fabricated a vast experience and knowledge of the motor racing world and its various personalities, name-dropping to infer intimate relationships.

Each of the girls was, for varying reasons, captivated by his outrageous tale which ended nonchalantly with: "It's just a job."

Jim had the pick of the crop and arrogantly indulged himself in their infatuation, even though he had long since made his choice. "So what are you drinking, Angel?" Angelina, the dusky beauty was somewhat taken aback by the fact that he knew her name and enquired how he had come by such knowledge. Jim flashed a piratical grin. "I work for the press."

No further explanation was apparently required. Angel relaxed. "I'll have whatever you're drinking – thank you."

Angel's companions were becoming increasingly aware from Jim's actions and the view of the back of his head that he had hit his target and their welfare was no longer of importance. Some spiteful remarks were hurled at Angelina whilst Jim was at the bar and her friends shuffled their seats in disapproval of her selfishness. At this point Jim returned with two bottles of beer.

"Oh! You're not leaving so soon are you?" Sarcasm was clearly a tone understood in any language, and the exiting female group jeered as they dispersed onto the street.

"Well, now then." Jim moved closer. "Do you enjoy racing?"

"It's my first time," she replied gazing into his liquid blue eyes. Jim coughed.

"Perhaps I could give you a few tips." He drew nearer, planting a light kiss on Angel's cheek. Noticing that she was again without refreshment, Jim offered another drink, suggesting she might like to try something more exotic. "I know a particularly soothing cocktail."

The conversation was moving a little too fast for a girl of such tender years, and despite the fact that Angel's main objective had little or nothing to do with any enthusiasm for motor sport, she was nervous and missing the support of her pals.

Jim returned from the bar precariously balancing a large glass which resembled a bowl of fruit rather than a drink. Coloured umbrellas and novelty swizzle sticks protruded in all directions and Angel clearly wondered where to start, if at all, with such a concoction. But she got stuck in anyway. Jim watched as the glass emptied, and confident that his endeavours would pay off, broached the subject of accommodation. Angel willingly offered an address: "It's only a few blocks from here." She hiccoughed.

Jim's secret recipe was taking effect, Angel admitted to feeling "a bit squiffy."

Jim leered as unsteadily she rose to her feet. "Nice ass," he thought to himself "I think I had better take you home." He offered his arm in support; they staggered the few hundred yards along an uneven sidewalk to a gloomy block of rented rooms. As they boarded the lift, which surprisingly, was still operational, Jim asked if she was sharing the so-called apartment. Angel giggled. The lift jolted as it began to move. Angel lost her footing and fell back against the wall. She smiled provocatively. "What if I am? Can't you cope with more than one at a time?"

Jim was riled by her inference – placing his left hand over her shoulder, the other around her petite waist, he pinned her to the side of the lift, their lips met and he caressed the edges of her mouth with his tongue. The lift shuddered to an abrupt halt. Angel rocked as Jim pulled back, casually brushing her pert breast with pin-point accuracy.

Stepping out into the corridor, Angel fumbled in her handbag for the key which she dutifully availed Jim of. The room was small and stuffy but, much to Angel's delight, unoccupied. Before their brief encounter in the lift, she had half hoped that one of her girlfriends might have returned early, but not now, Jim's flippancy had made her feel quite the opposite. She wanted more and was already moist with anticipation.

Jim stripped off his faded denim shirt and loosened the top button of his jeans. Angel watched as his masculine form was revealed. She had not been with anyone like this before. Jim took a step towards her. In one swift, well-practiced manoeuvre he took her in his arms, slipped his hands beneath her shirt and lifted it clean over her head. Angel's long dark locks fell across her face but this was quickly swept away. He cupped her breasts firmly whilst guiding her back toward the bed and as Angel's calves made contact with the mattress, her legs buckled. Jim unzipped her tightly fitting shorts and slid them and her panties over her hips and down her glistening thighs. He stood above her and dropped the blue jeans, there wasn't anything else. Lowering himself to the floor, Jim pressed his palms firmly between her knees and parting her legs; he advanced between her soft tissues. Letting his hands run riot over her rounded belly Angel let out a whimper as he entered her body with some force. He pushed again and Angel begged for deeper penetration – again Jim buried himself deeper and deeper until his final thrust brought a rigid ecstasy that left Angel gasping.

The entire act was over in minutes and having taken his pleasure, Jim's brain clicked back into gear. "Shit!" he yelled, "What time is it?"

Angel, still moaning, rolled over in ignorant bliss. Jim grabbed at the watch on his wrist, to his horror it read seven forty-two. "Christ! Marti." Leaping from the bed, he scrambled into his clothes and dashed for the door.

Angel meanwhile had raised herself on her elbows to get a last glimpse. "Can I see you again?"

"Sure!" shouted Jim as he disappeared down the hallway. He was still buttoning his shirt in the lift, much to the disgust of two elderly ladies who had got in with him.

Jimbo crashed through the hotel entrance, leaving its doors swinging in his wake to find Marti in the lobby. She was furious.

"Where the hell have you been?" Jim was about to explain when Marti retracted her question. "On second thoughts don't answer that – your face says it all."

"You can tell by my face?" Jim was surprised and just a little disbelieving of her intuition. He then began to rock playfully from side to side, hands in pockets and grinning. "I'm famished!"

"So what's new?" Marti said glancing down. "You might want to zip up your jeans too, before you terrify the restaurant staff."

The couple sat down to dinner and Marti decided that a few ground rules should be set out before they proceeded any further. She didn't care what or who he did, but pointed out how thoughtless it was of him to leave her hanging around in a strange place. "There's nothing worse than waiting for someone," she said dejectedly. "All sorts of horrible things were going through my mind!"

Jim could see that she was upset and understood her reasons. "I'm sorry."

Marti accepted his apology. "It's OK – this time. Just don't promise me anything – if I'm not expecting you I won't worry for you either."

Jim freely agreed to the rules and offered no excuses in his defence. He looked glumly at the plate which he had just been scraping clean.

"You're priceless!" Marti quipped, hopelessly shaking her head. They finished their meal and retired to their respective quarters. An early start was expected in the morning.

Marti changed her jeans for something loose and cool; the dry heat made her feel listless. She pulled up a chair in front of the open window which overlooked a bustling square – the perfect backdrop for some people watching. Making herself comfortable, with one leg draped over the arm of the chair, she settled down to dream.

Initially her mind was drawn to the following day's events. Apprehensively she wondered what new experiences might be in store. She was nervous – she knew 'he' would be there. But then, 'he' was hardly likely to notice her with hoards of beautiful women milling around – not to mention the ever-tracking press. Now there's a peculiar notion. Marti sniggered as it occurred to her that she would be both one and the other. Well, perhaps not so beautiful, she thought catching her reflection in the dusty window pane.

Resting her chin in the palm of her hand, Marti gazed longingly at the world outside. Dusk was falling. In the distance she saw a dark stranger; his wavy, unkempt hair fluttered in the warm breeze. He wanted for nothing – yet an empty sadness filled his soul and Marti sensed that a great many of life's simple pleasures had been missed. For sure, he was a loner, openly admitting that he liked to be alone, but there is a substantial difference between, *alone and lonely*. Marti enjoyed her own company and was never at a loss to find a means of entertainment, but she usually had at least one confidant to trust – a sanctuary surely we all need, no matter how strong our sense of self-perception is.

Marti knew. She didn't know how, but she knew in her heart, that inside his sturdy physique there was fear. He was lost, hurt and extremely vulnerable. Marti continued to follow the tragic figure. She wanted desperately to hold him, believing that a person needed to be loved most when they deserved it least. She stirred stiffly in the wicker chair, unsure whether she had been sleeping or not. "Ouch!" Well her leg was asleep, if nothing else.

Marti hobbled across the room trying to resume circulation to her one, numb limb and climbed into bed taking her stranger with her. Her dreams were sweet, yet crammed with detailed, facts and images. As she cradled a new born babe, the Spring Equinox dawned but the brightest of our night's stars was still clearly visible. One in particular, high in the east, drew her attention as she swooned over the warm bundle clasped close to her chest. A shock of soft dark hair brushed his forehead, forming a natural quiff, just left of centre, which would be apt to annoy him in later years. His nose was a little wide and his ears stuck out a little too much but he had the most beautiful, deep chestnut eyes and to Martha he was perfect. He had long spidery fingers which seemed to fascinate him as he stretched and curled them, gripping at her clothing with an urgency that sought maternal, protection.

Home was a farm. The land belonged to her father but the area was too vast for one man to work and had been divided into rented small-holdings. One of those plots was a gift on her wedding day. She was sixteen.

Marti woke with that strange sensation of confusion. For a few moments, as her head focused on the day in hand, she was unable to decide whether she had been dreaming, if this was a past reality or even if it was now?

That morning, Jim and Marti began their work in earnest, arriving at the Hermanos Rodriguez Circuit just before eight o'clock. They were sporting Press passes but as Jim braked suddenly at the main entrance; both had that feeling of uncertainty as to being allowed access. They could well imagine an official rejecting their documents and turfing them out. It would not have been a first for Jim, who had been thrown out of far less desirable joints. Marti also! On parking Jim immediately wondered off, leaving Marti to collect her camera equipment from the boot of the car. "Charming!" she thought purposefully hanging back. Then just as Jim was opening a small wire gate to another enclosure, she sharply tapped him on the shoulder. "You can't go in there!" He stopped dead in his tracks, turned on her and began a tirade of abuse whilst clutching the Press Pass hung around his neck. Marti beamed, delighted by his reactions.

"I'd like to clip you round the ear at times!" In jest Jim motioned a swipe at her, but only the wind made contact.

It was early, but there was already a great deal of activity and most of the pit garages were open for business. Although the faint smell of recently fried bacon and eggs was still detectable. Marti and Jim spotted Philip Rheutemanne, an up-and-coming German driver in his first season but he quickly fled back-stage. Marti felt awkward – there was a distinct feeling of apathy from many of the teams. Together they walked from one end of the pit lane to the other. Jim looked at Marti:

"This isn't easy – where do you start?"

The couple sat apprehensively on the wall, in the hope of catching sight of some other Press people. As luck would have it their wait was not prolonged, for a middle-aged man sporting a white trilby, perched jauntily on his head to shield his eyes, stumbled into the garage opposite them. Marti and Jim scurried after him. The man walked up to a mechanic and bluntly asked him what he was doing.

Simple! – Marti and Jim hovered at close quarters, trying their best to be inconspicuous. The mechanic however, was unwilling to divulge any information and made this clear with a stream of rapidly fired foreign expletives. As the un-offended journalist turned to vacate the premises, he bumped right into Marti and Jim, who were only a few feet behind him.

"Sorry," they blurted, simultaneously, almost tripping over each other in their haste to get out of his way.

The experienced hack immediately realised their intentions and called them back. "Wait a minute, you two!" he shouted in a Cockney accent.

Marti suggested that they ought to stop but Jim urged her to walk on briskly, pretending that they hadn't heard him. They were almost running as they rounded the corner from the pit lane. Taking refuge in a small temporary cafe, Jim suggested a coffee.

"Good idea." Marti agreed.

As they took a seat and collected themselves, the gentleman appeared in the chain-linked curtained, doorway.

"Keep your head down," Jim said furtively, "it's him!"

The man went up to the counter and ordered a large mug of tea. He scanned the room beadily. Surely he wouldn't approach them? In the hope that he would not the pair fixed their view in the opposite direction.

"Mind if I join you?" He gave a rather chesty cough and tilted his hat.

"Err – well – umm." Jim stuttered.

"Not at all." Marti pointed to a spare seat feeling perhaps that a friendly approach was best.

Jim grimaced. "What the hell are you saying?"

"Not a bad morning," the man said jovially, "but it's going to be very hot later." He removed his hat, uncovering a few wispy strands of hair and waiving it at them as if to beg the reason for his attire, clumsily plonked himself next to Jim who flinched.

Nervously Marti continued the conversation on the subject of the weather, but the man interrupted her to introduce himself. "My name's Jack." He paused for a moment, pending a corresponding reply, and when none was forthcoming he thrust a hand across the table announcing himself again: "Jack Brenner."

Marti acknowledged his greeting and he continued to explain his identity. "I cover various motor sports for several newspapers back home."

Jim eventually looked up from the table, realising that some form of etiquette was required, and introduced himself and Marti. The two men shook hands. Jack was reluctant to let go and spoke with a broad smile. "I tried to stop you in the pit lane but you appeared to be in a hurry." Both Marti and Jim were embarrassed by their naive actions. "Typical Brits," Jack said, "We're all the same you know – can't do a thing before that first cuppa."

After slurping his tea through a greying bristly beard, Jack rattled on. He was a true Londoner and well suited to his work.

"I haven't seen you before – have I?"

Marti felt honesty was the best policy. "No – we're new at this game."

Jack laughed aloud. "I'd never have guessed!" He joked. "You were eavesdropping – weren't you my luvs?"

The fledglings admitted their crime. "It's a good job you picked on me – a lot of others would give you a real hard time. You see the trick is to try and squeeze out that little tit-bit of information that nobody else has – you'll do well to remember that." Jack had worked in media for longer than he cared to remember and was no longer protective of his abundance of skills.

Marti and Jim thanked him for being so understanding and he stood up to leave replacing his hat before venturing into the glare of the sun. "I must be off, the drivers will be arriving soon and they're the ones that the general public really want to hear from."

"Phew!" Marti let the tension go from her shoulders.

"He was OK, quite helpful in fact," remarked Jim, harrying Marti to finish her drink. "I think we'd better start afresh, don't you?"

Marti, gulping the last of her coffee, nodded in agreement.

On their return to the pit lane which, with first practice due to commence at nine, was now a hive of industry, they noticed a tight huddle of journalists clamouring around one section of the pit wall. As they tentatively approached, the reason for the fuss became clear. The reigning World Champion, Marcus Veridico, had decided to give an impromptu press conference. Jim quickly switched on his tape recorder, but being a late arrival and at the back of the crowd, he was fearful that his microphone wouldn't pick up Marcus' comments.

"Listen hard to everything he says!" In his excitement Jim let the words out too loud and was probably on everyone's tape. However, it caused a distraction for a few seconds as the hacks turned upon the culprit. Jim offered a mute apology whilst Marti, ever the opportunist, seized the opening and, with the assistance of a firm hand from Marcus, scrambled onto the wall beside him.

"That was a good move," he said quietly as he gazed into her eyes. Marti smiled nervously, he was delectably calm and for a second a multitude of sins rushed through her mind in imagination of a few moves she fancied making with him. Captured by his charisma, Marti felt that nobody else existed.

"Thanks," the word came out with one breath. "Do you mind?" Marti pointed at the camera.

"For sure." A thin smile traced his lips and she clicked...

Marti and Jim were thrilled with their first interview, particularly in view of the fact that it was with the main man. Unfortunately, the tape was hardly audible.

"Not to worry," said Marti. Taking a small, tatty notebook from her rucksack she began jotting down a few key points. Jim watched attentively, impressed by her adaptability. "I am a secretary, remember? Besides, I had to have a good memory, because my shorthand was never up to scratch."

"You used to be a secretary." Jim gave a sigh of relief, suggesting that they go and see who else was about.

This time as they wandered about the pit lane they felt more confident.

"We ought to find a British driver," prompted Marti.

The great British hope was David Westwood who drove for the Javelin team, themselves a British contingent based in Surrey. Marti recalled seeing their garage earlier, at the far end of the lane, so they made their way along the line, being conscious at all times of the need to be looking and listening. Disappointingly, David was '*not available for comment.*' The mechanics seemed peevishly guarded and Marti and Jim sensed that they were not welcome at this particular moment in time.

Having collected what they thought was a fair amount of information, and as the sun was by now, 11.30am, very warm indeed, they decided to take a lunch break. There were so many kiosks and refreshment tents with little tables and chairs set out like make-shift patios, that the choice was difficult. Each table was equipped with a brightly coloured umbrella and Marti and Jim sought shade under one of these. Marti ushered Jim towards the table nearest a busy hospitality suite. "You're getting into this," he muttered deviously.

They were as close as possible. "I'll get the beers in." Jim always moved swiftest when in the vicinity of a bar. Marti sat quietly, absorbing her surroundings. It was unbelievable, dozens of luxury motor homes lined the tarmac to the rear of the garages all with aerials, satellite dishes and goodness knows what else attached, and each embossed with its own sponsors' logo and team coloured canopies, pinned and painted on all sides. '*Another world.*' No expense had been spared to accommodate their respective fast and famous stars. Marti knew that there was money in motor racing but, until seen from inside the fence, it's impossible to equate just how much 'dosh' is involved.

Jimbo returned with the well-appreciated drinks. "It's packed – and the price!"

"I'll bet – look at this lot next door." Marti nodded in the direction of the fancy mobile homes.

"Wow!" Jim peered morosely through the fence; shaking the wire, he said bitterly, "Is this to keep them in or us out?"

Our intrepid duo watched the world scurry by as catering staff and attendants fussed endlessly over their appointed dignitaries. Judging by the health warnings carried on the local food and water, Marti hoped that the teams had supplied their own nourishment to minimise the possibility of any internal upsets.

Jim was transfixed by the hospitality suites. Marti waved her hand in front of his face. He jumped slightly, truculently advising her that there was some, "Tidy trim in there."

"Perhaps I should tell them to build a higher fence," Marti said.

"It wouldn't work." She tried not to smile because it only encouraged Jim further, but she couldn't help herself.

Suddenly Marti spotted David Westwood and he was coming straight towards them. Neither had noticed it, but the suite next to them was for the Javelin team and sponsors and was obviously Westwood's destination. 'How could they be so dull?' Marti quickly set up her camera, testing for light and distance on the crowd in front of the unit. David was escorted to a table reasonably close by.

Westwood, on seeing Marti with camera at the ready, posed arrogantly. "Yuck," Marti gagged, "get me a bucket." They were about to go on their way when they heard raucous cheers of adulation from the two gentlemen with whom David was conversing.

"Perhaps we'll have another drink," Jim suggested.

It transpired that young David had only just arrived at the circuit, having unfortunately been delayed by 'a couple of blond bits with legs up to ...' No wonder his team were a mite tetchy this morning. Marti and Jim stayed long enough to get the gist of the previous night's conquests. Naturally, enthralled by Mr. Westwood's account of events, Jim wished to remain for longer, but Marti felt the information probably wasn't relevant for a motor racing magazine. Or maybe it was? It might even improve sales, appealing to a wider audience! Perhaps she should suggest this to the Editor on their return? Marti's mind was now going off on another tangent altogether. "Get back on track!"

For some reason, Jimbo suddenly became despondent and Marti enquired of his reasons. "I want to be on the other side of the fence."

She clutched hold of his arm affectionately. "Come on," she said leading him from temptation, "I'm sure you'll find a way – I have faith in you."

"Have you?" Jim grinned impishly, and admitted to having mentally noted a few chassis numbers in case an opportunity should present itself over the weekend.

The couple studied the sleek, single seater cars as they zapped round and round the track with their paintwork glinting in the afternoon sun. Marti's thoughts were returning to the hospitality suite. "Do you reckon any of the 'upper crust' is actually interested in motor racing?" she asked.

Jim scathingly replied: "Pretty unlikely, I doubt that half of them know one end of a car from the other."

He then got up and announced that he was going 'walkabout'.

"I'll come with you." Marti was scrabbling to her feet when she realised that her company was not required. "Oh – OK then, shall I wait for you, or meet you back at the hotel later?"

They arranged to meet in the evening; Marti had the car keys and Jim said he would make his own way. From the speed with which he took off across the gravel, it was obvious Marti had unnecessarily detained him with her questioning.

The reason for Jim's sudden disappearing act was that he had espied two smartly dressed young women from the Javelin team's HQ. He was anxious not to lose them in the crowd, and caught sight of them again on the stairs to the main grandstands' VIP Viewing enclosure. Jim followed, flashing his press documents he managed to bribe his way past the Mexican official on the gate, who understood very little English and was actually probably about twelve years of age. Jim took up his position, one row behind the ladies, and lay in wait. Both girls were extensively adorned with shimmering metal and stones of all colours and sizes. Jim listened attentively to every syllable uttered, awaiting the opportunity to pounce.

"Who's driving car number 8?" the blonde enquired of the brunette in a rather posh plummy accent.

Jim was in there like a shot: "Roberto Pasccari, he's Italian."

"Oh! – thank you," the blonde lent back, "is it a Ferrari he's driving?"

"Yes!"

The blonde again: "Do you know a lot about this sport?"

"Oh well, you know, a bit." Jim feigned lack of interest in the racing, preferring instead to change the subject.

"What's your name?" It was a direct approach and one he was well versed in. Over the years he had got away with it and in some respects it projected his basic honesty. Jim never made any secret of the fact that he was trying to pick a girl up nor did he hide his reasons for doing so.

The blonde introduced herself as Andrea, pointing to her friend, who had not said a word and was probably hoping that if she ignored Jim he'd disappear into thin air. After a short embarrassing silence, Andrea nudged her companion and giggled, still no response.

"This is Stephanie, we're sisters."

"This could be interesting," thought Jim as he clinically studied each girl individually and then in comparison to each other but, he was at a loss to find a likeness. Pointing this curiosity out, Jim finally received a response from Stephanie.

"No!" she snapped, "Mummy gets bored every once in a while."

Jim was wickedly intrigued. "Perhaps I could meet Mummy sometime then?"

Andrea giggled in amusement, but Stephanie's malign expression immediately dissuaded Jim from pursuing the topic of 'Mummy' any further – for now at least?

"So who's your favourite driver?" asked Jim chirpily.

Again, it was Andrea who replied: "Roberto."

"Thought it might be – I can tell you like a bit of dark meat."

Jim had Andrea eating out of his sticky hands. She had a certain coyness and persistently swept her long straight hair from her face, tossing her head backwards as she ran a set of perfectly manicured fingernails through it with child-like nonchalance.

Stephanie, on the other hand, was defiantly unimpressed.

"I'm going to see if Daddy's back yet."

This idea seemed to unsettle Andrea; she tugged at Stephanie in an attempt to persuade her to stay. "Don't go yet, it's only a bit of fun." Stephanie obstinately brushed her sister aside and left with a great flurry.

Without her sister's domination, Andrea appeared less nervous. Jim slid onto the seat next to her. "Is she older than you?"

"Yes," she snarled followed by a confiding outburst. "She's so up-tight about everything all the time and she's so self-righteous you just wouldn't believe it."

Stephanie was definitely 'Daddy's girl.' In his eyes she could do no wrong and she was therefore protected by all his might. Andrea was the one who bore the full brunt of his considerable wrath.

Jim stayed with Andrea for a while and chatted about anything that came into his head. She was quite interested in the racing, unlike most of her type, and was keen to learn more. They felt comfortable together and were enjoying each other's company so Andrea invited Jim back to her father's hospitality tent. Now this of course had been Jim's original objective but, having been exposed to a brief family history, his initial instinct was to refuse the offer. In fact, in past situations of such complexity he would already have fled for the hills. But he felt a growing affection for Andrea that was totally alien to him.

"Please," she begged alluringly. Jim, swallowed up by her large sapphire blue eyes, succumbed to her request, agreeing open mouthed to escort her.

Inside the suite, Jim felt acutely conspicuous; in truth he was way out of his depth. For a start, all the blokes were in designer gear and he was clad in torn Levi's and a faded black T-shirt with "Carpenters know all the angles," pasted across his chest.

He started to speak: "Which..." His throat seemed to swell,

strangling the words. A lack of lubrication was evident and he coughed several times before being able to proceed, and even then the pitch of his voice was highly strained.

Jim wanted to be sure of her father's identity, so as to be prepared for any confrontation that might arise. He had a sneaking suspicion that 'Daddy' could be none too pleasant a chap if upset.

"He's by the bar, he drinks a lot," Andrea replied to Jim's eventual question. Jim noticed that Stephanie was with her father, playing the part of the devoted daughter like a real pro. Daddy was bigger than Jim had first imagined both in stature and in the fact that he was the Top Dog in this outfit, a point which was clearly demonstrated by the way everyone in his proximity kowtowed to his every word and movement.

Jim tried to usher Andrea as far away from her father as possible; he was also not keen on Stephanie seeing them together. It was too late, however. She was gliding across the boarded floor toward them. Jim felt a shiver run down his spine.

"Hello Andrea." Her tone was coldly demeaning: "I see you have returned and – oh look, you have your new friend with you, how nice. What's his name again? I never did quite catch it."

"That's because you didn't have the courtesy to ask."

Jim, although faintly attracted by the girls' exchange of words, wished the ground would open up and swallow him. "These two are never right," he thought.

"Come and meet Daddy," Stephanie hissed.

Jim was sure this wasn't a good idea. "No – um, it's OK, he looks to be tied up at the moment, and in any case I really must be going, I'm already late for a very important appointment." Jim was running low on excuses although Marti did flash through his brain.

Meanwhile, amidst his ramblings, Stephanie had beckoned her father, whose formidable figure was now encroaching on their space.

He was a tall man of heavy build like that of an ex-rugby player with silver-grey hair cut a little too short, as though he had just stepped out of the barber's and wished he'd never gone in. His carved granite features were cold and unwelcoming.

"Hum," he grunted, "where have you been?" His question

was directed at Andrea – Jim didn't appear to exist in any shape or form. The interrogation continued.

"Why didn't you come back with your sister?" Before she could answer, Daddy fixed his hostile glare on Jim. Not a single muscle in his face moved. Daddy probed further: "Is he the reason?"

Andrea was frantically trying to appease her father and save Jim from further emasculation.

"Come on Daddy," she smiled sweetly, "I only asked him back for a drink (which Jim never got), he has to go now anyway, he has work to do."

"Hum." This second grunt seemed to come from the pit of the old man's stomach. "Work!" he jeered, "a waster like him!" The old man flicked a gnarled hand at Jim's chin; he braced himself to check his natural reactions. "They're all after the same thing, my girl, and they're not getting it!"

Andrea tried pathetically to argue in Jim's defence. Her disobedience enraged her father further and he raised a fist to her face.

Jim was about to step in, but decided enough was enough, he was off. Cutting his afternoon's recreational schedule short, he said his goodbyes to anyone who was listening and made a hasty retreat.

Andrea chased after him. Close to tears, she apologised profusely for getting him involved in such an awful scene. Jim took her hand, squeezing it gently. "Maybe I'll see you again, tomorrow or sometime."

Jim eventually found Marti, after some time searching, sitting on the pit wall, happily scribbling with pencil and pad. He had a job to get to her, as access to this area was limited this late in the day, even to journalists, or maybe especially to journalists.

"What are you doing here?"

Marti was bemused. "What do you mean?" Jim explained the difficulties he'd encountered on gaining access. "But I've been here for ages," she said with surprise, "nobody has bothered me – anyway, how come you're back so soon?" Jim conveniently let her question pass him by.

Marti had been quietly sketching the scenery and as she hadn't been poking her nose into anyone's business, nobody had thought to ask what she was up to. But while she may not have been noticeably prying, she had been keeping an ear to the ground and had picked up snippets of conversations from passersby, which concerned her. 'He's not on the ball,' was one? 'He's not interested this season,' was another. Marti had focused her attention on one man in particular. He seemed to distance himself more than most, and Marti perceived a highly toxic mix of emotional turmoil bubbling within his insular framework. She detected a sense of failure, uncertainty, and a weariness in his body which suggested that he was not ready for this race – it had come upon him too soon. However due to the fact that Jim had now gained entrance to the pit lane by revealing Marti's presence to track officials, the pair were soon ousted.

"What happened to you this afternoon then?" Marti waited for the rundown and the now-familiar grin that he would flash whilst recalling his conquests.

"Oh God – you won't believe it!" Jim gave a heavy sigh, burying his head in his hands.

"Try me," she chirped, expectantly.

Jim traced his jaw line with a finger of unaccustomed seriousness. "Yeah, yeah," knowing exactly what she was thinking. "You'll be surprised to learn that I didn't get laid."

'Was he ill, or something?' She thought, 'what if it's the water?' – Marti offered him the car keys which he declined. *Shock horror!* As she drove back to their hotel, Jim proceeded to tell the tale of the two sisters and Daddy – "There's something weird about that guy." Jim was sure of it.

Later that evening, a splendid reception had been organised for sponsors and press alike. Marti and Jim donned their glad rags to attend, though Marti was sceptical of her choice of attire. Back home whilst packing, the thought of being glam hadn't really occurred to her. But she had stuffed into her case a white, cotton halter-neck frock, which, with the aid of a hurriedly purchased, multicoloured scarf and matching flower from the hotel boutique, she used to decorate her waist and secure her wayward hair. Jim was still in jeans but had acquired a jacket. The bash was held in a large function room, something along the lines of a 1930s Hollywood set; which though still regal was a little the worse for wear. The couple mingled with the jet set, champagne flowed in abundance and every other person seemed to be a waiter offering another glass.

Suddenly, Marti felt a clammy hand on her shoulder. It was old Jack. "Boy! Am I glad to see you." Jack and Marti got chatting, but Jimbo had clocked Andrea.

He surveyed the immediate area in case any undesirables were lurking and, satisfied that the coast was clear, made his excuses and set off to beat his way through the gaggling 'haw-haws' and ever eagle-eyed press. As if to add spice to this hazardous journey, Jim collected two, full glasses of champagne whilst still in transit. Just as he was nearing his quarry, David Westwood showed up on the scene.

"Damn it!" By the looks of Andrea's warm greeting of the young driver, they were obviously well acquainted. Jim could feel his hackles rising and viewed the new 'speed king' as an instant rival. To aggravate matters, Westwood had also brought refreshments, but he had a magnum of champagne and two glasses. Jim stared mournfully at the remaining contents of the vessels in his hands. He frowned, downed one, dumped the empty on the next passing tray and prepared for battle. His head was spinning. "I'll bet Daddy doesn't come crawling out of the woodwork to tell this smooth bastard to piss off." It was uncharacteristic of Jim to adopt such a high moral stance, normally he would simply pick up the next bit of skirt available but something had definitely got under his skin in this relationship and he was rattled by the uncomfortable stab of jealousy. There was a little voice in his head telling him that she wasn't going to get away with this.

Jim's collar appeared to be getting smaller. He adjusted his borrowed bow-tie and confidently moved in. "Hi Andrea; Daddy about?"

The poor girl turned scarlet. "Oh – Jim," she stuttered, "I didn't expect to see you here."

Jim nodded courteously in acknowledgement of Westwood's presence. "No. Well, I have a habit of popping up at the most *unexpected* times."

At this point David, who had been affording Jim glares of degradation, butted in: "Do you have a problem with this guy darling?" He put his arm protectively around Andrea, which incensed Jim further. He was livid. "If so – I could sort it out for you."

Jim wasn't totally stupid. "Oh yeah! – What do you wanna do, step outside maybe? That would make a terrific headline on the eve of the season's first race!"

The two squared up to each other and those in close proximity edged away, sensing a confrontation. Andrea stepped between them, begging that they calm the situation. Jim however, continued to goad Westwood into throwing the first punch but realising Jim's intentions, Westwood backed off.

Throughout this fiasco, Jim had kept his wits about him, making a point of knowing, at all times, exactly where Daddy was. The hostile vibrations by now had reached him and he was making his way towards the fracas. An aisle opened up through the guests as the big man advanced. Jim had time for one last menacing jibe. "You'd better watch yourself from now on," he snarled, and turning threateningly to Andrea, added "I'll see you again!"

Before Westwood could retaliate Jim vanished, disappearing into the sea of faces, all of which had been focused on the turbulent trio.

As Andrea tried to keep track of Jim in the crowd, she felt the forceful hand of her father grip her upper arm. "Having some trouble, my dear?"

"No!" she replied abruptly.

"Ah – David Westwood I believe?"

"That's right, Sir."

'Smarmy little git,' Andrea thought to herself.

The indications were that the two men had never met and Andrea knew that the use of the term 'Sir', made her father ooze with superiority.

"It's good to see you enjoying yourself, daughter, and in such fine company for a change." The ugly beast then left them, probably to inflict pain and suffering on some other unsuspecting guests.

Race day arrived and all the teams were testing in full race trim during the early morning practice session. Rumour had it that Westwood had again failed to turn up. Knowledge of this agitated Jimbo somewhat and once again, leaving Marti to fend for herself, he made off in the direction of the hospitality units.

Obviously Jim was unable to get past the British steward on the gate, but he did manage to glean from him the fact that Andrea had also not been seen that morning.

Jim was furious but at this stage was unsure whether his pangs of anger were purely the result of being up-staged or caused by some other, foreign sensation. Whichever it was he was definitely miffed.

Suddenly, there was a commotion at the far end of the pits: Westwood had just put in an appearance. Jim, who had now returned to be with Marti, thought better of going to investigate and anyway assumed that Andrea would also show up soon. He kept a vigilant eye on the sponsors' suite; he wanted to catch her before she had a chance to get inside the tent.

Sure enough, here she came, gaily flitting across the tarmac. Jim ran towards her, grabbed her by the waist and dragged her behind one of the burger stands. "What on earth do you think you're doing?" she protested.

Jim had a good hold on her and she was struggling fiercely to break free. They were causing quite a spectacle and Andrea's screeching attracted some disapproving attention. Under pressure, Jim was obliged to release the girl, but he blocked her escape as she tried to run past him.

"So aren't I good enough for you? Daddy wouldn't approve of a poor boy, would he?" Jim's eyes were bulging with rage as he continued his attack. "It's OK to spend the night with a rich dick is it? – Is that the way it is?" Jim was struggling for control of his temper. He would have liked to hit her.

"It's none of your business what I do!" Andrea sobbed.

A small group of onlookers had gathered and were becoming increasingly concerned about the situation. Acknowledging this Jim stepped aside. Andrea fled in tears and Jimbo returned trackside to find Marti.

On their reunion, she clearly stated her disapproval of his behaviour. This constant disappearing had to stop. Jim apologised. Marti had been doing most, if not all of the work whilst he had been off chasing his ego.

Marti had worked out, with some assistance from Jack, the

best vantage points from which, she hoped, to be able to get some good action shots. She had even marked them on a map of the circuit. Jim's inadequacy brought on a terrible sense of guilt which he tried to compensate for by continually apologising until Marti, sick of his contrite wittering, finally told him to shut up.

There was barely half an hour to go before the race began and the cars were already appearing on track. With the circuit situated at an altitude of 7,500 feet, a Formula One car is capable of two hundred miles an hour. The race duration was 67 laps, equalling 184 miles, and for those who completed the distance it would last for approximately, one and a half hours.

There was a long start/finish straight and Marti wanted to be positioned at the end of this for her initial photographs, as there was always the possibility of an incident when cars entered the first corner, with all the competitors frantically trying to secure the best position on the track. The other place she particularly wanted to be was at the exit from the famous Peralta curve: a banked, sweeping 180 degree bend traversed at frightening speeds.

The pair jogged along the trackside sporting hi-viz Press emblazoned vests and arm bands, to the first pre-selected position and Marti went about setting up her camera in readiness for the start. It was extremely bright and she didn't want to be shooting directly into the sun. She fixed her sights on one of the cars in the front row of the grid and zoomed in. Its driver was motionless, with eyes half closed in a squint. He appeared for all-the world to be asleep and completely unaware of the fuss continuing around him, as his mechanics made their crucial final adjustments to his shiny, spaceship like projectile. He seemed to be alone; and this solitary state, to a certain degree was protected by his manager, who discouraged on-track media interviews, taking on much of the press attention personally.

A horn blasted and the track was soon cleared of all unnecessary bodies and equipment. The parade lap would come first, providing an ideal opportunity for a dry run with the lens. As the engines whined, Marti kept her camera fixed on the first two cars on the grid, drawing the lens back as they encroached. "Click, click, click," she made the noise to herself. They were at the corner and she panned the race line with them, "Click, click." Although the velocity would be far greater when they pulled away for real, Marti was confident that she could take enough pictures to ensure some amount of success and was satisfied with her calculations.

All this time Jim had been sitting on the parched ground moping. He knew he hadn't been playing his role and as Marti appeared to have everything under control, was feeling somewhat left out. "Come on sad sack, you don't want to miss the start after all this." Jim scrambled to his feet with child-like clumsiness, brushing the dust from his backside and Marti asked one favour of him: "Just keep behind me." With only one crack of the whip she didn't want a bunch of snaps featuring the back of Jim's head.

The machinery lined up on the grid with engines screaming; the pitch rose higher and higher as the red lights came on held for a few seconds then – Go! Go! Go! The noise was incredible. With the sun glaring down and a heat haze rising from the semi molten tarmac the cars appeared to materialise before her, like gladiators on a vital galactic mission. Marti managed to take the amount of pictures she wanted but what was captured on film would only be revealed on development. She felt good about it though. As the cars sped away, Marti allowed the camera to drop to her waist and took in a large gulp of air to compensate for the fact that she had stopped breathing at the precise moment the throttles opened.

"Wow!" exclaimed Jim excitedly, "they're quick – do you think you got them in focus?"

Dubiously Marti smiled at him. "We can only hope!?"

Each lap took roughly a minute to complete but it seemed only seconds before they were back in view. Marti wanted to move to the far side of the first set of bends for a few more shots before moving onto the Peralta. Half a dozen laps had been covered without incident and the defending World Champion was leading, closely pursued by Westwood in his yellow and black Javelin. This formation continued for three quarters of the distance, until Marcus was forced to retire with a mechanical failure. As commonly expected, the Peralta produced a spectacular crash when the Austrian ace Paul

Ericson, team-mate of Marcus Veridico, spun out of control and smashed into the tyre wall right at Marti's feet! She felt the shudder go through her body like a shock wave and almost toppled from her precariously mounted viewpoint. Fortunately Paul was unhurt and clambered from his cockpit, shaken but none the worse for his detour. He even removed his helmet and posed for Marti with a huge cheesy grin.

Westwood won, with Philip Rheutemanne second and Roberto Pasccari came home in a well-challenged third. Marti and Jim made a mad dash for the pit lane, as did several hundred spectators, where the presentations were to be made – more pictures were to be taken and it would now be Jim's turn to act by attending the post-race conference, where he would obtain the drivers' views of the race and also an insight into the next event on the calendar. Brazil.

CHAPTER 5

On their return to London, Marti and Jim reported directly to Head Office, as owing to the close proximity of publishing dates, there was hardly any time to edit material before the monthly magazine went to press. Having submitted their documentation they returned, by train, to sleepy Roebuck. By the time they reached home, both were exhausted, and confused by the six-hour time delay. The cottage was cold, having not been occupied for several days, so Marti threw some old newspapers and logs on the burner, just enough to take the chill off. The fire thus set, she searched the small wood-panelled porch for post.

A large brown paper parcel sat on the doorstep, another returned manuscript. Opening it tentatively, Marti slipped out the enclosed letter. "Not commercially viable – considered unsuitable for our U.K. list."

Seeing the beginnings of tears, Jim put his arms around her. "Never mind – there are plenty of others you can try."

Marti knew he was right, but the list was endless. Her story was of immense significance to her and she did not want its contents distorted. She realised her stubbornness would restrict the chances of getting her book into print, but if it was going to succeed, it would be done on her terms.

The next few days were passed almost in silence as they went about the normal daily routine of sleep, food and exercise. No word came from Power Play and neither Marti nor Jim wanted to make mention of the fact. Surprisingly it was Jim who broke the silence: "I hope everything's alright!"

They were each as nervous and indecisive as the other. Marti suggested one of them phone Andy at the office, but then both decided that no news was good news, they left the situation hanging. The suspense however, was not to be prolonged, for at midday the phone did ring.

"You take it!" Jim blurted, making the excuse that Marti was a better communicator then he.

Marti took the call while Jim hovered on her shoulder, bending his ear in an effort to pick up some of the dialogue. "What did they say? – What did they say?"

"Calm down – apparently," Marti began with thoughtfully measured words. Jim's features contorted with the tension. His look was agonisingly painful and Marti, unable to sustain the pretence, promptly put him out of his misery. "They're really pleased!"

Jim collapsed to his knees, clasping his hands together skywards in prayer. "We did it!" He cried aloud for the entire neighbourhood to hear.

Knowledge of their acceptance relieved the anxiety of the past few days and Jimbo now felt a celebration was in order.

"Later," Marti said quietly. She needed to be alone for a while to mull over what had gone before and also to contemplate what may still be to come. "There are beers in the fridge."

Ever the eternal dreamer, Marti flicked the keys for Morris from a red and blue parrot-shaped hook by the back door and set off for the wilds. It was a bright day, and although only mid-March was still quite cold. Marti had however dressed accordingly and even had her faithful wellies in the boot. Morris trundled sedately out across the Somerset Levels to a quiet riverside hideaway, a place Marti frequently visited when in need of solitude and space.

Looking northwest from the narrow cattle bridge, a spot from which Marti had dived and skinny dipped on many occasions during the long hot summers of her youth, could be seen the Knoll, The Isle of Frogs, a small flat-topped mound complete with Iron Age fort that was situated close to the river's estuary and her cottage. Because of the fact that the surrounding countryside was low-lying, and indeed prone to flooding, this landmark dominated for miles. For Marti it provided a sign of safety in that she always knew where home was. Having spent time travelling in her past she was sure in her heart that this was the place she belonged, she could never imagine not seeing it again. From the other side of the bridge, the Tor was visible: a magical, mystical point surmounted by a single limestone tower that could tell many an intriguing tale and another key requisite for her existence. If she stayed really quiet and still, with eyes closed and heart open, it was possible to absorb the vast energy emitted by the multitude of ley lines which connected these and many other historical sites.

Marti did just that. She sat motionless on the time twisted, rusting iron railings of the little bridge as the murky waters flowed gently beneath her feet, her reflection dancing on the rippled surface in the afternoon sunlight as it followed its journey to the sea.

Quite some time passed before a second reflection appeared. The image was that of a boy, not quite a man. Inside she felt the presence of a troubled soul. He was crying fretfully and his slight chest heaved with every sob expelled. He rubbed his eyes. "Not so hard," Marti advised caringly. The young man tried to speak but was unable to find the language to make his feelings understood. Frustrated by this inability, his sobbing grew stressfully louder. He was frightened and felt that he was in hostile territory, wide-open to ridicule. But there was an arrogance in his nature and Marti surmised that the situation was, in part self induced, that he was, for some reason, forcing himself to go through with whatever it was he was doing here?

"Why do you cry so?" Marti asked slowly, to aid his comprehension.

His reply was stilted as he searched with difficulty for the correct words. "I want – to be – home – but I have to take something with me."

"Why? And what?" Marti enquired of the little fellow, who seemed surprised that she didn't already know the answers to her questions.

With some resentment he supplied the missing ingredients: "To prove – I am – also worthy of love." He went on: "My family have provided everything I need, I have had a better education than most in my circle and with privileges, and it is now up to me to repay them, so that I may receive love."

His face was ageing, albeit only by a few years; it was fuller, and the chest was stronger. However, the torment and anguish was still clear – indeed having deepened and grown in their complexities.

He spoke again, this time more fluently and with urgency: "I want to be first, I want them to look at me first." He was crying uncontrollably and Marti herself could physically feel his anger. He wanted desperately to be home, but when he was there, all was not as he wished. Something vital was missing, and that 'thing' had created a massive void, his understanding of which was limited. He possessed a burning desire to correct this situation, believing that if he pushed himself hard enough and far enough he would, one day, receive the acceptance and love that he craved so, from those he loved so.

Marti came too, almost falling into the river. She grabbed at the rails with both hands to balance herself. The days were still short and the sun was already setting behind her. She pondered her apparition. Who was he, this man, setting himself on a course for self-destruction in the mis-belief that he was "not worthy of comfort"?

Marti understood his craving for attention but it had to come from those who mattered. He didn't appear to lay any trust in colleagues or acquaintances and he seemed to be his own worst enemy at times, slamming doors shut if anyone came too close. His self-worth appeared practically non-existent and she feared there was an inability to grasp the meaning of love or friendship in any shape or form without suspicion.

Suddenly, Marti remembered Jimbo. He'd be wondering where she had got to. Cocking her legs over the railings she slid to the ground, and hurried to the car. "Wait a minute," she checked her pace, "What am I rushing for? It will do him good to get some of his own medicine." Humming along to her favourite music tapes, she took the longest possible route home.

Returning to her cottage Marti found Jim sound asleep on the settee. "Why do I bother?" she said rather loudly in the hope of causing a disturbance, 'nothing.' She went into the lounge and shook him just enough to jolt him from his slumbers.

As Marti strolled to the galley-style kitchen, she found Jim following, yawning. Still stooped from his resting position he stretched himself in the doorway, and with arms bent, raised his torso gracefully by finger tips on the top edge of its thick, stained wooden frame.

"Hope you weren't worried about me." Marti quipped sarcastically.

"No." Jim squinted in an effort to bring his wrist-watch into focus. "Is that the time?" he asked, through gaping mouth. It was a little after six. Wearily Jimbo enquired where Marti had been.

"Just for a drive; to a few old haunts." She knew there was no point whatsoever in discussing her experience with Jimbo and besides, didn't want to reveal the whereabouts of her secret sanctuary. It was a private place and none of his business.

The couple went out for the evening, as earlier planned, to a local restaurant. Jim drank a little too much and Marti ended up putting him to bed, before attending to the revolting task of sluicing away the sick that now splattered her door step

The next assignment details for Brazil arrived and the excitement again began to bubble. That was until they were boarding the aeroplane at Heathrow, when Marti suddenly discovered she had an acute aversion to long-haul flights. Taking off and landing were terrific but the bit in the middle was just a waste of time. It would be fine if she was flying the thing. Once in the air, Marti felt stranded. She couldn't stop, she couldn't get out and she definitely couldn't change her mind about her destination. For transportation purposes, she remained convinced that the freedom of her own vehicle was still unbeatable and no matter what the price of fuel nor how much governments tried to persuade Joe public that the use of public transport was fun, she could not see her opinion deviating.

Marti stared despondently through the porthole at the ever-diminishing land below. Concerned as to the future progress of her book, she had sent a full copy of the manuscript to her editor at Power Play, Derek Bennett, in the hope that he might be able to offer some advice, or at least some constructive criticism. It had become acutely clear to her that she would require a certain amount of expertise and inside knowledge of the publishing world. However, as the plane climbed higher she began to have reservations about the virtue of her plan.

Marti and Jim arrived at the Autodromo Jose Carlos Pace,

south of the industrial city of Sao Paulo, on Friday morning, just as the teams were preparing to begin their first practice session. Jim was intent on seeking an interview with Mr. Westwood, although Marti had suspicions about the reasoning behind such a meeting.

Jim took a direct route to the Javelin team quarters and his prey. Meanwhile Marti clicked away with her camera. A continuous line of immaculate arch-topped workshops stretched the entire length of the pit lane. There was always so much going on, it was difficult to be selective with one's choice of photographs but she supposed, in time, this skill would come. Marti followed Jim's trail. David was sitting in his car and she took a rather dashing portrait of him. He was fair, blue-eyed with a square jaw and was particularly photogenic, although nothing that Marti personally would write home about. Her preference was for a little more mystery, with just a hint of danger.

Jim inflated his chest and strutted up to the British Number One. "Hi David – just like to ask you a few questions." Jim's words were friendly enough but he was standing over the side of the car with one hand placed on the air intake above David's head. His lean frame intimidated from this high angle and on the other side of the car a mechanic tinkered with what appeared to be a tiny on-board camera, so it was virtually impossible for Westwood to escape from his snugly-fitting seat without causing a fuss. "So!" Jim started contentiously, "you've made a good start to the season – winning in Mexico, I mean. Just like to get a few comments on your expectations for this one?" Jim's pretentiousness made Marti cringe; she could sense trouble and so left him alone to continue his personal vendetta.

Moving to the next garage, Marti ventured inside. The atmosphere here was also tense. Its tenants for this weekend were Team Centaura and their star driver was giving his manager a particularly hard time. Apparently he was disenchanted with his vehicle's reliability in Mexico and judging by his erratic gesticulations, its performance had not improved with testing. Marcus caught sight of Marti with her camera and glared accusingly. She froze. Marti had made no attempt to take his photograph and now doubted her ability to do so. His deep set staring eyes made her insides quiver. Sensing the discomfort caused, Marcus eased off and moved with his manager to a more secluded area at the rear of the garage, where another member of Centaura's support team was waiting to hand Marcus a message. Its arrival appeared to bring Marcus some relief; it also seemed to bring some comfort to his Manager. Marcus pushed the letter inside his overalls for safe keeping.

By this time Marti had managed to take a step backwards but in doing so she trod on some bloke's hand which caused him to let out a small yelp as he gathered up his spanners. Realising that she hadn't taken a single picture of the team, she snapped nervously at one of the cars whilst bleating an apology to the poor chap who was trying to get some feeling back into his fingers. The noise and her flashlight created further attention from Marcus but this time the faintest glimmer of a smile was cast in her direction. Coyly, Marti took her leave.

Emerging from their respective garages simultaneously, Jim asked how she was doing.

"Fine," Marti's reply was aloof and there was a short pause: "How about you?"

"I'd like to punch his lights out if you really wanna know!"

"Ah!" Marti sniggered, "isn't that a little excessive?" Her criticism was not appreciated. Jim shrugged off the comment, obviously unwilling to discuss the matter in any greater detail.

Marti suggested a break. Whilst they were sitting in the shade by one of the snack wagons, Jack Brenner happened along. They chatted freely, although on this occasion Jack was not revealing any secrets. Jim's attention was constantly drifting so much so that Marti kept kicking him under the table, humiliated by his impertinence. It didn't seem to bother Jack but after he had gone Marti asked what his problem was.

"No one – nothing!" Jim growled.

His petulance goaded Marti: "Am I supposed to believe that?" You're behaving like a total dick and there's *nothing* wrong? Fine!" she stormed, and decided to take a walk around the circuit in an attempt to get acquainted with its lay-out, leaving Jim to sulk.

The afternoon practice session was in progress, thus providing another opportunity to picture man and machine in unison, hopefully – although Marti's thoughts flashed back to the Centaura pit. Having walked some way, she assumed a vantage point on Curve Two and took a few shots. Her mind however, was still elsewhere.

Marti was flying, high above a forest, its lush green canopy obscured the ground beneath and she marvelled at its immense beauty. But the landscape changed dramatically as her flight continued. Now banking left, she was cruising at low altitude over a city – the largest city in the Southern hemisphere. Its grimy factories belched toxic dust from towering chimney stacks and it was barely possible to make out the slums below. Marti was appalled by the sprawling mass of makeshift tin and timber shacks. She was not alone however and turned to her pilot to ask the significance of their journey. His answer was simplistic: "It is not always possible to see with your eyes what is good or what is not."

In the meantime, whilst Marti had been flown around the globe, Westwood had flown around the track, securing provisional pole, and Jim had been flying after Andrea.

During the final timed session on Saturday, Westwood successfully defended his grid position, despite enormous efforts from the Local Hero, during which, in pushing himself and his machine beyond the bounds of credibility, he had a coming together with a slower car. He had taken a hefty thump into the wall and was helped from the upturned wreckage by numerous marshals whilst an ambulance stood ready. He appeared to be unscathed, apart from his ego and not in any serious trouble. But of course the pit-lane gossip suggested that he would be in doubt for the race and would now; anyway have to drive the spare car. It was all very dramatic but Marti was confident that he would be on the starting grid, one way or another.

On returning to their hotel in the early evening, Marti and Jim washed and changed for dinner. As they came out of the lift, they were surprised to see Andrea in the lobby making enquiries at the reception desk. Jim politely asked if she would like to join them for a meal. At first Andrea declined, but with further consideration and in view of the fact that she was a non-resident she gratefully accepted the invitation.

Seated in the large airy dining-room, Marti felt awkwardly

conspicuous and somewhat in the way. Jim was fervently gathering information on why, where, who and anything else he thought would bring enlightenment to his reports, whilst Andrea's uncooperative, laconic responses were causing a significant degree of atmospheric discord.

As they finished eating, Andrea observed David Westwood entering the room. Carefully folding her napkin and placing it on the table beside her, she promptly excused herself.

"OK," Jim said, casually.

Marti raised a sceptical eye brow: Jim's foot was tapping furiously under the table in direct contrast to his expression of calm, cool ease. "You know why she agreed to have dinner with you – don't you?"

"Of course I do," Jim snarled, shoving his chair back. "I don't care what she does – I'm off out anyway."

Marti was concerned, "Don't do..."

Jim cut her sentence short: "Listen! I'm a lot of things, but stupid isn't one of them!" He stormed out, informing Marti in no uncertain terms that he would see her in the morning.

Once more alone, Marti strolled outside and made herself comfortable on a poolside sun lounger. The evening air was humid and she loosened her blouse. A waiter smartly arrived to take her order and she was soon indulging in a large gin and tonic. It was served on a silver tray in a tall crystal glass with plenty of ice and a thick slice of lemon. No prompting was required and Marti admired it, as tiny bubbles sparkled and flitted off the liquid's surface, causing a tingling sensation before fading on the back of her hand. Huge exotic flowers, like tangerine flames, surrounded and protected her from observation and this, together with the reflection of tiny coloured lights dancing on the cool waters of the pool, near mesmerised Marti to a state of pure tranquillity. Her peace, albeit gently was however disturbed.

"May I sit with you?"

Immediately she recognised the soft accent and without the need to see his face, reached out and drew up a nearby chair. He was shy and projected this through jerky movements as he shuffled the chair backwards and forwards, several times before being able to settle beside her, even then having to make clenched fists around the ends of the chair arms, in an effort to secure his body. Softly, Marti stroked the back of his hand, which brought relief of sorts as some of his tension ebbed away.

During this time Jim had been hot on the trail of Stephanie the 'snooty' sister. Armed with the data gleaned from Andrea, he found himself in the bar of the hotel where the sisters were staying. Pulling up a high backed stool he prepared to wait. A few beers later, Stephanie made a grand entrance. She was stunningly attired in a scarlet opaque lace cocktail dress which emphasised her shapely rear. She spotted Jim immediately, making a bee-line for him: every head turned as she crossed the high gloss parquet flooring and, well aware of her audience, Stephanie accentuated her wiggle that bit more. "Well hello stranger!"

Stephanie's voice contained ambiguous undertones and Jim was quite taken aback by her uninhibited advances as she pressed her hips firmly between his knees. Their conversation degenerated over a couple more drinks, until Stephanie provocatively suggested a nightcap in her room. Once inside she closed the door and slid the bolt across.

Unexpectedly Jim was lost for words as he unzipped the back of her dress, peeling it off slowly to reveal an uninterrupted sun tan. He gazed with delight as she stood before him in nothing but black patent stilettos. Stephanie then began to undress him – slowly at first, but then more urgently and with aggression. She pushed him back on the bed, tugging at the legs of his jeans to remove them. They writhed and wrestled in a frenzied tangle of arms and legs. Jim whimpered in pleasure at the strength of her oral investigation, culminating in a full embrace of his manhood; he hadn't expected such pace and had to change up a gear to compete. "Touch me! – touch me!" She pleaded for stimulation. Jim's fingers ran from her knees up the inside of her thighs; as they did so, and she spread her legs, Jim laid himself across the supple limbs to prevent them from coming together. Stephanie was moaning as she reached the point of no return. Jim rubbed firmly until she begged for his entrance. He let her hang momentarily, as he raised his body over hers, penetrating exactly as she climaxed. Her back arched: "Push! Push!" she panted with every thrust. As Jim came with a final lunge, their bodies convulsed and she clasped her legs around his waist, pulling him ever further inside.

Jim awoke to blazing sunlight streaming through an open window. He could hear water running and turned over to feel for Stephanie, but she wasn't there. He tried to open his eyes, the brightness impaired his vision. Gathering his senses one by one, he rolled from the luxurious high, soft topped mattress and glanced at his watch. He winced, it was ridiculously early, then he realised Stephanie was taking a shower. Jim leered from the bathroom door; while unaware of his presence, she seductively lathered every curve of her rich brown body. Jim had caught her off guard and his first touch made her jump. He pressed her against the wall. "Augh! – it's cold!" she squealed but Jim took no notice. He lifted her feet clean off the shower tray, pinning her to the shiny cream and gold tiles with each thrust. Jim completed the task and on returning her to terra firma withdrew and left.

As Jim stood proudly on the hotel's marble entrance steps, re-arranging his jeans, he met Andrea returning. "You're up early," he chirped, with a Cheshire cat grin. Andrea was tight-lipped and offered no response. She simply glared and brushed him aside.

"Oh well – guess you can't have 'em all, but one should never stop trying." Jim's conceit filled his entire body as he strutted, peacock fashion, back to his own hotel.

Andrea stomped directly to her sister's room, very upset. Stephanie was getting dressed, contently stroking her freshly cleansed skin in the process, until she was rudely interrupted by an impatient hammering.

"Let me in!" demanded Andrea.

Stephanie opened the door and was almost knocked to the ground as her little sister stormed through. Andrea flounced around the room for some while until, exhausted, she threw herself, untidily into a chair. "Do you know where I spent the night?" she raged.

"No." Stephanie was totally unruffled by her sister's churlish behaviour, the memory of her good start to the day still fresh in her mind.

"In the bloody lobby of Westwood's hotel!" Andrea's tired

face was reddened, her make-up was smudged and she was close to tears.

"I take it you didn't see him then?" Stephanie's complacency was beginning to arouse suspicion in Andrea as she continued to inform her sister that, though she had seen Westwood, he had flatly refused to spend the night with her on account of the 'bloody race!' Stephanie smiled, but she couldn't understand her reason for staying in the lobby all night and asked for an explanation.

"I wanted to see who turned up!" This was a slightly misleading statement. Slowing her verbal ranting for a moment and allowing her brain to catch up, Andrea looked at Stephanie, properly for the first time since entering the room. She observed the cool smile. "What's with you?" she demanded, turning dejectedly towards the window and continuing her story yet again: "The only thing I got last night was a free meal out of that bloke, what's his name?" – Andrea waved a hand in the air vaguely – "Jim." She turned back to Stephanie whose smile of contentment had broadened.

Suddenly the penny dropped. "You bitch!" she yelled, so loudly that her comment was overheard by a passing chambermaid who hurriedly scuttled into a vacant, opposing room to avoid being seen by Andrea as she sprinted down the corridor to the lift.

Jim had arrived home just in time for breakfast. Marti was already seated and David Westwood was dining at a nearby table, in the company of an extremely attractive young lady.

Jim bounced in: "I'm starving!" pause, "She's fit," he announced. He was, puzzled however by Westwood's unknown companion; he had been working on the assumption that Andrea would have spent the night with David. (God knows how his brain operates, Marti thought.) "Hey Marti, who's she?" He winked and nodded conspicuously in the loving couple's direction.

Marti wrinkled her nose, "I don't know." To be honest she didn't much care.

Jim examined the food which had been placed in front of him before proceeding to wolf the lot down in ten seconds flat. He scraped the empty plate with the edge of his knife, which made

Marti's teeth stand on end, his brow furrowed in deep contemplation of the situation. Looking again at Marti he asked if Westwood and the girl had spent the night together.

She stopped eating, put down her knife and fork and sat back in contempt. "How," she paused, "the hell should I know? What do you think I was doing all night, spying through keyholes?" Marti shook her head in dismay and continued her breakfast.

Jim just couldn't let anything go. He lowered his head to make eye contact but Marti avoided it. He lowered it further until his chin was almost resting on the table. "Did you..?"

Marti lifted her gaze slowly to meet his gleeful expectance. His face beamed with anticipation, but it soon dimmed as she told him, defiantly that it was none of his business.

"Spoil sport..."

To deflect attention from her personal life, Marti returned to the original subject of Westwood. She asked Jim why, if he didn't care about Andrea, he was so interested in what Westwood was up to. Jim had an annoying habit of ignoring things when it suited him, and again questioned Marti on Andrea's whereabouts that previous evening. Had she seen her?

"Not since we had dinner together. Anyway, I thought you were knocking her off so I really wasn't looking for her." Marti's bluntness perturbed Jim, he looked away. He fancied himself to have a little more finesse than her phraseology suggested.

On their arrival at the autodromo, bang on nine, Jim marched off towards the pits, amazingly, and possibly to do some work or 'duff up' Westwood perhaps, whichever opportunity presented itself first. Marti, meanwhile, set about the preparation of camera angles.

At noon they met up to compare notes and swap gossip. Marti wasn't particularly hungry; it was far too hot to eat. Jim however, went for a burger – he queued for ages.

Marti was sitting on a small patch of lush green grass close to the hospitality tents. The atmosphere was clammy and she could hear raised voices. At first it was difficult to tell from which direction the vibes were coming, but on further investigation and by moving a few yards nearer to the source, she observed Andrea and David, cowering behind one of the motor homes.

Andrea was violently hurling abuse at him and prodding him in the chest with a vindictive finger. With acute hearing attuned, Marti managed to establish the sequence of events that had led up to this argument. Laughing to herself, she moved back to her original spot on the grass.

Jimbo eventually returned, stuffing his face with something disgusting that had been squashed into a bread roll. Actually, everybody seemed to be eating which made Marti feel quite nauseous. She put her hand to her mouth.

VIPs were being wined and dined and the whole place was bustling with waiters and waitresses. Considering the amount of activity though, it was relatively quiet. No engines roaring, no tyres screeching and no hideous music blaring forth from randomly placed loudspeakers, precariously strapped to the tops of over-flexed wooden posts.

"So – um, how's Steph?" Marti picked this little quip right out of the blue. Jim almost choked on his burger; he was coughing and spluttering, unable to speak in defence. "I know what you're up to," she teased mischievously. Taking full advantage of his temporary speech impediment and slapping him on the back, she proceeded to tell him of the fracas she had witnessed behind the motor homes.

Jim grinned impishly and Marti enticed him further: "Your plan is working!" His face went into various contortions in annoyance that his strategic operations may be discovered.

"Don't worry." Marti assured him that she wouldn't blow his cover and he settled once more to devour his lunch.

Andrea reappeared, this time with Stephanie and at the front of the tent. As they came out into the open, Stephanie saw Jim and Marti, she lowered her over-sized sun-glasses so that they perched on the end of her nose and shepherded her oblivious sister in their general direction. On the pretence of their meeting being purely accidental, Stephanie blurted an overly surprised greeting. Andrea, pre-occupied with David's whereabouts, burst into tears and rushed back to the relative safety of the tent. Stephanie asked Jim if he would like to join her for some refreshments, adding cynically that Marti do the same.

"No thanks." Marti refused the invitation, leaving Jim to continue with his unwritten play. Although only having met

Stephanie briefly, Marti felt this woman was artful and detected the distinct smell of deceit in her expensive perfume.

Once more within the confines of Javelin's hospitality, Stephanie paid great attention to Jim, almost to the point of fawning over him in her attempts to further humiliate her little sister. Stephanie was, however, suddenly called away by an elegant middle-aged brunette. "It's Mummy – I won't be long," she promised Jim, who was now looking exceptionally vulnerable.

Andrea, had been watching proceedings from a secluded corner, and knew well the sadistic capabilities of her mother. But, together, mother and elder sibling took on a much more sinister witch-like aura; for though far from ugly externally, she was certain that inwardly they were concocting an evil spell.

Stephanie stealthily returned to Jim and, slipping her hands into the torn back pockets of his jeans, pulled him close with a gentle squeeze of his buttocks and suggestively whispered in his ear. They left the party through a gap in the canvas which had been conveniently unlaced to allow more air to circulate. Jimbo could hardly believe that even his luck could be this fortuitous. Stephanie led him like a lamb to the slaughter, beyond the countless snack bars, past the paddock to the members' car park, and stopped beside a sleek black limo with mirror windows. As she opened the back door, Jim jokingly asked with a nervous laugh if she had any Mafia connections. The door was promptly closed behind him and another woman gracefully entered the car from the opposite side. The vehicle was like an oven, it was all Jim could do to breathe, let alone perform to the best of his ability. There was plenty of leg room though and Jim straddled the burning leather seats. Groaning in the heat, the woman attempted to quieten him in case anyone should hear – a quite absurd exercise as it was blatantly obvious to anyone who may have been passing what was taking place; the car was rocking around like a Mexican low-rider with hyperactive suspension.

Meanwhile, Marti was going nuts. The race was about to start any minute and there was no sign of Jim. From her point of view this habitual tardiness was becoming bloody annoying.

All of a sudden, here he came, footloose and fancy free with hands in pockets. "What you checking for?" Marti chided indignantly whilst pointing in the region of his groin. Jim's jaunty step halted and his brow furrowed across the bridge of his nose. "Augh," Marti sighed and thrust the tape recorder into his hands.

Taking up a pre-selected site for her initial photographs, Marti sat in readiness. The lights went from red to green and the race was on! No major incidents occurred; in terms of accidents, although Marti reflected that we were all victims of our own obsessions, no matter how vehemently we tried to defend or justify them.

It was a good result for the Brits, with David Westwood taking the chequered flag for the second time. At the official press conference, however, Jim was still having severe problems in his love-hate relationship with Westwood; neither liked to take second place and there was some ambiguous questioning on Jim's part.

The sun sinking low in the evening sky cast shades of yellow and pink around the now peaceful track as the last of the spectators drifted away. If the tarmac could speak, what secrets would it reveal of the day's events, having been graphically scarred and torn by searing rubber and steel?

Marti had shot the victor and was now sitting on a wooden bench with attached table. You could barely see the ground for plastic cups and empty paper packets, all of which seemed to be attracting swarms of insects as they hunted for their favourite nectar. In the distance a gaggle of fans hounded the defeated local boy, like disciples – or were they wolves dismembering their prey? He willingly gave autographs and his physical form was intact, but what of its contents? Marti momentarily raised the camera to her face but couldn't bring herself to record such scenes of mental rape. For the time being at least, the boy escaped gracefully and still in possession of his dignity, through a tight gap at the side of his motor home, where he safely incarcerated himself. Marti was saddened and deeply embarrassed to have been present at the kill and began, despondently, to dismantle her camera equipment. As she did so there came a scratchy sort of tapping on her back which was slightly raw from an over-dose of sun light: it was Andrea.

She seemed jittery. "Quickly!" she said in a hushed voice, "before someone sees." Marti surveyed the area; there didn't appear to be anyone of any significance around. "Give me Jim's address!"

"Please," Marti said emphasising the 'p'. Andrea, in her urgency or was it ignorance, didn't notice the quip, so Marti relented with the manners business and rather than an address, gave the girl a phone number, her own. This information was divulged partly to get rid of Andrea and partly to expose Jim, which in retrospect was possibly a little harsh – but he'd pissed her right off today.

Eventually Jim surfaced from the press room, along with many other journalists from around the world. He was sporting a broad smile, having managed to get close enough to the trio of drivers to obtain a clearly audible recording. "There's some really great stuff on here!" he announced excitedly. Marti was tired and hungry now that the air had cooled and after all his messing around, found it difficult to share Jim's enthusiasm.

On returning to their hotel they made their way straight to the dining-room, where a lavish buffet-style meal was laid out to perfection, the centre-piece of which was an ice carving of an F1 race car. Choosing from the international array of dishes was tricky. Both Marti and even Jim, whose food preferences were generally quite conservative, tried as many tastes and textures as possible. Marti revelled in it – a little bit of that, a little bit of this – it suited her appetite and cravings down to the ground. Having now consumed sufficient to be satisfied, she decided to take a walk before retiring.

The night sky was clear and displayed its stars for all to see. She began to count them, starting with the biggest and brightest and descending in order; an impossible task for sure even though there weren't as many as back home, but they were extraordinarily bright and it brought Marti comfort to indulge herself in this pastime. She studied them for a while before picking out her special light. It was, by far the most beautiful, and the warmth it generated, flowed across her skin like the gentle breathing of a loved one as they lay sleeping beside you. It was a secret private refuge amidst so much violence. Marti held on to this star for a short time, not too long for fear of being rejected for her possessiveness, and then gently returned it to its celestial home.

The back of her neck was sore from gazing upwards and as she turned her head carefully from side to side to ease the tissues of her spine, she realised she'd been crying, an unusual phenomena for her. Whilst wiping her eyes and examining the tears on her fingertips to make sure that they were genuine, sadness traced her lips. She touched the corners of her mouth with her tongue and could taste the salt. They were real.

Slowly Marti wandered back to the hotel. Seeing Jim at the bar with some chaps he'd met earlier, she sheepishly nipped across the hallway to the lift and went to her room. Their return flight was scheduled to leave early the next morning and a couple of hours' sleep was welcome. As she lay in her bed, the memory of her precious star buried itself within a special place in her heart, where it would forever remain.

Dawn broke and chaos reigned. Jim had overslept and now that he was awake was suffering from a severe hangover, incapable of doing anything remotely useful. Marti had no sympathy for his self-induced incompetent state. She threw his clothes into a suitcase and dragged him, still complaining, down the hotel steps to a waiting taxi. Making it to the airport in the nick of time, they boarded the plane and almost before its wheels had left Brazilian soil, Jimbo had fallen asleep – out for the count.

The on-board, packaged breakfast was served about half an hour into the flight and Jim managed to stir and stay conscious long enough to scoff the lot and part of Marti's, his appetite completely unaffected by the alcoholic consumption of the previous evening. "His insides must be like a dustbin," thought Marti as she stared in amazement. Having finished eating Jim returned to the land of nod. For Marti, the rest of the journey, approximately twelve hours, was like an endurance test in tedium.

She wondered if in the future, man would be able to transport himself from one continent to another at the press of a button, like Captain Kirk. If the technological gadgetry and enhancements being applied to some of the Formula One cars was anything to go by, it probably would be possible, but then she wondered if 'faster' formed a healthy definition of 'better'? Perhaps it wouldn't be such a good idea after all. Right now however this fictional notion did appeal greatly.

Six hours passed: half distance. Jim had now fully recovered and was downing complementary coffee as though there was no tomorrow, whilst busily writing up his report for Power Play. He paused now and then to examine and correct his wording. Rather annoyingly when he did this, he tapped his pen on the pull-down table top, for too long on occasions, prompting Marti to give him a nudge. His concentration was immense; it tickled Marti to watch him during this thought process. She hadn't seen him so engrossed in anything since they had first met at Thruxton when he was tinkering under the bonnet of a car. At last he was putting in a serious effort, though how long it would continue was another matter.

The aircraft touched down smoothly and Marti and Jim came through customs, unchallenged to catch the underground directly in to the City Centre. It was late afternoon. Battling their way amongst the masses on the streets of their capital forced Marti to make a direct comparison with the sunny, warm colours of the country they had just left. It was damp and cold here but the predominant inner city ingredients remained the same.

It was all systems go at Power Play. With a print deadline for late Tuesday, Andy was waiting anxiously to receive the report and more importantly the films for processing. He rushed them straight to the lab. All the company's employees were prepared to work through the night if required to achieve their scheduled target date. Marti and Jim stayed long enough for tea and cake in the canteen, but both were jet-lagged and to be truthful, were slightly disorientated by the hullabaloo of the office, so they decided to head home.

It was late before the comforting sight of the Knoll came into view, but eventually as Marti opened the stable-style door to her cottage, which always stuck a bit and needed a shove at about knee height, she was greeted by the warm, unmistakable scent of burning willow. The lounge was aglow with golden shadows. Her neighbour finished sweeping the excess ash from the hearth, and placing Marti's back door key on the mantelpiece, cheerfully bid them good-night.

CHAPTER 6

Our reporters slept well into the next day, Tuesday. Specific reference needs to be made to the day as Monday ceased to exist. In actual fact it took until Thursday to resume any kind of normality and on this morning the telephone rang.

Marti woke with a start and for a moment couldn't work out whether she had been dreaming or not. The ringing continued and so, deciding on the latter, she stumbled down the wooden staircase. Mid-way she stooped and glanced at the video clock. It was only six thirty and she frowned contemptuously at the phone. Marti picked it up but hesitated to speak, having had weirdo calls before at unearthly hours.

"Hello, hello!" came a rather impatient, loud voice. Marti held the receiver away from her head – it was Andrea.

"I'll get him," she said sleepily. Marti woke Jim and returned to the comfort of her bed.

Andrea wanted Jim to go to London for a few days; she was desperate to talk to him in person and said it was imperative that he agreed to a meeting. Jimbo wasn't keen. Although his original scheme had been to make Andrea jealous, he was quite enjoying his secret liaisons with her sister Stephanie and another. He attempted to make excuses but they were weak. He didn't exactly have any pressing engagements in the immediate future. Andrea continued to plead her case and Jim finally folded and agreed to her demands. Having hung up, he also returned to bed and in no time at all was back in deep-sleep mode.

Eventually the pair of them resurfaced. This habitual late rising was a most enjoyable experience, and one to be savoured after years of monotonous regimes, involving timekeeping and duty. Marti had put in a good fifteen years' unbroken service on the nine-to-five shift and although she was ultimately an optimist she was also a realist: "nothing lasts forever." Therefore the good times were to be treasured and carefully, stored away to sustain her on darker days which, unfortunately and inevitably, come to everyone from time to time in our increasingly rapid, changing world. Marti felt however that not all these changes were for the better. "Being first and fastest isn't always best." In the past she had frequently stated her opinion to the established hierarchy only to suffer persecution for her questioning but, unperturbed Marti ardently defended her beliefs to the point of self-sacrifice: "there has to be a better way!"

Marti and Jim went to the Crown for lunch. During the meal, Jim broke the news of his pending visit to London. He was, however, concerned as to the source of Andrea's contact information. Marti owned up, "I was so mad with you at the time – sorry."

He shrugged: "I probably get what I deserve." Ironically, Jim then asked if Marti would be all right on her own which appealed greatly to her sense of humour.

"I'll manage," she replied satirically. In fact Marti welcomed the prospect of once more having her own space in which to fully relax. Besides she was never alone and her head was stuffed to bursting with any amount of interesting though possibly useless subjects, simply dying to be let loose.

The following morning Marti took Jim to the station. She waited with him until the train arrived and once he was on his way, returned to Morris and allowed the wheels of motion to dictate her destiny.

It wasn't long before she found herself at the foot of the Tor. This, of course, was not purely accidental, the simplistic enigma of its ancient tower never failed to draw her curiosity; it was as if someone were reeling in an invisible cord from which she could never totally be detached.

Marti climbed the slippery slope to the top, a keen wind caught fresh on her cheeks. The sky was clear blue and she walked the circumference, carefully checking that all the towns, villages and points of significance were in their correct positions. The tiny cathedral city of Wells lay to the northeast, with its twin towers rising dominantly out of their lush, green footings.

Satisfied that all was in order, she sat down on the age-cracked, grey, slate slabs with her back to the old stone monument. She faced southwest: below her the antiquated cottages of the medieval town of Glastonbury squashed and huddled against each other for support. Beyond, the low wetlands glistened in the sunlight and looking further, the flat topped Knoll was visible; beyond that, the coast, and beyond that the dream.

Marti stayed pressed against the weathered limestone for several hours, the peaceful atmosphere contained a beauty and strength above compare, and time was willingly spared to absorb these qualities.

It was only the fact that she was beginning to feel numb with cold that brought her down from this mystical mount. A mist had drawn in on the moors; like a huge, soft blanket pulled over them to retain the precious heat, provided by the few allotted sunshine hours and protect their secret knowledge. Marti had to drive carefully, but she felt no fear in a place such as this.

Marti's sleep was pleasantly invaded, although her intruder did not wake her. She was back on the farm, which now belonged to her alone. Her baby had grown into a chubby, boisterous toddler with an insatiable appetite for strawberry jam sandwiches and chocolate in any shape or form. He also possessed a kite with a Red Indian's face emblazoned on its canvas, accessorised with a long thin green feather. They had also acquired a golden retriever puppy, called Bella, who incessantly chased both the child and the kite, until all three became tightly bound. The task of untangling wriggling bodies from twine then fell to Marti.

Sometimes they would make the short drive to the coast. He adored picnics and after the initial, breathless shock of the water's cool temperature, the sea held no fear, until a hefty wave caught him unawares from behind, sending him crashing to the shifting sand. Marti scooped him up just as a loud wailing was about to emit. Wrapping him in a large towel, she cuddled him close. His powers of recovery were unique and he soon proceeded to plaster Marti with endearing kisses. It was then that she discovered that jam and sand did not mix! He had exceptional natural strength and indeed his few weaknesses only materialised whilst asleep. His breathing would on occasions become intermittently stifled, and Marti applied lavender oil tenderly to his chest and back to soothe the discomfort.

Jim had arrived at Paddington station to be greeted by Andrea. She flung her arms around his neck, hugging him tight, as though he were a long-lost relative, returning from some expedition into unknown territory. Actually, he was about to enter it.

Andrea had her car, a silver Porsche 911, waiting on the street outside. She drove to her apartment which was a large open plan, upmarket flat furnished in glass and shiny tubular steel, with numerous, inanimate objects thoughtlessly scattered about. The decor was black and white, nothing in between.

Andrea informed Jim that they were going to attend a bash: "Just a few friends," she said, making it all out to sound very innocent, but Jim sensed she had some scheme up her sleeve and didn't entirely trust her statement. As events turned out his judgement was correct.

On their arrival, by chauffeur-driven limo at a plush hotel in Mayfair, Jim was greeted – well, just about acknowledged – by Andrea's entire family, the Fairbrothers: marvellous! Father, mother! and Stephanie were in attendance and it was blatantly obvious from their surprised and slightly enraged reaction, that they were not expecting Jimbo. To compound matters, were this possible, David Westwood was guest of honour.

Jim felt deeply intimidated, something he disliked immensely and a suspicion of manipulation burned inside him, but that was exactly where he kept it. Although he fleetingly considered leaving there and then, this action would have provided the Fairbrother clan with far too much satisfaction for Jim's liking, so he doggedly stuck it out.

The gathering was an extremely formal affair and once again, Jim's dress code was way off the mark. Service was provided with the utmost efficiency by fifty or more catering staff, neatly attired in black and white, chequered waistcoats and aprons. As Andrea's guest, Jim was seated at the main table with the rest of the family and Westwood. A factor which irritated both David and the head of the Fairbrother family Sir James, who were obliged, in the presence of so many sponsors and governing body dignitaries, to afford an acceptable amount of respect and civility towards him. In view of this light, there was little anyone could do about the situation without causing unwanted attention from the wealthy guests.

The function room itself was adorned on all sides from floor to ceiling with elegant pink drapes; an ornately carved cornice was depicted in gold leaf and four large, smooth marbled pillars dominated from the centre, providing a cubism effect although the actual space was not symmetrical. Jim did not feel comfortable at all. He was unsure of Andrea's motive for his invitation and felt also that his own plan could backfire at any moment.

When the meal was eventually over, Sir James stood before his selected audience and made a pompous speech about how wonderful it was to have his family and friends around him, and how close they all were, etc. etc... Jim found it increasingly difficult not to laugh out loud. Next it was David's turn to procure the affections of the crowd. He was uncharacteristically nervous and kept stopping mid-sentence to lubricate his larynx with a specifically requested, bottled mineral water. In all probability, Sir James had pre-written the script for David as he menacingly simulated under his breath, every utterance the poor young man made. Jim comically lifted the starched white linen, peering under the table to see if he could see the strings, which caused Andrea's pale complexion to turn crimson.

Pomp and ceremony completed, the tension diminished slightly as people mingled freely between tables. Those seated in the centre of the room were inconspicuously re-located to the outer-circle and a dance floor was revealed beneath the thick piled, royal blue carpet. Music could be faintly heard, though its source was unclear until the largest of the drapes slowly drew back and a full orchestra emerged. Andrea urged Jim to dance with her. He looked glumly at the sombre musicians – not exactly Rock 'n' Roll! But by this stage, he'd do anything to escape the foul air which had been circulating around the top table. Once on the floor he felt easier and it was possible, amidst fellow revellers, to evade the evil eye of Sir James.

After several laborious dances, Jim guided Andrea to the back of the room and escorted her swiftly to the lounge bar. He was anxious to get to the bottom of this. Unfortunately Andrea was still playing the innocent, insisting she had no ulterior motives and that she only wanted to be with him. Jim might have accepted this, if only to boost his ego and the chances of getting laid; he could be a sucker for a pretty girl at times but, as he had said before, he didn't consider himself to be stupid.

They had been in the bar for about half an hour when Stephanie showed up. Apparently she had been searching all over for them, as everyone was so worried that something may have happened to them – both. *'How sweet'*. Jim smiled scathingly at the irony implied.

The three of them, Stephanie now having taken an uninvited seat, chatted and laughed together in a reasonably adult manner. The complimentary champagne flowed effortlessly and, as ever, the conversation got down to the subject of sex.

Stephanie gloated over the wonderful night and morning which she had spent in Jim's uncompromisingly, virile company, even managing to imply her assistance of the impromptu arrangements for the episode in the back of Daddy's car. Jim was flattered by her recall of events, yet in the back of his mind he pondered Mummy's satisfaction. Leaning over he whispered suggestively in Andrea's ear that she might enjoy the experience better, first hand.

Andrea giggled and fell into his lap. She had had far too much to drink and Jim, advantageously quipped: "How shall we start?" The girl was not in control of her senses and Stephanie was encouraging her to go along.

Sauntering to the hotel lobby, Jim procured the services of the concierge, who promptly called for a cab. When he returned to the bar Andrea was alone.

"What happened to Steph?"

"I don't know," she hiccoughed, "she just went."

Jim helped Andrea to her feet and into the waiting taxi. As the car pulled away, Stephanie appeared from the hotel's revolving entrance on the arm of David Westwood. Jim tried in vain to avert Andrea's attentions but it was too late. Even in her inebriated state she had recognised the figures and the short ride to her apartment was undertaken in virtual silence – apart from the few jokes Jim tried cracking, which, much to Andrea's disapproval, amused the cabbie tremendously.

Jim had the suspicion that his chances of scoring were fading rapidly, although he did not intend giving up just yet. Heaven forbid – he had a reputation to up-hold. He tried the soft approach, cuddling her protectively but she fell limp against his chest. Either he was in, or she had passed out.

When they arrived at Andrea's flat she seemed to have sobered up considerably; she walked unassisted and pretty well straight to the lift. They stood there in the tin box side by side, neither catching the other's eye, staring at the yellow numbers as they flicked across the semi-circular panel above the doors. As the lift rose through the floors Jim felt the heat of the moment diminishing and fully expected to have his suitcase thrown at him. However, contrary to his theory, as the sliding doors opened, Andrea took him purposefully by the arm and offered him the keys to her flat, which he willingly accepted.

Upon entering, Andrea suddenly became agitated again, unsure of what she was doing. She offered Jim coffee, in an attempt to stall proceedings, which he declined. He sensed a naivety in her mannerisms. This was yet another attribute with which he was not familiar. Most of the girls he had bedded knew exactly what they wanted in the same way that he himself did. "No strings" had been his strict rule. Jim felt a burning desire in the pit of his stomach; he wanted her badly but feared the consequences.

Tentatively he moved closer, placing his hands gently on her hips. Closer, the first kiss was soft and Andrea responded favourably; slipping her delicate hands under the lapels of his jacket, she fumbled nervously with the small buttons of his crumpled shirt. They embraced and a longer kiss ensued, growing more passionate with each breath. Jim carefully caressed her fine frame as they moved towards the bedroom. A large, modern, tubular four-poster took centre stage. Slowly and methodically they removed each other's clothing. Jim nuzzled her neck, sensually nibbling her earlobes as her sweet aroma filled the air, soothing him; her pale, silky skin took on a transparency in the subtle lighting, Andrea ran her fingers through his sun-bleached hair and when ready drew him to the edge of the bed. She lay back and for once, Jim took time, to appreciate the full beauty of the female form, projected on black satin sheets before him. He went to her and the act was tenderly uninhibited.

Morning broke and the bedroom door flew open crashing back against the wall.

"Daddy!" screamed Andrea as she leapt from between the covers, dragging the top sheet with her.

Jim was completely exposed, not to mention confused.

Sir James came towards him, his black booted footsteps echoing on the bare floorboards and his face was like thunder. "What the hell are you doing with my daughter?" His booming voice ricocheted off the walls.

Jim tried to defend himself – but with what? Words wouldn't come quickly enough and Andrea had bolted herself in the en-suite bathroom.

Sir James seized him by the throat. Jim fought back strongly and managed to loosen the man's grip but Sir James was coming again.

Jim was now standing, still starker's and deftly avoiding the punches which were being thrown at random. Sir James was going crazy, hurling venomous insults and accusations whilst Jim was still dancing round the room in an effort to dodge the tirade being rained upon him, he didn't want to hit back.

Jim knew his own power only too well. The last fight he'd gotten involved in landed him in prison for grievous bodily harm and he couldn't handle that again. Anyway this guy was twice his age. However, the ranting of Sir James continued and the temptation to flatten the bastard was becoming harder and harder to suppress.

Sir James stormed on violently swiping at Jim. "Don't think I don't know what you're up to, I've seen shits like you before and had them dealt with. You're only after my money! You're a no-good son-of-a-bitch and you forced my daughter to have sex when she was under the influence, and against her will!"

The final straw was broken, when Daddy inferred that he would file for rape. Jim snapped, letting out a mighty roar he charged the old fool down. The force of their collision carried both men to the ground and it was now Jim's hands that were firmly clasped around the belligerent, sagging grey goitre of Sir James.

Jim straddled the arrogant fool's chest; he could feel Daddy's windpipe pushing against the palms of his hands. Mercilessly, Jim drew back his right fist and was about to throw one almighty punch when Andrea rushed in screaming and crying for him to stop.

Jim paused. He was shaking, partly in rage but more overly at the realisation of the damage he could have inflicted. He got up and began dressing.

Andrea knelt beside her father, sobbing. Jim looked back at father and daughter as he buckled his jeans; he noticed that the old man hadn't moved.

"Jesus Christ!" he cried, dashing to the motionless Sir James. Andrea was hysterical. Jim frantically loosened the old man's collar, checking for a pulse whilst Andrea kept up the screaming and flapping.

"Shut up!" Jim yelled. "Shut up!"

The bastard's heart, thank God, was still pumping. Jim turned him face down and sat back, holding his head between his knees, his own breathing stifled in fear. Slowly Sir James regained consciousness, but Jim couldn't believe it, the maniac was coming at him again!

Andrea intervened by flinging herself in front of her father; Jim held up a defiant fist and this time the old man relented, collapsing again to his knees.

Sir James struggled to his feet, using a nearby table for assistance. He leant over it, his face etched with pain. Still to catch his breath, he supported himself on one arm and wagged an accusing finger. "I'll get you, boy!" he gasped.

Jim, remembering the threat of charges, looked to Andrea for back up: she must have heard everything, even if she hadn't witnessed the scene. But Andrea averted her eyes and tended to her father. Jim was gobsmacked! His shoulders sank and he let out a desperately, agonising groan. "For Christ's sake, Andrea – say something!"

Sir James having regained his composure, though still perspiring, prepared to leave. At the door he rounded on Jim one more time, and whilst in the process of re-buttoning his collar, informed him of the fact that he was a man of his word. Sir James glanced toward his daughter with a smug expression, secure in the knowledge that she would not dare defy her father. With that he confidently left.

Jim was infuriated by Andrea's lack of compassion and begged the reason for her apparent, unconcerned attitude. "Why did you let him humiliate me like that? You know he's wrong. Why didn't you speak the truth and stick up for me – for us?" There was a long silence; Jim was almost crying – "Speak to me, damn it!"

Andrea was either disinterested or totally unaware of the severity of the allegations which had been made against Jim but she did, after much pleading, speak.

"It's OK; I'll sort it out later." She didn't appear to think that the matter called for any urgent action; she was now calm, damn near serene. It was quite unbelievable that only a few moments earlier she had been a gibbering wreck.

"Just like last night," Jim thought. It was as if she had an on/off switch which she could operate at will to suit her own convenience. Jim didn't think he could trust her and hadn't felt this needy since he was a kid. He clocked a phone on the bureau in the lounge. He really wanted to call Marti but there was no privacy.

Andrea carried on for the rest of the morning as though nothing untoward had taken place, while Jim sat mournfully staring at the giant TV. He wasn't watching any of the programmes, simply flicking through the channels with the remote control.

Then, quite gaily, Andrea suggested that they go out to lunch. Jim was stunned by her relaxed attitude, demanding to know when she was going to speak to her father: "My future hangs in the balance here." He could just imagine the police breaking down the door any second.

Andrea finally sensed his concern and, smiling warmly, told him not to be so anxious.

"What?" Jim was unconvinced but, it made him wonder if this was a regular feature in the Fairbrother saga.

Unfortunately, however, Jim was not in a position to do much about the situation and being naturally hungry, the couple went for lunch at a small wine bar on the Embankment. It was pleasant enough – no beer, but Jim was adapting to this and didn't make a big deal of it; relatively speaking it was a minor problem.

A few days passed without interference from Sir James or any other family members, so perhaps Andrea was right, maybe he had only been making idle threats in the heat of the moment. She certainly didn't appear bothered and took Jim to all the major historical landmarks and places of interest offered by the capital. He was beginning to relax and enjoy the break, even the theatre trip was fun, if different, to Jim's normal source of entertainment. They were becoming close as a couple, at ease in each other's company and discovered many similar passions, (including hamburgers). Jim found they could discuss any number of topical and philosophical subjects comfortably, without either one turning the debate into an argument. He also felt that he didn't want things to end.

Andrea and Jim returned home late one evening, having enjoyed the entertainment of a heavy rock band at a west end pub, to find her apartment door slightly ajar. Jim tentatively, pushed the door open to find Sir James sitting directly opposite in a large, deliberately sited rocking chair. They halted. As the door slowly swung back on its closer behind them; Daddy's dark figure loomed ominously.

"Oh God," thought Jim, a lump lodged in his throat: "Judgement Day!"

The young couple cautiously entered the room. Sir James' glare was unfaltering. As Jim heard the latch on the door click shut, he wondered in a moment of silliness, whether if he were to go out and come in again, this would not be happening. The past week had been so wonderful; he'd started to believe Andrea was right about her father not being a tyrannical beast – that this was only an impression, he liked to impose on his minions, to keep them under control and that – just maybe – he and Andrea had a future.

"So – you're still here," Sir James grunted. Jim looked to Andrea for support but again she had fled. He was utterly devastated. They had been so close – then all of sudden Daddy appears and she's gone.

Jim sat adjacent to Sir James, keeping the coffee table between himself and his aggressor. The old man glowered menacingly. He sat bolt upright in the rocker, like some self-made potentate dictating his rules for what seemed like eternity. Jim stuttered an explanation, though goodness knows why, vigorously protesting his innocence. Sir James didn't flinch, not even so much as a blink.

Receiving either unfavourable grunts or no response at all, Jim's concentration waivered; at a loss for words he simply sighed, slumped back on the settee and told Sir James bluntly, to "Ask Andrea."

At the mere suggestion of this, the father became grossly agitated and lent forward, yet again pointing in Jim's face with a thick finger. "Leave her out of this!"

Jim couldn't begin to comprehend. "How can you leave her out of this?" He was beginning to get the impression that the whole family was completely bonkers.

Sir James, also deciding enough was enough, stood up to leave. However, always commanding the last word, he informed Jim in no uncertain terms, that if he left within the hour, he would forget the earlier incident in the bedroom but if he was intent on staying at the flat, he would have to face the consequences of his actions. From this, Jim presumed Sir James was referring to his threat of legal action, which was an acutely terrifying thought considering Jim's previous record and the fact that Andrea, if not prepared to stand up to her father in her own home, was highly unlikely to stand up in a courtroom.

Sir James made clear his intentions to return within the allocated time of one hour, and the moment she heard the door close, with a dull thud that echoed all the way down to the basement of the apartment block, Andrea re-emerged from the bedroom, carrying Jim's suitcase. He glared at it, then at her, and begged her to do something. If she would only talk with her father, surely the whole absurd mess could be sorted out?

"Just go." She wept pitifully. Unfortunately Jim feared that her tears were for self-preservation.

Jim slouched back on the settee, trying to fathom out what her father's intentions were should he stay. He had never been one to run from trouble, for reasons both good and bad. He also had growing sentimental reasons for wanting to stay, and after the joy they had shared these past few days, hoped that Andrea had developed similar feelings for him.

Jim persisted with her to give him some insight into what Daddy might do.

"He'll do something terrible to you if you stay!"

"Like what?" Jim shrugged flashing a hapless smile.

"Please," she begged, "you must go – he will be here soon and won't be alone."

Jim's eyebrows lifted sharply to a peak above his nose. "I can handle myself," he said with naive arrogance.

Andrea shook her head with concern. "They carry pieces!"

This could be the deciding factor. "You mean..."

"Yes, now go home please!" Anxiously Andrea glanced at the clock on the white marble mantle-piece, "Go – Go!" She was fighting back tears of frustration as she pushed him towards the door.

"Don't you feel anything for me?" he asked dejectedly as he opened it.

Tears were now streaming down her porcelain cheeks: "Don't ever think that!" She bit her lip in an effort to contain her sobbing as she forcefully, pushed him out into the hallway. Her goodbye was faint as the door closed on him. Jim could hear her on the other side, still crying, but there was no more time, he could hear the lift coming.

"Oh shit!" He panicked, the only other way down was via the emergency staircase but the door to this was next to the lift. Scuttling to the end of the passage in the moonlight shadows he peered nervously around the corner. "Phew!" Jim let out a massive sigh of relief on discovering the lift occupant was only a neighbour, though the man did give him a wide berth and a very weird look indeed.

Jim wandered slowly along a narrow back street, dragging his case behind him. It was cold and the dim lights, glimmering on damp pavements, made them shimmer a silver grey. The atmosphere was eerie; it was now the early morning hours and not too many ordinary people walk the streets of London at this time of day. Jim carried on for a while, aimlessly but was becoming increasingly agitated; his mind was working overtime on the possibilities of what Sir James and his henchmen could have done to him and he began to suspect that he was being followed. He crossed every alley-way with trepidation, fearful that someone was lying in wait.

Jim's imagination was running away with common sense and finally, on reaching a more populated part of the city, he submissively hailed a cab to take him to Paddington. On arrival at the station, Jim rummaged in his pockets for some cash. The taxi driver watched, somewhat unsettled by the wait but Jim eventually, managed to scrape enough together to pay the man. However this did leave him short on the train fare. Why did he not have his bank card like Marti had advised him? He had enough money to travel as far as Reading.

Jim plonked himself on an iron bench next to a rank of wall mounted phones, dithering over whether he should call Marti or not. "She'll be really pleased," he thought to himself. Jim was tired, cold and alone. "She wouldn't really mind – would she?"

He picked up the receiver, fingers crossed, he even reversed the charges. Marti answered and Jim knowing her dislike of unearthly timed calls spoke immediately. He was pleasantly relieved by the warmth of her greeting, Marti was obviously of a much happier disposition then he, or perhaps she felt sorry for the sombre voice on the other end of the line. Whichever it was, she promptly agreed to pick him up, on one condition: that he never, ever took the mickey out of Morris again. This evoked a chuckle from Jim as he accepted the deal.

As the train drew into Reading station, Jim could see Marti already waiting on the platform. He was so glad to see her that momentarily, he forgot his tiredness and ran to greet her with the tightest hug imaginable.

It was by now 4.00 am and had been one of the longest nights of Jim's life; he dearly hoped he would never have another similar experience. Jim soon dozed off in the passenger seat.

"He's so sweet when he's asleep," thought Marti who, in contrast, was wide awake and enjoying the nocturnal adventure.

She loved driving at night, the tarmac rolled effortlessly under the big blue bonnet and she wistfully wondered where it went. She couldn't see it in the rear view mirror, which meant there must only be one way to go – ever onwards. Marti was prone to peculiar notions from time to time and feeling spirited, she set the wavering needle as near to seventy as possible. 'Not speedy I know,' but she had undying faith in this old car and was confident that she could keep it there, all night and day if necessary. In fact, the further they went, the better they ran.

Marti pulled into the gravel drive at the side of her cottage to be met by her neighbour who offered a cheery "Good morning." He never ceased to amaze her either, it didn't matter what time she came or went, he was always there. She guessed he was just one of those people who didn't need much sleep. Besides it gave her comfort, providing a sense of security which she appreciated when the property was empty.

Marti had to wake Jim to get him inside. He was pretty groggy and heaved himself stiffly out of the car. Once indoors, he dropped his belongings in the middle of the lounge and hit the sack.

Jimbo was extremely withdrawn over the next few days, it wasn't at all characteristic of him and Marti was beginning to worry. She had tried to enquire as to the source of his problem on several occasions but he was stubbornly unwilling to discuss it. Marti didn't push him.

From personal experience she knew there was nothing more upsetting than somebody persistently asking what's wrong, when you blatantly do not wish to talk about it. Jim spent a lot of time in his room over the next few days and Marti let him be, although she caught him using the phone once or twice, when he thought she wasn't around.

Marti had her own troubles anyway, which would never be possible to discuss. Her dreams were becoming more frequent and increasingly worrying. In the latest episode they were returning from the coast, having hurriedly abandoned a picnic amidst a freak tropical thunderstorm. Driving conditions were treacherous and visibility was poor, when suddenly a large black shadow crossed the vehicle's path. Marti felt the wheel snatched from her control and they spun, violently as if trapped inside the funnel of a great tornado. Whirling faster and faster, its powerful vacuum sucked them down, deeper and deeper; the pressure on her chest as it compressed her lungs was unbearable. Down, further still, it was pulling them into the depths of the earth. But as she desperately fought to save the crumpled body of a tumbling child, her vision faded.

Marti woke abruptly in a cold sweat. She was shaking and horrified to find that she had temporarily lost all sensation in her legs.

Something else bothered her too, although not to such a frightening extent. A soft voice inside would speak out, quite unannounced at any time of day or night. On odd occasions he would be chatty. Though timid at first, if she showed him some affection, Marti could coax him out of his shell. He learned quickly how to grab her attention and once he felt he had secured it, he would sit beside her, always to her left, telling her with profound confidence, what he had done, what he was up to and most importantly, what he was going to do. For one so young, his ideas and dreams for his future were seriously defined. He had experienced some of the worst poverty in the world first hand, though he himself was not poor, and he vowed to aid the society which had created his being. Although, at this early stage of life the methods of attaining such a goal were unclear, he was nevertheless determined.

Unfortunately these happy moments were few and far between, more often he would be sadly mournful. In the beginning this upset Marti but in time she found she was able to comfort him. Most often he would come in the evening, around ten o'clock when he would be extremely emotional, tearfully scrabbling into her arms where he would settle and proceed to ask many questions. The nature of his conversations could become heavily involved in matters that should not concern an infant and Marti had to dig deep for appropriate answers. Of course, all too frequently she had none. He would linger for an hour, sometimes longer, depending on the level of distress he was suffering – a pressure, which in turn, determined the length of time required, before he was content enough to close his eyes and allow sleep to take him.

Marti had been spending most of her waking hours down by the river, alone, and sometimes wondered if she had invented the little chap for company. But then again if a woman of thirty something was going to have an imaginary companion, surely they would be a protector, not one seeking protection or asking so many awkward questions – "Oh, I don't know!"

Of course, Jim's supposedly secret phone calls had been to

Andrea and he was becoming distraught at his failure to make contact. Every time he rang, all he got was the bloody answer phone: "I'll get back to you..."

It was the weekend now, though they didn't seem to have the same meaning any more, as they now no longer had to hit the 9 – 5 regime. Marti had been out shopping and on her return found a thickly bearded Jim beside himself with worry – he was in a real state, repeatedly dialling a number then slamming the receiver down and generally out of control.

Quickly, Marti took a can of beer from one of the numerous shopping bags she had just lugged in from the car, and thrust it into his waving hands. "Calm down, just calm down before you smash the place to bits."

"Where is she?" he shouted in anguish, looking to Marti for an explanation. She patted the top of his head maternally, roughing up the straight straggly strands of hair.

Marti wasn't really feeling strong enough to cope with a further psychology session right now but, alas could not stop herself from offering a shoulder to cry on. "Do you want to talk about it?"

She was genuinely sympathetic and Jim poured out his heart. He was obviously aggrieved by Andrea's lack of consideration and being slightly in love – something he had not encountered before – was having great difficulty in understanding the emotion.

Marti suggested he went back to London to find her, and it was then that the story of Sir James and Co surfaced, together with the threatened rape charge so on second thoughts, with Daddy looming on the horizon, this probably was not a good idea. Jim's tense response implied a similar reserve. Marti pondered Andrea's implication that her father's employees were prepared to carry weapons and tried, ironically, to reassure Jim, that if this was the case, then he was not likely to want to involve the law, so the possibility of him pressing charges was considerably reduced.

He then went into his "I don't give a damn – she's nothing to me!" routine, accompanied by the obligatory slamming of doors, at which point, mouths appear to become totally disconnected from brains and the transmission of thought to speech breaks down completely.

Jim had gone outside and was pacing up and down the garden path in the pouring rain, by the time he had cooled down enough to come back in, he was soaked to the skin. Marti giggled in dismay. "You look like a drowned rat," she laughed again with less restraint, "do you feel better?"

He must have felt a bit easier, he could see the funny side of his soggy predicament and shook his head vigorously, showering Marti with drops of cold rain water before pulling her into a playful fight.

CHAPTER 7

The day was fast approaching when Marti and Jim would be en route to the next Grand Prix. The travelling circus was due in Europe, Portugal to be exact. The venue: The Autodromo do Estoril; the date: 21st April, 1992.

Estoril is situated on the west coast, not far from the capital, Lisbon and is one of the country's most popular resorts. The circuit is purpose-built, high in the hills. Exposed to the Atlantic, it takes the full force of the unpredictable winds that cross this great sea mass from the shores of another continent.

Jim and Marti arrived at the track on Thursday evening, after a nice, short flight. Jim was apprehensive at the thought of the Fairbrothers being in attendance, but they would not be there for a couple more days and Marti assured him that things would be OK. "Anyway, what's Sir James going to do here? There'll be far too many witnesses about for him to accost you!"

Jim smiled a crooked, nervous sort of smile. She did hint, however, that it might be sensible and in his best interests to steer clear of the lot of them. Jim pretended not to hear this.

Being mid-April, the sun held some warmth but the Atlantic breezes brought a chill to the air; you could see the changes in the weather pattern as the clouds rushed in over the coast, invariably crashing into the hills surrounding the circuit. Friday afternoon was therefore wet and windy, much like home really, although allegedly the weather in England was apparently more congenial. However, due to the poor conditions there was little or no activity on the track and the teams, having exhausted their technical data, could find little else to do. This brought about a relaxed atmosphere in the pits, itself a rarity and a willingness from some to talk freely of their conquests and desires.

Marcus Veridico was perched on a large, red and black,

wheeled tool cabinet, with overalls rolled down to the waist, swinging his legs and sipping frothy hot chocolate from a large paper cup, whilst Jim fired a volley of businesslike questions at him, never once stopping to notice the lack of focus in Marcus' eyes, as they continually searched the white garage walls for inspiration. Marti had many similar pictures of him. Secretly she took another photograph of the still reigning World Champion, wiping a creamy moustache from his top lip with the sleeve of his exposed, fireproof underwear. But as with the rest, it was never her intention to publish such images. She had acquired a secondary camera, strictly for her personal use; she also had her own questions to ask, so when Jim finished his interrogation, Marti took over.

Marcus seemed to become nervous at her approach, rubbing the tops of his thighs. His fingers and palms were heavily taped with white Elastoplasts. Marti offered to leave but he said no, so she began.

"What happened to your hands?"

Marcus pulled at the tapes. "I get blisters from the heavy steering and many gear changes."

"Do you still enjoy racing?"

He shrugged, "Yes."

His mouth twitched, "Yes – but..." He stopped. Marcus' ideal scenario was to get up on a Sunday morning, arrive at the track, secure pole position, race, win and return home. But those days were far behind him.

"Is there anything in particular that worries you when racing?"

"Yes – I wouldn't want to lose the use of my le..." Before he could finish, his team-mate Paul Ericson burst in on the action. He was particularly forthcoming and animated in his accounts of practical jokes and funny incidents which had befallen both himself and some of his professional colleagues, including Marcus.

Ericson was highly regarded as F1's resident comedian and he jostled his team-mate. "Remember when I hid your gloves?" Marcus smiled timidly.

"He went crazy you know!" Ericson laughed raucously and rocked about wildly on an empty oil drum.

Marcus held himself uneasily and beneath the obligatory red

and gold, wide peaked cap, Marti could see his agitation. Ericson also sensed his colleague's embarrassment.

"My partner is very shy," he stated in defence of his friend, "but he does have a sense of humour – I think!" Marcus gave them both the benefit of a fleeting toothy grin, but his left hand was gripping his knee, uncomfortably tight.

"Relax!" said Ericson.

That was too much; Marcus politely excused himself and sought refuge in the team motor home. Though, privacy was difficult to sustain on race weekends.

"Do you like working with Veridico?" Marti asked Ericson.

"Yeah, he's fine – different, but fine." The Austrian paused. "He knows how to get the best from his car and himself – well on the circuit at least, he is a very loyal friend." Mr. Ericson dodged the subject further by the subtle employment of a somewhat ironic sense of humour, which Marti found pleasantly enlightening. Others, however, were less open, preferring to limit their responses to obvious facts and figures, for fear, maybe, that their words would be misinterpreted or, perhaps the fear was of intrusion. Whatever, all were pleasant.

David Westwood gave an in-depth communal interview in the press room. He had after all won the opening races of the season and understandably was in high spirits. He had every confidence in his own ability and also in that of the machinery provided for him to complete the task and fully expected to feature well on Sunday.

Marti went outside; it was still raining so there was no chance of any further testing being carried out at this late stage in the day. Some of the drivers had already left, to return to their hotels with their wives and or girlfriends. Jim was still in the pressroom talking to David. Race talk presumably? His anger towards the guy appeared to have subsided.

Marti interrupted to inform Jim that she was also going to return to the hotel. He said he wasn't worried, he'd find his own way back. Marti raised an eyebrow, "Are you sure? – I'll give you the phone number if you like!"

Her cheekiness brought a similar response from Jim. "Get out of here," he said, playfully slapping her on the behind with a rolled-up programme.

Back at the hotel, Marti went straight to her room to rest. Making herself comfortable on the bed, she flicked inanely through the TV channels, even with Sky there was nothing on that caught her imagination, so she switched it off again. Stretching out on her back with her hands loosely connected across her chest, Marti gazed at the white embossed ceiling tiles. There patterns formed a haze and a peaceful serenity seemed to fill the room.

Then it came, a sobbing, hardly audible at first and punctuated at random, with sniffles and gurgling sounds, as tears overwhelmed.

"It's – my – fault." The short sentence was stuttered by intermittent gulps as his frail chest struggled to force air into its lungs.

"What is?" Marti enquired sympathetically as the little chap cuddled into her side.

What ensued caused great alarm. Apparently, the frightened soul, approximately five to six years of age, had been accused, or thought he had been so, of causing some awful fate to befall his brother whilst supposedly in his care. The boy had been savagely scolded for leaving the baby unattended.

Fleeting statements made in moments of stress can cause so much grief and confusion for years to come. The poor child was inconsolable. Marti tried, with all her heart to gain an acceptance of her explanation, assuring him that the injuries were not of his making. But as the youngster had been denied any form of parental acquittal at the time of the incident, or indeed in its wake, it was extremely difficult to convince the distraught six year old that the implications were not, or so she hoped, directed on a personal level. Grownups just don't understand the simplistic nature of a child's mind. Seemingly, we forget so soon.

He held on tight, hands clenched in tiny fists as he clutched at Marti's blouse. His presence was so strong it was suffocating; she could actually feel his pathetic, skinny body trying to hide inside her. It was impossible to let him go and she endured a night of restless sleep as if constantly checking on a sickly babe.

Morning however, did come and none too soon. Marti met Jimbo for breakfast. He was exceptionally bright and breezy, recounting the jovialities of his evening at the bar. For once there was no mention of any female encounters, just a simple night out with the lads.

The pair set off for the track, stopping briefly in a small fishing village to collect some local produce. The tiny harbour bustled with activity as restaurateurs haggled and bartered over the recently unloaded catch of the trawlers which, for such small vessels, were abundantly stocked. They dashed around the market stalls collecting fresh fruit, fish and bread, desperately avoiding the little, black-shawled old lady who was trying to sell them some lace or knick-knack. "It'sa very good!" she insisted in broken English' "you buy, you buy, is good pricio!" Marti was sure she was right but they couldn't really spare the time.

Saturday provided a hectic schedule. After the previous day's washout, no significant times had been recorded and grid positions were still to be resolved. Much misleading technical data, not to mention tactical talk was bantered around the pits, and it was considered quite an art to proficiently undermine the opposition.

David Westwood was setting a blistering pace. As he came off the track into the pit lane, bringing his car to a halt in front of its respective garage, an entire platoon of mechanics trooped forth from beneath the half-raised aluminium doors to toil like soldier ants, totally engulfing both driver and machine. Of course, Javelin weren't the only team behaving in this manner and, sometimes when a particular garage space was approached, the shutter doors would be sharply rolled down in front of the lens. Marti took what pictures she could of these secret industrial haunts.

Sponsors had been arriving thick and fast throughout the afternoon, especially the main men providing the purse for the power, and it could be said that after a colourful day, the general public had got their money's worth.

Jim and Marti returned to their hotel and after a quick wash and brush up, joined the gaggle of media personnel in the bar. There was a distinct air of hilarity about everybody it seemed, each trying to wheedle out of the other, tit-bits of information – all in good faith, naturally – and likewise being rebuffed. It was the accepted pattern of behaviour at the end of a working day, everyone hoping that somebody would have one drink over the odds and let slip that vital snippet of gossip. Young Brit, David, whom Jim was referring to like a blood brother, was also present, he was accompanied by Roberto Pasccari, who had partnered David at team Javelin the previous season and become a close friend. Although neither drank on duty, both liked to join in the afterhours antics, bringing some respite to the intense concentration and dedication required of their chosen sport.

Marti was being paid particular attention, in view of being one of only a few women present, in this male-dominated arena and she was enjoying every minute of it. She could hold her own technically and also with the sexist comments, they didn't bother her at all; it was only if they became patronising that the hairs on the back of her neck would start to rise.

Word began to creep around the bar that Westwood was dating Andrea Fairbrother. When it reached Jim, Marti saw the devastation on his face. He hid his angst well from the others by keeping the rumour hot. Later, however, he came to Marti. She could see he was almost fit to explode. "Hold on tight," she said to contain his emotions, "it's only gossip."

Jim found this hard to swallow; he'd got it into his head that somebody was deliberately setting him up and there were no prizes for guessing who he thought the instigator was. "You don't know that, don't be so paranoid," she told him. She also told him not to bite. "Anyway, who else knows your current circumstances?" Jim nodded sharply in Westwood's direction. "Oh come on! I thought he was going with Stephanie?"

Sir James and his entourage were staying in the same hotel; therefore at some stage, sooner or later, there was likely to be an encounter.

The hack pack were having a great time, even Jimbo who earlier had been unnerved, was faring well. That was until Sir James arrived with wife and daughters.

Jim had his back to the door and couldn't see their entrance. Marti waited expectantly, while Daddy set about his outrageous publicity stunt, spouting phrases learned in a book or more likely written by some upstart, commercial consultant at one of those awful company seminars, held to teach us all how to talk in the same techno-speak language, where letters override proper words. Because apparently we don't have time to converse in a conventional manner and it also makes us feel very important, if we actually understand what the hell they are saying.

"Champagne for everyone!" he boomed with an ugly gruffness.

Jimbo spun round on his stool quicker than any F1 car could do a donut on the track. "Oh God – here we go!" he thought. The Fairbrothers are celebrating and the entire world had to know about it.

Jim made a rather bullish exhibition of his exit, clumsily bulldozering through any furniture that happened to block his path, causing a momentary silence.

It was just as well he left. The lavish festivities were in aid of Andrea's upcoming engagement to Westwood and the little darling was flitting from table to table, flashing an extravagantly oversized diamond and sapphire ring, which newly adorned her left hand.

Marti had decided to stay on in the bar, despite the fiasco, as she herself was receiving vast amounts of lascivious flattery from an Italian photographer.

He was tall, with dark, swept-back straight hair, a smooth, swarthy complexion and a nature to match. His name was Osvaldo – or Ossi as he was more commonly known. Their conversation was enjoyably flirtatious but as it grew later, Ossi began to question her relationship with Jim.

"It's purely business," she stated clearly; but unfortunately Ossi misunderstood this and took it mean that she was available. Marti deterred his advances politely. "Please, let's not spoil a good night."

Ossi got the message. "Maybe another time – ay?" He was hopeful, but didn't pursue the issue and accepted her mild refusal graciously.

Time was getting on, the crowd was thinning; Westwood and Pasccari had long since left the party and Marti, feeling just a touch heady, wandered outside to catch some fresh air. The tall French style doors opened onto a colourful, tiled patio area, surrounded by intricate bamboo trellis-work, the new season's plantation of which was just beginning to bud. The leaves still supple and freshly coloured with a sweet scent of honey dew. She gazed wistfully at the royal blue heavens in search of her treasured star. The knowledge that it was out there, somewhere, brought her immense comfort.

Having absconded to his room hours ago in search of solitude, Jim now heard a gentle knocking on his door and believing it to be Marti, opened it and slouched back to his bed, before properly checking the identity of the visitor. Jim was staring gloomily at the ceiling and only on hearing the lock click, did he bother to find out who had entered. He was mortified. "Oh fuck! What the hell are you doing here?" Jim demanded that she leave immediately. "I've had enough of you lot! Get out!" He was going berserk.

Stephanie however, refused to budge and stood with her back to the door. Jim tried to reach for the handle, but she obstructed him, making the task impossible without making physical contact somewhere in the region of her hips. Jim backed off. "Come on," he pleaded, "just leave – I want nothing more to do with you, or any other member of your family."

This sentiment was gravely sincere.

Stephanie however had other plans. Jim made another attempt to grab the lock but again she positioned herself between him and the door and his hand caught her waist. "Changed your mind, have you?" Stephanie spoke with a sinister calm and proceeded to leave.

Jim was initially relieved but as she was half in the hallway she mentioned carelessly: "I think I'll go and have a word with Daddy."

Jim, instantly horrified, dragged her back and slammed the door. The sharp noise made him flinch with the thought of who else might have heard. Still holding her firmly by the arm, he forcefully sat her down in a chair. Stephanie remained quiet whilst Jim paced the floor contemplating his next move. Then he faced her and immediately recoiled at the beguiling figure confronting him. Lying back in the seat, with legs clasped around each of its arms, Stephanie was sensually caressing her thighs, lifting her flimsy skirt higher with each stroke. Jim, wide–eyed, was powerless to stop her. She was pouting, seductively tasting her lips with her pink tongue. Her fingers went higher. Jim watched agape as a droplet of sweat trickled between her scantily covered breasts. She was moaning in ecstasy as she fondled the dark crevices of her own body until reaching a climax. Jim was devastated by her self-satisfying portrayal of sexual desire. Stephanie then raised herself slowly from the chair and without a word or so much as a second glance left.

Jimbo crashed out, burying his head in the pillows. His emotional patience had been stretched to its limit and further. Just then there was another knock. Jim froze: "I can't take any more!" He lay silently rigid, anticipating the next sound.

"Jimbo – you OK?"

"Augh!" Relief! – This time it was Marti, he couldn't let her in quick enough.

"Why are you shaking so?" she asked. Jim told her that Stephanie had popped in and graphically described the scene – which was a little too much information to be honest.

Ordering a couple of coffees from room service, which were swiftly delivered, Marti tried to take Jim's mind off things.

"Hey, have you noticed anything about this hotel?" Jim stared glumly, he couldn't think of anything specific.

"The plumbing!" Marti prompted.

"I hadn't noticed it."

"Precisely!" she said.

"Hum." Jim forced a smile, and his thoughts drifted back to their first hotel room in London. It was all so easy. "It was a nice night." He recalled with a regretful whisper.

Marti could feel her cheeks blushing and got up from the bed. "I'm tired," she excused herself with a yawn and went to her own room.

Marti was sympathetic toward Jim's plight, she didn't like to see him hurt but couldn't help thinking he might have avoided such turmoil by operating with a little more restraint, but there, that was Jimbo.

Marti's dreams were enjoyably peaceful; she was on a disused airstrip, miles from anywhere. Palm trees dotted the surrounding green hills and in the distance she could see the figure of a boy. Her appearance startled him, although he deliberately stopped himself from looking up. Scattered on the concrete, around his bare knees, which were scuffed and dirty from kneeling, lay an assortment of toy cars and aeroplanes. One of the models was broken and help was required to make its repair. Marti obliged and, once working, it was a case of I play – you be there, so she watched, with some amusement as he delighted in the mechanics of his possessions. After a while, she became bored as a spectator, and suggested that she would have to go soon.

This caused great distress. A panicky, high-pitched squeak came back at her instantaneously with the now familiar phrase, "Please don't leave me!" and a frantic search was conducted to find a means of making her stay longer. Marti refused to respond to his pleading, dark eyes which in an effort to mitigate the likelihood of impending separation, were beginning to fill with tears.

Marti stood firm, although the desire to hold him securely was intensely difficult to quell. This time, she decided, it would have to be worked out with the use of his own initiative. No assistance. Eventually, and with much deliberation, the desired response came, though it was still extremely cautious. "You can play with my toys," pause for more thought, "if you want." Marti gladly accepted his offer and all was again happy, although little more was said. Suddenly, in fact in an instant, tiredness overcame and sleep was required immediately. He was gone.

Race day arrived with its early morning free practice session. It was raining again as the curtain rose for the final dress rehearsal. Undeterred, several drivers took to the sodden circuit, presenting the opportunity to capture some spectacularly graceful spins, as cars went skating through corners in the hands of fortune.

However, as if to emphasise the truth of the dangers involved, one pilot was not so lucky and had to be taken to hospital with a suspected fracture of his right leg, after the gravel trap failed to retain his vehicle and it crashed into a tyre wall. Word filtered through later, that apart from his injured leg, he was as well as could be expected but of course it would not be possible for him to compete.

Finally the rain relented, and provided no more fell; the surface would dry in time for the race. Unfortunately the bad weather had caused havoc for the backroom boys on the show ground, who were busily making good sopping, windswept tents and tarpaulins, lifting the brightly coloured canopies with brooms, to disperse the vast amount of water collected upon them. Like a cloudburst, it cascaded down, drenching the ground beneath. A catch-22 really; do you let it drop on customers heads or let them paddle around in it? Perhaps it would dry before the beautiful people arrived.

Westwood, being on pole and rightly so in his opinion, was required to give the pre-race interview. Keen to promote his newly acquired status of lead driver in the championship stakes, this caused no problem, except for Jim, who understandably wasn't inspired at all. It showed in his write-up later. Marti stayed close to him, just in case a valve blew.

With this agonising task complete, Jim went off for a drink with a couple of other reporters. Meanwhile Marti went for her now customary walk around the track perimeters. There was a Formula Three support race due to start shortly and she thought it would be a good opportunity to check her camera shots. Selecting what she perceived to be a good site, she sat on the wall to sort out an appropriate lens. She was rummaging through her kit bag when she heard a voice: "Over there, it would be better!"

"Hum," she thought with a wry smile. Initially, Ossi sprang to mind and she swung round fully expecting to find him behind her. No one. She pensively moved through a full circle. There was no one near her, certainly not within earshot. "Strange – the voice was so clear. Oh well, I must be going crazy."

Marti continued with her camera adjustments. "It won't be so good here – honest."

This time it clicked. Through his persistence, she felt herself being guided further along the trackside. Albeit, only by a matter of a few yards. Marti indignantly consulted her viewfinder and was perturbed to discover that this small distance, had in fact created far more drama and a wholly superior shot.

Carefully, placing her waterproofs on the ground to prevent

111

any embarrassing damp patches, Marti sat down with her back resting against the crash barrier. A rich, warm glow consumed her entire body. Her little companion had returned, though his voice had deepened an octave or two, suggesting he was on this occasion, no longer so little.

"I could show you some other good places to take pictures!" He was excited and there was a wanting in his nature to be of use. Marti agreed, picked up her gear, and they were on the move again. His speech was spirited and seemed to bounce along beside her in time with his brisk rhythmical step. He was exceptionally inquisitive. "Why are you here? Do you really like motor racing? Why did she?" So on and so forth, and hardly with a moment's breath for her to slot in a reply.

However, there were some curious questions, haphazardly tossed in between those more superfluous, perhaps in hopes that she wouldn't notice. "Do you mind me talking to you? Is it OK to be with you? Do you have children?" And even "Do you like me?" the latter question seemed of the utmost importance and he allowed her time to respond.

"Of course I like you!" Marti gave reassurance to quash any doubts and his colourful enthusiasm exuded once more. Marti pondered the sequence of his questions and the way that he arranged the words. It was if he was trying to develop his ability to communicate on a more personal level. But, a foreign language was creating a stilted, slightly childlike conversation.

"I like to be with you – it's safe," he added with a coy sideways glance.

Marti felt extremely honoured by his last, humbling, remark. Though with it also came a huge weight of responsibility.

The F3 event was now underway and as they walked on, his voice became more serious – businesslike in fact, as he reeled off the position of cars on the track in relation to a given point. Where best to pass, how the manoeuvre would be executed – the speed, the timing, the gearing, the judgement required: on and on with meticulous attention to detail and telemetry. Marti listened with intent but she really didn't understand half of what he was saying. It was as though he was reading from a script, they were actually in the car and the technical feedback of every lap was coming fast and furious. Marti had long since lost the ability to absorb much of the data, the sheer power and flight of the experience was taking on another dimension. Strangely, whilst travelling at such speed, she encountered no sensation of fear and was, absolutely confident that the skilled hands of her conductor would not allow error.

Suddenly the speed reduced dramatically and she found herself, alone, on the far side of the circuit. The support race had finished, its winner was being announced over the loudspeaker system, yet Marti couldn't remember seeing or hearing anything of it.

Looking at her watch, to her astonishment an hour and a half had elapsed! For a moment she couldn't recall what she was supposed to be doing here at all. "An hour and a half!" she repeated to herself in disbelief, simultaneously making a concerted effort to collect her wits. The time was actually coming up to 1.30 pm. With a shock like a kick up the backside it came to her: "The Grand Prix!"

It was due to commence at 2.00 pm and she would have to get her skates on if she was going to catch the green lights. Marti made it just in time, though out of breath. Jim was waiting in the paddock, demanding an explanation. "You're a fine one to talk about cutting things close," she gasped, bending over with hands on knees in an attempt to slow her heart rate.

The cars were on the grid and there was no time to discuss her whereabouts, even if she had been prepared to do so. As they parted company yet again, Marti noticed the corner of Jim's mouth was bleeding but there was no time for enlightenment, she was dashing for first base – a prone position on the trackside, perilously close to two over-inflated, black rubber rings. A pair of large brown eyes glared at her from the mysterious depths of a yellow space helmet with 'Boss' boldly stamped across its chin guard. Marti wasn't sure he was real, but smiled apologetically and sprinted off for Turn One to get the required photographs of the start. Then having taken them in such a hurried fashion, she realised the quality may not be too brilliant.

She set off down the track in preparation for her next series of pictures, automatically drawn to the exact position pinpointed by her earlier accomplice.

As Marti watched the race unwind, lap after lap, the accuracy of his description was downright uncanny. One car in particular seemed to be following the instructions to the finest detail; she could even anticipate its next move as it swept smoothly and surely through the curve on which she was sitting, leaving a rooster tail in its wake of the residual rainfall, each time he passed a little closer to the car in front. Mesmerised by this extraordinary phenomenon, many laps had been completed before she'd taken a single frame

There were only five laps remaining, the leader appeared on the horizon with his pursuer next to him; wheel to wheel they approached in a colourful haze of changing hues. Sparks flew as Westwood was forced to relinquish his now customary lead by the brilliantly flowing control of his rival. Marti jumped to her feet in ecstasy as the two of them zapped past; trembling with anticipation, she anxiously awaited the return of her hero.

Sadly, her wish was not to be granted; some technical failure had caused his untimely retirement from the race.

With the pressure removed, Westwood was again the victor. Marti felt an overwhelming reluctance to return to the mêlée of the pit lane. She could well imagine the imminent portrayal of false integrity on the podium. Her only wish was to hold her star, to press it deep and safe within her body, but she couldn't quite reach it, the distance was still too great.

Loneliness ensued and she desperately wanted to tell someone of her earlier experiences but knew in her heart that this was not possible. The information entrusted to her was intimately delicate, precious in its honesty, and to treat it with contempt, would only serve to cause pain and suffering to the soul who had engaged her trust. This she could not do; she would never betray him.

Marti eventually wandered into the paddock, two hours after the race had finished. Jim was furious. The presentation and press conference had long since finished; in fact some of the teams had already left the site or were soon about to. Marti's face was totally blank; there was no explanation for her absence. She offered an apology but it sounded so inadequate, she could barely be bothered to listen to it herself and it simply petered out.

Just then Ossi appeared on the scene. Quick thinking was called for. Marti's resources were not entirely spent. Skipping off across the car park to catch up with him, she called out his name. Ossi turned round and waited for her to catch up, he must have thought his luck had changed. "Hi Ossi!" she called again with a vibrant wink which Ossi found irresistible. He greeted her with a warm custom, placing a kiss on each cheek. Marti slipped her arm in his, turning him back towards the paddock: "I need a favour."

Jimbo was angrily put out by her antics. He hadn't seen her all day, she hadn't done her job and now she'd disappeared again; besides his face hurt like hell.

Ossi gave Marti a lift back to the hotel, during which time and without compromise, she managed to persuade him to send her some negatives of the finish and post-race conference. This wouldn't pose too much of a problem; Ossi was freelance, in control of his own destiny and he was outlandishly generous. He did however mention the possibility of a fee but failed to name a figure.

The couple reached Marti's bedroom door; as she opened it, Ossi peered inside. "This is nice!"

There was a suggestive undercurrent; Marti paused for a moment's physical examination. The packaging was of good quality but she decided the price was too high. Instead, she invited him to join her and Jim for dinner at around 8.00 pm, which Ossi graciously accepted.

The trio got on well. Although at first Jim was off-hand with Ossi, the Italian's charm and continental humour soon won the day and both meal and company were pleasantly enjoyable. Having finished, they retired in the normal course of events to the bar, establishing a small ring of stools, and the spontaneous chat and laughter continued, though Jim at times did look a little uncomfortable.

David Westwood then arrived, sporting a shiner of a black eye. Marti looked directly at Jim; his lip was badly swollen and purple bruising was now evident under his chin; she glanced back at Westwood. You didn't have to be a genius to work out the connection. Jim's bottom jaw was now resting firmly on his chest. Marti made no comment, for which he was truly grateful.

Later however, within the confines of Marti's bedroom the truth was extracted. Jim's earlier anger again brewed as he reconstructed the episode. "He started it," Jim grumbled broodily.

Apparently Westwood had taunted him over Andrea which, as a testimony to his self-control Jim had ignored, albeit with difficulty. Westwood's remarks were cynical and he continued to fire a barrage of malevolent hostility, designed to emasculate. The insinuation that country boys were inferior was the one at which Jim let fly with a crashing right fist.

A struggle had ensued, with both men wrestling in the dirt and generally giving each other a good beating. Jim lifted his shirt to show Marti his battle scars. His back was severely grazed and the front-left-side of his ribcage bore the imprint of a set of knuckles, clearly defined in various shades of blue. Marti tentatively touched his injuries. Jim winced; the soreness was beginning to come out. Marti asked if anyone else had been present at this turbulent incident but as far as Jim was aware, no one had seen the fight.

All this had taken place prior to the race and Marti wondered, if Jim was in this state, what other damage Westwood had sustained? Jim for sure would give as good as he got; once provoked he wouldn't be the one to climb down. In Jim's own words, "I give him credit for his stamina and ability to still go out and win the race." A passing thought crossed Marti's mind at this stage. No mention had been made at any time, during or since the race, that Westwood had at one point, although admittedly only briefly, dramatically been robbed of his first place.

Jim was feeling exceptionally dejected and the way he continuously wrapped and unwrapped his bloodied hands in his shirt-tails, signified a need for sympathy. Marti ran a hot bath for him in which to ease his wounds.

Marti was not a believer in painkillers; they seemed to her to defeat the object of the pain in the first place. However, she was interested in homeopathic medicines, a system of treating like with like. Having tested several remedies for personal joint and muscular injuries caused through years of abuse, and discovering that they actually worked, she made a point of carrying a few of those which she had found most useful with her. Arnica was good for bumps, bruises, strains and stress, so she started Jimbo on an immediate course. Reluctantly he took the first pair of little white pills whilst still submerged in the tub.

Marti then proceeded to explain the philosophy of homeopathy. "It kick-starts the body's own immune system into action, thus enabling it to take care of the damage itself."

Jim didn't much care for this at all. "How does a tablet know where to go?" he demanded contentiously.

It was a plausible question but Marti didn't want to become involved and simply rolled her eyes. "Oh hush," she said softly whilst brushing his damp hair from his forehead. Jim stirred at her touch and Marti vacated the bathroom.

The initial course was deliberately intense and she woke him every couple of hours to administer the recommended dose. Jim didn't believe this was possible, until his third awakening at 3.30 am.

Estoril is an excitingly, active European resort with many nightclubs and casinos, and Paul Ericson, after much persuasion, had managed to drag his less exuberant team-mate Marcus out for a rare evening's entertainment. Neither man had featured well in the day's race and Paul's cure was to forget all about motor sport and enjoy himself – something which he liked to do with tremendous zest, as evidenced by his vibrant gyrations on the dance floor. Twirling coloured lights lit and dimmed the immaculately painted faces of his numerous young partners.

Marcus meanwhile was hunched over a table in a darkened corner of the club, cogitating. Ericson bounced over to him: "What's up?"

"Nothing!" snapped Marcus.

"Then come and dance, there are loads of girls."

Ericson gave a wicked smile and elbowed his chum who, after deflecting the impact, continued staring into an empty glass. This lack-lustre response aggravated Ericson.

"What the hell's wrong with you? – even you can't win every time!"

Marcus felt his stomach churn and glared at his friend, he was deeply hurt and resented Ericson's implication that being first was his only objective in life, but his wound was widened by the self-knowledge, that this was the impression he projected. Ericson hustled him again: "I thought we were going to play around – have some fun!"

Marcus raised his eyes. "Aren't you forgetting you have a wife and child at home?"

Ericson fumed, "You're a fine one to give moralistic advice – a divorced Catholic!"

Both men were hitting well below the belt.

"I don't want to play around!" Marcus snarled defiantly. "Besides," – his voice softened, "someone once told me that making love was the ultimate human experience. Fucking somebody's only marginally good while it lasts."

"I'm just dancing!" Ericson was neither surprised nor perturbed by his friend's theoretical outburst. They had known each other for some years and had been team-mates for two. Their off-track relationship, was bound by much personal knowledge and more than a good share of fun. Ericson knew Marcus could be intensely serious but of late, his outlook on life had become worryingly pessimistic. Paul wanted to help Marcus by getting him *'out there'*, and it saddened him that his efforts were being rejected. Once again Ericson returned to the sea of boogying bodies, while Marcus sloped off alone.

Marti and Jim treated themselves to a lie-in the next morning, missing breakfast. Their flight wasn't due until midday, an unusual treat. Normally they flew home as soon after the Grand Prix as possible, but there had been some mix up with the tickets and so they were still in Portugal.

On waking, Jim rose swiftly from his bed – well, Marti's bed actually, and examined his ribs. It still hurt if he pressed hard enough but he was pleasantly surprised by the results.

Having returned to England, only one slight hitch remained. The lack of photographs! From Heathrow they telephoned Andy at head office, making the excuse that Jim was unwell and they would have to go straight home. This would allow Ossi if he was still willing, to send the evidence. Marti cut Andy's conversation short, not allowing him time to question further. True to his word Ossi's negatives arrived early Tuesday morning. Not a bad service!

Jim had written up his report and cycled to the village post office to send the parcel, together with the tapes by first class to London. With luck, they would arrive in time before going to print. This was after all their third Grand Prix and should mark the end of their probationary period one way or the other but both knew that their Editor, Derek Bennett, was away on holiday. Marti phoned Andy again that evening at the offices, knowing full well that it was after hours. She left a message on his answerphone, pretending that she had mislaid his private number and assuring him that their portfolio would be with him first thing.

CHAPTER 8

Marti's 'friend's' visits were becoming longer and more frequent. Often he would spend the entire day with her, hardly speaking, but nevertheless present. On other occasions he would be fraught with uncertainty as to his direction. She deduced that an awful lot had been sacrificed to gain his present status and doubts were now creeping in as to the virtue of such abstinence.

Detachment is dangerous, even when not totally self-induced. It's hard to come back when you're so far out. Having one's shell continuously stripped away layer by layer and the context of every utterance or movement, scrutinised to the point where the subject ceases to exist, only drives a deeper wedge of insecurity and ultimately, creates an inability to show true colours. Care was needed to nurture these suppressed attributes, which had been lost through years of condensing to a minimum.

Happily however, in their dreams, Marti discovered that he still had the potential to enjoy himself and relax. But in contrasting the two alarmingly different and separated sides of his character and, coupling this with the fact that he was rarely above pre-school age when content, Marti derived that his true feelings had been screwed down, initially by others at a very impressionable age, perhaps through an inability to cope with his strong artistic nature. If he wasn't understood he would pose a threat and would therefore need to be controlled by any means available. But the creativeness never stops; it goes on, inside, hidden from view and therefore publically acceptable. "Only the heart sees clearly," muttered Marti whimsically.

This constant turmoil inevitably has to find an escape route and when it does, the shock waves can be detected for miles; and thus opens the door for further intense examination and ridicule; and so the spiral continues and its speed increases.

The task of extracting him from this ever-accelerating whirlwind was daunting, although, as the relationship developed, Marti was able to discuss the situation with the man in a rationally, constructive manner. Help was desperately sought and he was willing to listen to any suggestions, advice or even criticism. His predicament had become obstructive to his profession and therefore his life.

Meetings of such a high level of intensity would leave Marti drained and exhausted, but there was also immense pleasure as she watched over his spirit and accepted the responsibility of guardianship with honour. The weight now having been more evenly distributed, his face would soften and his breathing would become light and regulated, as he gently drifted into the land of dreams. Peace for the time being was restored and Marti was also able to sleep though she never left him.

Shortly after her return from Portugal, Marti experienced a particularly harrowing episode; it was nevertheless extremely enlightening as to the cause of his personality distortions.

Marti's sleep pattern was literally shattered by anguished screams of terror and the sharp convulsions of a fragile body next to her. This was normal to a certain degree, for if she was not roused by audible means, she would feel a jolting, as air was gasped into his crushed lungs, as he fought to keep the silent order imposed. But on this night, they were excessively violent and his stress level was at a peak not before experienced. Marti had to search for him, eventually finding him, to her horror, locked in a dark, damp room no bigger than a broom cupboard. He was in a pitiful state. As she opened the door, the light caused his eyes to squint and they were immediately covered by grubby hands, his clothes were also in a poor state of repair and cleanliness.

"It's alright – I'm not going to hurt you!" Marti assured.

He was cold as ice. With knees bent, huddled tight to his chest and head buried, he rocked himself back and forth on the flag-stone floor. Marti was appalled by the vision of this tragic figure. He was shaking uncontrollably, terrified of who had entered his solitary domain.

As Marti knelt before him, he peeped cautiously at her from between tiny fingers. She reached out to him but he shied away, rebuffing her contact. She stopped him firmly, reasserting her intentions and tried again, speaking softly, "Don't be afraid, you know who I am."

With encouragement and time, he allowed her to touch him. Marti applied soothing circular motions to his forehead, which brought a hesitant yielding, until he made a final rush for her waiting embrace. A tremendous amount of trust and courage was required on his part to make this commitment; a trust that they had built up with every meeting, until he was sure he would not be rejected or scolded for his actions.

Marti hugged him tight and rubbed his back in an effort to restore some heat. "Let's get you out of here."

His reaction to this was one of extreme panic: "NO! NO! I must stay, he will be cross! Don't!" His eyes were wide with fear, like a little frog.

"There's no one out there," Marti told him calmly, "and if there was, I wouldn't let them hurt you."

Convinced by her unwavering persuasions, she managed to carry him out. He clung like a limpet to a rock, and it was doubtful that anyone would have been able to prise him off her if they had been there to try. His skinny arms and legs held such enormous strength as they entwined her neck and waist.

Perching him on the kitchen worktop, Marti set about cleaning him up. He was filthy and his fine features were reddened and swollen from hours of crying, unattended in that hole. Marti asked how he had come to be locked in. He was mute. "Were you playing some sort of game with someone?"

He was bemused by this notion and his glazed, innocent eyes fixed on her for an explanation. He repeated her words carefully: "Play with?" It was as if it was the first time he had heard such a phrase.

Now clean, she snuggled him in a blanket and sitting with him on her lap cradled him close to her breast. Perhaps in this safe environment, he would feel able to tell her of the reason for his confinement? Marti posed her original question once more and patiently awaited his response. When none was forthcoming, she tried the direct approach. Acutely aware that this course of action could set the whole upsetting sequence off again, she prepared for the worst.

"Who put you in there?"

His eyelids instantly flashed open, revealing once more, those two intensely dark eyes the size of dinner plates.

"Can't say, mustn't tell." The sentence was minimal.

Marti urged him to say more but he argued stubbornly. She hoped if she could keep him talking for long enough something might slip out.

"Pappa!" That was it, his lips clamped tight like a vice holding the next word.

He stopped breathing. Marti shook him! Nothing – again – harder. A gurgling came from somewhere deep in his tummy; unable to hold it any longer, he burst into tears and pathetic apologies, begging forgiveness for the mention he had not intended.

"Don't tell please don't tell!"

This request was of the utmost importance and he was beating her chest with clenched fists to force her allegiance. The punches were quite hard and she had to employ considerable strength to stem the flow. As she managed to grab one flailing arm and pin it down, the other flew instantaneously to his mouth and he began biting down, viciously on the back of his hand. Marti was almost wrestling with the mighty little chap, sprawled across her lap, legs kicking and still biting that hand. His fury was incredible, accentuated by the colour of his cheeks – almost blue!

All Marti could think of to get him to stop gnawing himself was a sharp shock. She tried shouts but, his tenacity was not to be fooled that easily. Eventually she sharply pinched the tender flesh on the inside of his upper arm with such pressure that he emitted a short yelp! Marti quickly pulled the by now, bloodied hand free. Severely weakened by his exertions he lay limp and trembling, silent tears filtered through thick lashes, soaking the front of her shirt. Marti bandaged the shaky, damaged paw in her handkerchief and now that the fight in him had diminished, once again made him comfortable.

It may seem cruel but Marti had to find out what had been said or done, in order to extricate this soul from his demons, so that some form of order could be resumed. However, not even Marti could have been sufficiently prepared for the grotesque account that followed. As she cradled the boy, the man narrated his childhood story.

At the age of four he had gone to live in the smart city suburbs with his father, where he discovered a brother – older than him by six years; and another arrived shortly after this move.

He felt like an outcast, emotionally starved and found it difficult to integrate with his new family, although he had more than what was needed materially.

"I was nine." The man bowed his head in shame; taking a deep breath, his speech quickened.

"I tried to hide." The fearful, humiliating recollection of his nightmare was indelibly etched into his features. Punctuating his sentences with heavy gasps, he continued his account.

"I was afraid," his face contorted in agonised, memory of the excruciating pain and he frantically mopped his eyes and nose with his cuffs. Marti took his hand.

"It's all right – you don't have to..." His body became rigid.

"I want to tell you!" He spluttered, gripping her fingers. "It felt like he was tearing me apart – I dared not scream, because others would hear then..." His voice dried up and was taken over by sobbing. Marti stroked the back of his neck.

"I thought I would die – I wanted to die!" He cried out and Marti reached for him, his body vibrations transferred to her own and lessened. The man took another, deep relieving breath.

"He raped me!"

Marti was horrified and felt physically nauseous. This incident had taken place at a boys' club, where instructors and highly regarded members of the local diocese took kids out on activities and held lectures, supposedly to bring independence and diversity into their lives.

Marti envisaged the violated child, helpless, half naked and unable to speak out. She wondered what in this world reduced a human being to a level capable of inflicting such hideous torture on another of his own. No other creature would act so and the only difference between man and the rest of the animal kingdom is that, Man, in his intelligence, has a choice.

A deeper residue of psychological problems, stemmed from the fact that 'Pappa' was a genuinely, revered member of a staunchly religious society, and in the home his word was law.

The father and adult had no patience for these allegations and refused all discussions, shutting his son off from any support or explanation. The boy fearfully respected his father; therefore in adolescence, he dutifully subdued a burning hatred of occasional abusive attacks, for fear of losing all parental support. Hence, his life to date had been spent under the misconception that he was in some way evil, and entirely to blame for what had happened to him.

As he matured, he discovered that others had suffered similar abuse. The perpetrator had since died. Now a man, he had made it one of his life's missions, to do all that he could to protect the vulnerable.

A now calmly nursing babe nuzzled Marti's breast. Delicately she traced the outline of his moist lips with her finger, which was softly gathered in for comfort. There were no external signs of his earlier, traumatic existence and Marti sensed an inner beauty and quality of unbroken faith. She was positive that, although dormant, he still possessed the essential balance required to exist as a whole.

CHAPTER 9

The next two Grand Prix on the agenda were scheduled for San Marino and Belgium, the later being first, on the 17th May at Spa Francorchamps, a road circuit set amidst the scenic, wooded lands of the Ardennes.

Having received their details and documentation, together with a brief covering letter from Andy, provisionally confirming their continued employment status in the absence of the boss, the journey followed its usual sequence of events, and Marti and Jim arrived at their hotel on Thursday evening. They were feeling pretty well relaxed, having adjusted their lives to meet their new found globe-trotting style. Naturally their first port of call was the hotel bar: many of the faces were now familiar and of course, Ossi was there with as charming a welcome as ever.

There was an awful lot of gossip to catch up on, both professional and domestic and Ossi provided the perfect source. "He must have radar," Marti thought. It was difficult to pick up all the details, particularly when masked by a highly excitable Italian accent. Marti had to interrupt him several times: "Slow down!"

Apparently on the domestic front, 'the happy couple' David and Andrea, had been seen at various 'High Society Galas' in just about every country in Europe during the intervening fortnight. They had certainly been in demand as far as the tabloid press was concerned; Marti noted that hardly a day had passed, without a newspaper being opened to be confronted with some 'lovey-dovey' photograph of them, headed up by some sick, journalistic notion of a romantic anecdote. Marti had thought, at the time of reading these articles, that for two people supposedly in love, the coverage of the relationship had been a little over the top, even for someone of Westwood's notoriety.

Marti could be cynical at times and with fifteen years' secretarial experience and an insight into office/colleague relationships behind her, had become proficient at reading between the lines. "Nothing in writing is ever what it purports to be!"

Ossi leant on the bar; arms folded, and gleefully continued his story. David and Andrea had already been seen in the hotel. Marti glanced at Jim to see his reaction but he was showing no adverse affects. It transpired that the common feeling amongst the reporting fraternity was that Sir James was instigating the marriage for his own gains. Ossi's evidence to support this theory was the fact that in all the pictures he had seen, and taken of the betrothed couple, neither made eye contact with the other. Who better than the top British driver/possible World Champion to front Sir James' multi-million pound organisation?

The company in question professed to deal in the high tech computer industry, a relatively new business in motor sport, as trends bucked and ebbed, but one increasing in credibility; as such electronic devices were gaining in momentum and importance within the team garages. However, many had suspicions of Sir James having his fingers in other pies, some of which were less desirable. His name had been associated on several occasions with spurious deals in the major financial capitals of the world, though it had never actually been possible to prove his association. It was all hearsay, really, which in turn gave rise to more sinister rumours of conspiratorial deceit and one-upmanship.

On retiring to bed Marti lay pondering the details of the evening's discussions. She felt a lot of it was highly unlikely and the question of relevance also sprang to mind. Still, never mind, it made for good entertainment – nothing like a few drinks to set tongues wagging and fuel exaggerated scenarios and even a little bit of putting the world to rights to round off the evening.

Friday began in watery sunshine and Marti and Jim arrived at the circuit (which mainly consists of public roads), in the early hours, to find a weary bunch of London mechanics making their way to the Centaura Team tent. Over the plates of bacon and egg, Jim, helping himself to the available fare, discovered that they had been working through the night in a valiant attempt to improve their cars' handling performance. A new technological system had been fitted to the suspension, back at their Oxford base but was still in the process of development, and was causing difficulties in satisfactorily setting the cars up to run on this particular track. The greasy gang were sceptical but hoped that their nocturnal endeavours would produce some success.

Back in the pit lane, Westwood arrived. Jim actually managed a civil acknowledgement of sorts, so Marti hoped he had got over the affair. He did, however, keep a healthy distance from the Javelin hospitality unit, even though Sir James was not expected on site.

Rain clouds cleared during the morning, enabling practice to go ahead in fair conditions. Paul Ericson, the little joker, was up to mischief, much to the annoyance of his PR colleagues. He had taken it upon himself to jolly proceedings along and was generally causing mayhem by spouting half truths, about what contractual deals were being secured and what other teams were up to technically, in an effort to cause confusion. All harmless fun of course – and mainly for his own entertainment, but nonetheless frustrating for those unable to cope so easily with his sociability.

Some competitors felt a need to be apart from social contact in order to function efficiently, believing friendship of this kind would hinder the conscious mind to the extent that it would have to distinguish friend from foe. Sadly, through this fear, for some, at least one of these emotions has to be obliterated in order to get the job done to one's own, personal satisfaction.

Back at base, Marti was enjoying the intimate attentions of Ossi who was still searching for a break. Jim felt out of sorts and didn't much care for playing gooseberry; apart from this an attractive older woman at the far end of the bar, had been giving him the come-on all evening. With Marti and Os deep in conversation, Jim sidled off, thinking that perhaps a woman of more mature years would provide the challenging motivation he needed to get back on track. Chances were her father wouldn't be around to cause havoc, which meant he wouldn't have to keep looking over his shoulder.

The woman introduced herself as Marion. She was reasonably good looking with wavy highlighted fair hair, brown eyes and obviously took great care physically; she had a stunning pair of legs and tiny ankles no thicker than Jim's wrist. He reckoned she was in her late forties. They got on well, chat came easily, she made no secret of the fact that she was married, ironically Jim thought this might be beneficial, believing that she would not want to publicise any details of a fling should one develop. No strings sex appealed to Jim.

Marion was friendly, funny and free willed. Jim sensed a familiarity but couldn't place the face. From the little mention of her husband, he got the impression that he was a workaholic and that the lady was seeking some light relief from boredom. Marion was insistent that she was not here for the Grand Prix and that sport, in any format held no interest for her. Jim took this to be a good omen.

Marion was staying at another hotel so Jim, being the gentleman, offered to escort her home. Marion readily agreed and before long they were between the sheets. She wasn't concerned with a lot of fuss and messing around and Jimbo obliged with a controlled performance.

Spa Francorchamps is well noted for its unpredictable weather systems. At times half the track could be awash from sudden downpours, whilst the rest would be bone dry. This, coupled with the unreliability of yet to be fully understood technical advances, and a new rubber compound being used for tyres, caused much distress for all teams and their respective supporters. The whole weekend was marred by minor crashes and suspension failures. Westwood once more took the top step on the podium but every team on the track, even Javelin, was relieved to pull down the shutters, load the wagons and move on.

On their return to England, Marion and Jim continued their relationship. Jim didn't know where she lived and Marion made it clear to him that the less he knew about her, the better it would be. They would meet at various locations. Jim assumed the position of chauffeur, which he didn't mind at all: Marion owned a Jaguar and Jim rather fancied himself in it. They would disappear for several days at a time. Marion paid for everything and showered Jim with expensive gifts, even a designer, TAG Heuer gold watch. Marti hadn't had the pleasure of meeting

Marion and was becoming curious but Jim refused to tell her what they got up to or where they went.

Finally Marti could stand the suspense no longer and on Jim's return from his mid-race calendar weekend excursion, she nagged him all evening, not allowing a minute's respite, until eventually and with some amusement he cracked up.

Apparently Marion was fond of the 'Arts'. "Oooo-urr!" Marti smirked sarcastically.

"If you're going to take the piss I'm not going to tell you anymore!"

Marti sat crossed-legged on the floor right in front of him like a naughty child. "Get on with it then! You have my full attention."

Jim smiled in disbelief. Marion's passions were definitely not shared by her husband and one would think not entirely up Jimbo's street, but then, she was paying. They would attend theatrical shows, art exhibitions and auctions, where Marion would spend thousands at a time on antiquities which, in Jim's humble opinion, having no taste for fine furnishings or the like, were mostly useless bits of old rubbish that he would have taken to the local tip. She would take him to all the best country retreats and restaurants; but they did go shopping at Harrods in Knightsbridge, which Jim thoroughly enjoyed and this was where Marion had purchased the watch which he was so proud of. Marti pondered the arrangement for a moment and then with a coy inquisitiveness asked what he did in return for such lavish gifts.

"Nothing!"

Marti rolled on her back in fits of giggles: "Oh – come on – you expect me to believe that?"

Jim blushed. "It doesn't matter whether you believe it or not." He paused, "I'm not sure I do but, it's the truth!"

Marti broke her laughter with the more serious suggestion that Marion simply wanted to be seen with a young, handsome man in tow. She in turn was now teasing Jim. "You know what that makes you?" Marti was still jollying along in a light-hearted frame of mind and although she sensed some mild embarrassment, she couldn't resist the opportunity of more fun. With eyes fixed on Jim's she wickedly blurted: "You're a gigolo!"

"Yes! – we have sex!" Jim's expression grew more severe; he leaned over her, hands poised in strangulation as they slid playfully around her neck, she squeezed out a few more words:

"This could be your next business venture!"

Jim fought and tickled her rompishly as she squirmed underneath him, pounding his back but he would not relent until both were breathless and hoarse from laughing.

"You'd be good at it – you got the body!" Marti encouraged, as Jim let her up, but he had already decided that for once, he was going to have the last dig. That was it – Marti had two ultra sensitive buttons, one each side around about the bottom of her ribcage, and he hit them bang on target! She collapsed in a senseless quivering heap. For a moment Jim thought she was hurt and hurried to help her up. A little play-acting did cross her mind as she felt the support of Jim's arms around her, strong yet tenderly careful, but she desisted. Enough was enough for one night.

Before long, it was off to San Marino, a tiny independent square on the top eastern side of Italy. The Imola circuit itself is actually 50 miles from San Marion but this doesn't seem to matter to the Italians. It is, after all, their second Grand Prix of the season and to a nation obsessed with motor sport, the precise geographical location is unimportant as the general heading of Ferrari covers the entire racing spectrum in this country.

It was now nearing the end of May and the weather was absolutely gorgeous. On the Saturday evening, Marti took advantage of a spare couple of hours to relax in the late sunshine by the hotel pool. She took a dip: the waters were cool and soothing. Allowing the clear liquid to take her weight, she floated effortlessly. "I wish life was like this all the time," she dreamed, "no pressure, just constant support."

Marti's transient euphoria, however, was totally destroyed when Jimbo, in his boredom, decided that it would be great fun to bomb her. He caused an almighty splash sending half the contents of the pool lashing against the surrounding fence. The two of them then proceeded to chase, push and duck each other in and out of the water, playing games and testing each others' aquatic skills. Who could stay under longest? Who was

BLIND ALLEY

A romantic novel by local Author Pippa Wood. Historically set in the 1990's, the story curiously, intertwines her love of the Somerset levels with the global excitement of F1 racing. Price £7.99. For more information email pippa9790@btinternet.com

quickest? – and so on, until they were shattered. Jim had to go to great lengths to beat her, even then, not winning every race.

The pair stretched out on a couple of sun loungers to recover from their exertions. They lay quiet for some while; then Jim suddenly uttered a thoughtful accolade: "You're OK!" he announced, slapping her thigh as he would a mate on the football pitch.

With a squint, she glanced sideways at him. The times she'd heard that. "Thanks!"

Sunday arrived and the pace of things was hotting up, mainly because of the exuberance of the Italian fans; they truly adored their motor sport with an undying passion. Their expectations demanded the highest level of performance and Pasccari, in flying form, had not disappointed them in the qualifying rounds. Cheered on by his home crowd he'd secured his first pole of the season, demoting the eager Westwood to a mere second position on the grid. The joke around the pit lane was that the only way currently of beating Westwood was either by locking him in his motor home before the race, or to confiscate his vehicle. The latter suggestion was somewhat cynical and one Westwood did not appreciate but he did participate in other banter.

Marti went walkabout. Dignitaries were being wined and dined and the track was empty, apart from a few stray spectators wrapped in flags, who were quickly rounded up by marshals. A sea of red engulfed the circuit, frantically lapping at its edges. Sitting on an embankment in the centre field, with legs outstretched to absorb the rays, Marti was about to take some photographs of the writhing masses when she sensed him slipping in behind her, as if easing himself into a tight cockpit.

His body moulded around hers forming the perfect monocoque. She was safely secured and as he nestled his face against her neck she felt his warm breath, man's purest manifestation, flowing softly across her skin. He reached forward and took control.

"I could take you right to the edge!" His words were darkened with the mystery of a foreign tongue as he took her – through every beautiful curve and corner, gently caressing the very apexes, as he flowed effortlessly into the sensually undulating straights. Delicately, he defined each rise and fall as the contour unfolded before him. On – into the next bend, his line exact, his timing perfect as he pursued his course further – further than any other, to another dimension creating perpetual motion with dedicated, intense care and precision. He was wildly sensitive and dominated her with a primitive power that she wanted to be dominated by. Marti's entire body tingled and her cheek was moistened by the tears he had shed at the ultimate point of simultaneous conception, which was reached through absolute awareness.

All of a sudden Marti noticed a marshal making his way toward her. She wasn't wearing her press jacket or badges and was certainly in no fit state to be confronted right now. Hurriedly collecting her equipment she scurried off in the opposite direction, still too flushed to even think of her destination.

Of course, her eventual landing place was the paddock, where she mingled inconspicuously with the gathering throngs of mechanics, drivers, wives, girlfriends, journalists, film stars and the usual selection of bimbos, parading themselves in the hopes of a worthy catch.

"It's one way out," Marti thought, though whether it be through tiredness, laziness or pure greed, she didn't know. "Someone ought to tell them that the hands grow cold." She surmised from the point of view of the rich and famous, however, that it must be extremely difficult to meet somebody 'normal'. Everyone present was either professionally or decoratively associated with the circus. Maybe if they had found a companion prior to fame, it could work, but she wondered how many crossed the line intact. "Still," she said to herself, "you could say that of any business. Life is but a breath, and not to be spent lightly."

The pit-lane area was beginning to clear and as people were despatched to their appointed viewing stations, it became easier to move and see what, or who was there; hence Marti bumped into Jimbo. He was in buoyant mood, not having encountered any run-ins, which made a pleasant change but then he had been deliberately keeping a low profile.

The competitors had taken up their respective grid positions ready for the off, although the managers appeared more nervous than any of the drivers. In reality, even with the employment of radio and telemetry, these chiefs have only marginal control over their precious men and machines once the race has started, and must pray that both come back in one piece. For the lone participant the anxiety is less oppressive: he knows what he's doing, or thinks he does. The related spectator, on the other hand, can only hope he knows.

Following the parade lap, the red lights glowed like a red flag to a bull. This is it – the moment when all else is deleted from the brain and nothing must distract from that single objective of reaching the first corner in a leading position.

Westwood made the perfect start, robbing Pasccari of his advantage on pole. They were close, very close; Pasccari angrily swerved in and out behind Westwood as they went into the Tamburello, a long sweeping left-handed curve which has been described by some as the most worrying bend in the world. On again, right; the Italian was pushing hard all the time. At the approach to Tosa, a tight left-hander, he almost had Westwood off the track. Westwood resourcefully recovered his faculties and henceforth dictated the pace of the race from the front, going on to take the flag. Unfortunately, after providing much of the action and whilst defending a well-deserved second place from Veridico, Roberto retired on lap 58 out of 61, having developed some problem selecting his gears. He was devastated.

As Westwood crossed the finish line, the scene in the Javelin garage was one of frenzied chaos and ecstatic jubilation. This latest victory brought the tally to five and placed Westwood firmly at the top of the championship table with a commanding lead over his rivals. An exemplary position to be in so early on in the season but of course there was still a long way to go in defence of this status.

That evening, back at the hotel, a 'society function' was being held in aid of local charities. Our intrepid duo, along with many other journalists, were in attendance, in full regalia. It would prove to be an interesting and informative event. The compère, Mr Edward Davidson, an advertising executive associated in some manner to Sir James, was a surprisingly humorous man, who conducted ceremonies with a rather wry, tongue-in-cheek attitude.

Mr. Davidson introduced Westwood, who was accompanied

by his fiancée, Miss Andrea 'Maud' Fairbrother. Jim sniggered. "Maud!"

Andrea appeared nervous, which was unlike her normal vivaciousness on such auspicious occasions. For most of the evening she kept her head lowered and spoke only when spoken to. The couple's arrival had prompted an extraordinarily mixed reception from their audience, arousing Marti's curiosity, but as the evening progressed further the reasons for the hushed, tart remarks become clear.

Journalists of all nationalities were present, including Ossi, and rumours were rife concerning family, professional and financial discrepancies. Apparently Sir James was well known for his business dealings in Italy, although one particular scheme seemed to have gone horribly wrong, leaving him massively indebted to a computer manufacturer. It was all very intriguing. Many felt Westwood was out of his depth and completely unaware of the dodgy circumstances surrounding his future father-in-law. He was, after all simply a hired hand and at the end of the day, all David wanted to do was drive a car.

Marti sat back for a few seconds from the group that had become huddled over the table, ensconced in debate. Whilst staring at the tops of the variously-staged balding heads, which amused her greatly, she puzzled over the question of the hired hand. Westwood wasn't daft; if everyone else knew what was going on then surely he did? Marti wondered if greed made one blind. She was convinced Westwood wasn't in love with Andrea and had grave doubts about her fondness of him also. Strings were definitely being attached and would, at some later date be pulled tight. That's when you need a hell of a good sense of balance.

Wine flowed freely and a more relaxed atmosphere prevailed. Marti had noticed Jim making eye contact with Andrea across the dance floor on several occasions, and in case he was having any ideas of chivalry, she sharply reminded him of past encounters, suggesting strongly, and in view of the further knowledge gained during dinner, that he stay out of it. "Daddy's threats may carry more weight than you think!" she advised imperiously. Jim nodded, but she wasn't convinced that he was listening. Andrea did look desperately unhappy and it was tugging on Jim's heartstrings.

When the meal was over, Marti noticed Andrea unassumingly leave the room and so seized the opportunity to go after her. There was only one obvious place to look. There she was, craning over the sink in front of a mirror, assessing the damage. Andrea didn't recognise Marti; they had only met on a couple of occasions and those meetings were brief.

Marti explained her identity and at the mention of Jimbo the sobbing began. She did her best to console the poor girl but was having a hard time believing her tales of woe. "There is always a price to pay."

As Andrea dabbed her cheeks with tissues and proceeded to replenish her foundation, Marti noticed a dark area under her right eye which she hastily disguised with more cream. Apparently, Jim wasn't the first boyfriend that Daddy, Stephanie or some other member of the family had seen off. Andrea was being put under enormous pressure to be seen in Westwood's company and it was obviously against her will. This perplexed Marti. Why was it so important that the onus be placed on Andrea? Stephanie had been associated with David and had far more cunning than Andrea ever had.

Unfortunately, Sir James knew only too well his youngest daughter's weakness: money. He'd threatened to cut off her allowance if she refused to obey and this, of course, would destroy her.

Andrea finished tidying herself up and with a heavy sigh, returned to the dining-room. Marti waited a moment, checking her own make-up, which didn't amount to much and for which she carried no touch-up kit, before going back herself to be greeted by an over-zealous Jimbo.

"Where've you been?"

"That's a little personal isn't it?"

He blushed – there were a lot of keen ears around. Whilst they were having coffee, Marti intimated that she had some news and would reveal all later, when they were alone. Her comment caused some heads to turn, so she and Jim continued with a trail of innuendos, which caused serious interest to be shown by several fellow journalists. "Do they ever stop working?" she sighed.

Marti and Jim had come to know each other's traits well over the past few months and were equally adept at weaving an elaborate web to entice anyone who paid the slightest attention. The more interest, the more challenging the game became, and therefore all the more wickedly entertaining!

Marti and Jim made their intentions to leave highly evident with a rustling of tablecloths, scraping chair legs and a great many tactile advances. From the doorway they glanced back to observe their associates once more huddled over the table. They giggled and scampered up stairs.

"I wonder what they're saying?" laughed Marti.

"We'll probably find out in the morning papers!" Jim jested pushing her into her room.

In the hilarity, Jim had not forgotten Marti's promise of news. "I'm flattered by your eagerness," she said, but Jim simply stared. Marti desisted; once inside, behind closed doors, she went on to explain the facts.

"Obviously, in her heart, Andrea doesn't want to be with Westwood and Westwood is still playing the field so therefore the feeling is mutual. Sir James is set on the marriage, for some reason, having threatened to pull the purse strings on Andrea if she fails to comply. This of course will hit her where it hurts most, because Andrea, the little darling, wants everything! Oh and she also has a black eye."

Disconcerted by the directness of her dialogue, Jim immediately became defensive. Marti reiterated her feelings, advising him to steer clear and backed it with a stern expression but, she could see she wasn't getting through Jim's thick skull. Despairingly she asked Jim to leave, adding: "I'm sorry if I've upset you."

Marti despaired as to the wisdom of Jim's intentions of further involvement, but he knew the score and although she herself had severe reservations, she felt less uneasy for having aired her views. Marti was a great believer that if something was bothering someone, they should state their case clearly; she also realised the risk of rejection that was run in doing so and as a result of her out-spokeness, had suffered persecution and isolation in the past. She had found that individuals, corporations and governing bodies often could not accept the facts and supposed, that short term, there was some truth in the saying that 'ignorance is bliss'. Marti's trouble was that if she did become involved in what she perceived to be incorrect dealings, she felt unable to shirk that responsibility because at the end of the day she had to live with herself. She could forgive but, not forget, and would accept the consequences if necessary. Anyway, Jim was a grown-up and she could do little else to stop him.

Marti refused to be disturbed by this dilemma any longer and as a little boy, who had crept in beside her, was gazing up at her with those saucer-like eyes, she could feel nothing but content admiration.

"I don't want to be alone right now."

"It's alright," she assured him, and he settled to rest.

Marti and Jim were grounded back at Heathrow on Monday morning. Jim's behaviour was jittery. He kept asking Marti what she wanted to do.

"I'm going home," was her consistent reply but he kept on and it was driving her up the wall! As they came out of the terminal, he asked the question yet again. Marti stopped dead. Dumped her suitcase on the pavement and sat on it. "What do *you* want to do?" she asked, directly.

"Nothing..." he said, shrugging.

Marti sighed in exasperation of this fib. "Oh come on Jim – I'm tired!"

She was finding it difficult to conceal her irritation and nervously, Jim half hinted that he wanted to stay in London for a few days. He cowered, fully expecting an ear bashing, but she simply said "Whatever," with a wave of her hand. Marti gathered her bags and they caught the next train into the city. Jim finally made the decision to stay and would deliver the reports and pictures to Power Play. Marti returned home, knowing full well Jim's intentions.

Having completed his errand at Power Play, which included the delivery of a letter from Marti addressed to Mr. Bennett requesting the return of her manuscript, Jim headed off for Andrea's flat. Of course he couldn't be sure she would be there and even if she was, that she would be alone. However he had heard on the grapevine that Westwood was still in Imola, testing a new car, and so convinced himself that she would be unescorted.

As luck would have it, she was at home and Jim's assisted intuition had served him well: Westwood was not in the country. Andrea was slightly uptight about Jim's visit, but nonetheless pleased to see him. Apparently Daddy was also out of the country on business, so they could both breathe more easily. This did, however, still leave the small matter of Stephanie to contend with and Andrea urged him not to stay too long. Jim honoured her wishes and, after coffee and a short chat, left. But he had no intention of returning to the homelands. Not just yet.

He found himself some reasonable accommodation. Power Play had paid him and he cashed his entire salary cheque. For once Jim was flush.

That evening he went out on the town, although this time not to paint it red. Jim was contemplating some detective work. He began by visiting all the restaurants and bars frequented during his fateful week's guided tour with Andrea. He wasn't really sure what he was looking for but hoped that someone or something would stimulate his subconscious. Whilst propping up the counter of a wine bar in Covent Garden an attractive young lady approached him.

"Haven't I seen you with Andrea Fairbrother?"

Jim was thrilled and immediately asked the girl, whose name was Joanne, to pull up a stool.

It developed that she had attended private tuition classes with Andrea as teenagers and still kept in contact on a casual basis. Jim couldn't recall meeting Jo before and was cautious with his dialogue which made for tardy conversation, rousing suspicion in Jo, who was well read when it came to the papers. Jim explained that Andrea was with someone else now.

"I'm not surprised." She smiled sympathetically. "It's been impossible to avoid the media coverage lately." Jo, realising Jim's disappointment at the situation, offered some constructive advice.

Joanne had known Andrea and the family for many years and was aware of Daddy's manipulative powers. "That's one of the reasons why I don't see much of Andrea these days," she confided.

Jim's knowledge was gradually building up brick by brick.

The subject of Stephanie also cropped up and he discovered that she frequented a night club just a few doors away. Fuelled with this enlightening information, Jim's mind was working at full throttle. He decided he would definitely check the club out but didn't want Jo's further involvement, and certainly didn't want her to sense his enthusiasm by rushing straight out the door in hot pursuit. Jim restrained his urges and spent an hour or more casually chatting with the pretty young lady, which suited his style no end.

The following day passed slowly. Jim kicked his heals on the city streets, drinking copious amounts of coffee and reading magazine articles and newspapers, frustrated by the long wait for night fall; but it came – as it always does, and Jimbo, dressed to kill, set off down town, for the bright lights. He was confident that Stephanie would be there, having convinced himself of this during the tedious daylight hours. However, his confidence waned somewhat as he stood in front of the club's entrance kiosk. The girl encased within this cubicle was stern and unapproachable, a fact intensified by the iron bars in front of her face. Jim fumbled with his wallet; the fee was extortionate and he had to bite his lip to refrain from saying something.

The disco's interior was almost entirely decorated in various shades of black with a few large mirrors, strategically placed and the carpet was as sticky and soaked with liquor spills and who knows what, as any other dive Jim had been inside. It was so dark that Jimbo wondered how he was ever going to recognise anyone. Fortunately there was a lounge area which was slightly better illuminated and it was from here that Jim took up surveillance. He waited for an awfully long time and was bitterly disappointed when, by 1.30 am Stephanie had not materialised. The club was almost empty and Jim was eventually asked by the stewards to vacate the premises.

A further day was squandered, in aimless wanderings (Marble Arch wasn't as big as he had imagined in childhood), until time dictated a return to his evening haunt. Now his patience was rewarded. Stephanie arrived but was obviously not expecting to see Jimbo sitting at the bar and was totally unprepared for his introduction; she dithered and stuttered as she struggled to restore her customary cloak of calculated calm. Unfortunately her defences had been breached, giving Jim the edge. He ordered a pint of beer and a dry white wine and as Stephanie went to accept the glass, he drew it away, leading her to a secluded alcove in the lounge bar. Stephanie, somewhat unwillingly, followed.

Whilst glaring in annoyance at the half-pint mug he found himself to be holding, Jim proceeded innocently.

"So I hear congratulations are in order!" Stephanie looked bemused, "David and Andrea," Jim prompted.

"Oh – yes!" she snapped impudently, changing the subject in an effort to entice Jim's affections.

Jim defused the situation by bluntly pointing out that he was under the impression that she had been seeing Westwood. Stephanie became agitated by his unsavoury insinuations and prepared to leave.

Jim acted quickly to delay her: "Lighten up! – It doesn't bother me who either of you see."

Stephanie settled back in her chair; this was more her level of commitment: get what you want and go! Naturally, for a woman of Stephanie's social status, there was no shortage of willing partners. She knew the rules and played them hard; no amount of cheap wine was ever going to get her to make a mistake. Jim was well aware of this fact and didn't waste the cash.

They danced for a while and Jim made his advances: Stephanie responded according to plan and they left for her apartment. The taxi drew up in front of the building and they went inside. In the lift Jim counted the floors and Stephanie led him right to the door. That was all he needed: "I'm out of here!" Jim made a mad dash for the lift; its doors were beginning to close but he made it safely by ramming his foot in the diminishing gap. Stephanie was absolutely furious; Jim could hear her obscenities as the lift descended. Back on the street, he hailed a cab and returned to his humble hotel room

Jim passed the next 36 hours as an undercover spy, watching Stephanie's apartment. Late on Friday afternoon, Westwood turned up. Jim had been expecting him but was still bitterly infuriated.

With finances running low, and having seen enough for one

week, Jim decided to return home. On his way to Paddington, he allowed himself one more sentimental visit to the Covent Garden wine bar. By chance, Jo was there – only this time behind the bar, where she was employed at weekends. It was early evening and not yet busy so Jo was able to talk without drawing the attentions of her boss. Jim told her of his plans to return home and she seemed genuinely pleased by his decision not to chase Andrea. As Jim was leaving, Jo was distracted by another customer. "Andrea's not his real daughter!" she muttered hastily, but before Jim could ask any more questions she had turned to continue her work with her boss looming in the background.

Jo's last statement resonated in Jim's thoughts and he mulled over the possible implications of the mitigating evidence. Before he knew it, the train was pulling into Bristol. The last connecting shuttle service, however, had just left: he could see its back end disappearing round the corner. "Typical! Only British Rail could organise this sort of hook up!" Jim growled, as he examined the contents of his wallet, which wasn't exactly healthy so he phoned Marti. There was no reply. Jim hung around a while before dialling the number again but there was still no reply. He tried several more times at evenly-spaced intervals. When there was still no response, he began to worry. "She was usually there." It was getting late so he finally concluded that his only option was a taxi.

The cottage was in darkness when he arrived: it was past midnight and he didn't have a key. Jim searched the shed in the backyard, which wasn't an easy task; everything including the kitchen sink was stuffed away in there. He could hardly see his hand in front of his face, let alone a key – which he was only assuming through experience, was amongst all the discarded plant pots and junk. Jim was becoming a touch frustrated as he tripped over various objects, while others fell on him from above. He almost died of heart failure when Gato sprang out of the darkness, spitting as she brushed past his face in a feline frenzy.

Jim had been none too quiet in his endeavours and Marti's neighbour came to investigate, complete with shotgun. He'd use it too, if necessary, and had let both barrels go on a previous occasion, when some kids were nicking petrol from local cars. His aim had been deliberately high, but it did the trick, the louts hadn't been seen since!

The old boy thankfully recognised Jimbo and offered some practical assistance by obtaining a ladder. Just as Jim, having gained a scrambled entrance through a tiny, upstairs window, almost breaking his neck in the process, reached the light switch at the bottom of the stairs; he heard a key turn in the lock. Marti, on hearing noises, was apprehensive and about to run for help when Jim yelled in anguish, "It's only me!"

"Was this supposed to be good news?" She thought as she went in to find Jimbo, with his face squashed against the living-room wall at the foot of the stairs.

"Why couldn't you have been here ten minutes ago?" he groaned in torment

Marti could hardly stand for laughing, and she needed the loo, she could well imagine his exploits and would have put money on her neighbour turning up armed! The old chap was now standing beside her, chuckling. But it took Jim somewhat longer to accept the funny side. "I was worried about you!" he stormed.

"So why didn't you call earlier in the day to let me know what you were doing? – I'm not a mind reader!" She remonstrated.

Jim scowled but understood her point of view and realised that he would have to get used to living on an equal opportunities basis if he intended to stick around.

"By the way," Marti added, "There's always a key under the dustbin."

CHAPTER 10

Marti's dreams were becoming ever more vivid, several times she had been taken to a large church, where an air of tranquillity prevailed. Standing at the entrance, the wide aisle stretched before her with towering pillars on either side, lined up like a guard of honour in support of a high stone cast vaulted ceiling. About halfway down on the left-hand side, she could just make out the figure of a man kneeling. Marti watched in awe for some while, somehow he was unapproachable, set apart in his own peaceful sanctuary, which he did not wish violated. When the time was right, he rose to his feet, and steadying himself on the back of the following pew, took the few faltering steps to the centre of the long passageway, bowed his head and crossed his chest. He turned to Marti with a look that suggested he knew she had always been there, she could see his features clearly in the flickering candlelight; and as he got closer he held out his hand. She was powerless to resist his offer of guidance and felt herself uncontrollably floating towards him as he led her to the great altar. His eyes traced the exquisite carvings which adorned richly decorated stained glass windows reaching above the tableau of religious artefacts gathered on this sacred table. Marti became transfixed by the mass of vivid hues created by the intense light as it reflected on every individual, angelic image as they seemed to smile down on them from another plane. The young man studied her reaction and was genuinely pleased. He asked for no gesture of worship and no pressure of acceptance was borne upon her.

He simply wanted to show her the beauty of his belief. What she chose to do with the information was entirely up to her.

Marti experienced a recurrence of this quasi-religious dream on consecutive nights. The sequence of events was identical but on each occasion the young man's incandescent image grew brighter.

In no time at all, further travel documents were dropping through the letterbox of the tiny unassuming cottage.

Marti and Jim were thoroughly and unashamedly excited about their next assignment, Monaco – the most prestigious venue on the racing calendar. A fairytale princedom, Monte Carlo itself rises defiantly out of the rocky slopes of the Alps, which seem to push its high-rise, architecture perilously close to the Mediterranean.

Marti and Jim flew into Nice and covered the remainder of the journey by hire-car. They opted for the coastal route and once out of the bustling city traffic, the scenery was absolutely fabulous; the intensity of the light on the Azure coast was beyond description. No wonder it was such an inspirational heaven for artists; they only wished that they had more time. "Perhaps... one day," Marti dreamed, as the narrow road twisted along the edge of the mountains, passing through Villefranche, Beaulieu, Cap-d'Ail and on into Monaco.

It was twelve noon, Wednesday; the weather was comfortably warm and after some difficulties in negotiating the tiny principality's clogged arterial road network – a problem that was aggravated by the thousands of extra, temporary inhabitants – they managed to reach their hotel. The accommodation was neat and tidy with TV, phone and bath. Marti opened the shutters to bring some light from the congested street below. Ironically, the use of a car seemed particularly pointless. Looking up and to her left, she could see the Pink Palace with its seafront sloping grounds, which housed the Royal Family.

Holding this fantasy image in her mind she decided to pamper herself in the manner accustomed to one of that ilk. Jim had cleared off on a reconnaissance mission, so Marti revelled in the private luxuries of her hotel room – in particular the large tub, which was the perfect answer after being stuck in traffic with the added heat of engines running. Filling it almost to the brim, she had complementary bubbles everywhere. Having taken a cream silk covered pillow from the bed to place at one end of the bath, she slid herself into the soothing waters. It was heavenly!

146

Resting her head gently on the soft cushion, she closed her eyes and opened her heart.

He soon came to her.

They were by a marina, extravagantly stocked with yachts and motor cruisers, some of which were registered to sub tropical continents and areas of deepest darkest desires. But Marti wasn't being taken to any of them. Instead he led her beyond the boats and ships to where it was quiet. Together they sat on the edge of a breakwater, kicking their feet in the sea. He was unassumingly attired in blue cut-offs and a faded yellow T-shirt which had once born a slogan for surf boards. "You can see fish in here sometimes," he informed her, excited at the prospect of sharing his knowledge.

He lay down on his tummy with his chin resting on the backs of his hands, gesturing that Marti should join him in this posture, explaining that it was not possible to see well enough from where she was sitting. He was adamant about this and became slightly upset when he thought she was not going to comply. Marti had always intended to co-operate but, obviously hadn't projected her intentions quickly enough for her friend's liking. He could be extremely impatient at times, but was becoming more aware of this tendency, and a certain glance from Marti was all that was required to remind him, gently, of this minor fault. Her mild reprimand didn't bother him; he was trying very hard to learn and truly wanted to.

Side by side they lazed in the sun, staring into the deep blue-green ocean. The hustling backdrop of the town was a million miles away as they drifted on their self-made raft. He wriggled closer to Marti and reached for her hand; he was shy and awkward and all the time watched, unblinking, for her reaction. Marti took the paw and tickled its palm which brought a chuckle from within. Embarrassed by his new found sensitivity, he hid his face under his arm. "Look!" Marti pointed with hushed enthusiasm at the sea below.

His head bobbed up immediately. "Fish – I told you!" he squeaked, thrilled that their wait had not been in vain.

Marti traced circles in the calm surface of the Mediterranean and woke to find herself making exactly the same motion in her bath water, which by this time had become quite cool. Laughing at her antics, she remembered her young man and smiled with contented pride as she recalled his naive attempts at physical contact. A single tear traced the contour of her face, reaching her lower jaw – whereupon it fell silently into the wasting bubbles.

As Marti dressed, there was a knock on the door: it was Jimbo returning from his scouting expedition. "Hi!" Marti was pleased to see him and planted a cheery peck on his cheek. "Tell me what's going on?"

Jim didn't share Marti's enthusiasm and in fact looked decidedly broody. He was sitting on the edge of her bed with the weight of the world on his shoulders.

"What's up?" she tried to coax him, but he just stared pensively at the purple ribbed carpet. Marti showed more concern and lifting his chin asked what had happened.

"The Fairbrothers are here, in force," he moaned morosely.

"Who did you expect in Monaco this weekend then?" Marti's surprised tone echoed little comfort and denied any sympathy, Jim stomped off to his room.

Marti allowed him a few minutes to simmer down before going after him. Eventually prising him from his depression she persuaded him to take her out to dinner.

Strolling along Quai Albert, past the swimming pool which forms part of the circuit, they stopped briefly by the harbour wall to admire the richly endowed, anchored flotilla.

Marti felt a strange familiarity with the area; turning to the imposing tower blocks behind, she wondered what it was really like to live here permanently, although she was well aware that many only used the resort as a posing playground. But it's a hell of a chat-up line: "Would you like to see my Monte Carlo apartment?"

"Umm..." Marti ponderously mimed the words: "Yeah," she decided with a wistful smile, "I'd probably go!"

Some settle here permanently but others use it as a convenient staging post from which to conduct business when home is too far away to reach. "Or do they go somewhere else? Somewhere their roots dictate."

They walked on, clambering over crash barriers that were placed along the street, defining the circuit. It would appear that all roads in Monaco lead to Casino Square. Marti and Jim found themselves hiking up the steeply inclining Avenue D'Ostende, past the back of the Hotel de Paris, which overlooks the port of Monaco, and as they rounded the corner they were confronted by the magnificent Baroque buildings that surround a beautifully appointed water garden in the centre of the square.

Jim had livened up somewhat, which considering the setting, shouldn't have been too difficult! Even he appreciated the sparkling fountains and crystal pools.

The pair decided to chance their luck in the American gaming room of the Cafe de Paris, which is situated directly opposite the hotel. It was crammed full of flashing slot machines, frantically whirring, in constant use by gamblers who fed them coins, in between sipping their drinks. Neither Marti nor Jim won a single franc and so left the hullabaloo in search of peace and perhaps some food; Jimbo's stomach was talking to them again.

There was a multi-national culinary choice all within close proximity. Peering through the half-curtained widow of a small restaurant, Marti recognised some famous faces and excitedly urged Jim to take her in. He became bashful, uncharacteristically pretending that the whole thing was no big deal. "Let's go somewhere else," he said; but Marti insisted and the next Jim knew he was sitting at a table ordering supper in a terrible mixture of Anglo French pronunciation.

Marti loved every minute and sat with her back to the wall so as not miss anything. Immediately she noticed that Philip Rheutemanne was not in the company of the same young lady who had attended the previous race meeting in San Marino; and in fact, on closer examination she looked distinctly similar to a woman who'd been seen with Westwood on numerous occasions, even since his engagement! A couple of other drivers were also present whom Marti knew to be residents of the town, so her expectations of the restaurant's service and cuisine were high. She wasn't to be disappointed, the meal was exquisite and the duo returned to their hotel full and satisfied.

Thursday proved to be work as usual, although one fighter pilot bounced off three barriers at Ste Devote and suffered shock and a very sore thumb. Friday was a free day, a day to relax and savour the party atmosphere that only Monaco can provide, with yacht and pool side activities accustomed to the wealthy. Marti and Jim grasped this day to relax and enjoy some sightseeing.

It was impossible to explore everything, even in a place this compact without being distracted and within the limited time available, but they decided to start with the Jardin Exotique, having been reliably informed that this was a good point from which to view the principality in its entirety. You can take a lift which rises up the side of the mountains, from whence stepping stones lead through an abundance of exotic flowers and vegetation, including some spiky varieties from South America. They also visited the Cathedral in the old town of Monaco, which is the resting place of Princess Grace from Hollywood fame. It was a tiring day, having negotiated the many hills, but well worth the effort and both retired to their rooms in need of a good sleep before racing began in earnest on Saturday.

It was all systems go from early dawn and a flurry of rumours hit the pit lane – of clandestine meetings between drivers, teams and sponsors. It seemed somewhat early in the season to be thinking of next year's appointments and job security but apparently not all shared this sentiment. Perhaps merit, or being in the right place at the right time, is not sufficient these days, and more manipulative means are required.

At the afternoon's timed practice, Westwood again secured pole position but all was not plain sailing. The narrow twisting street circuit was causing problems for many a man and machine. In particular, the less experienced Rheutemanne, the new whizz kid, could only manage eleventh on the grid after having several nerve-racking moments, clipping the walls lightly before doing the job properly and pitching his car into the Massenet barriers at about 150 miles an hour. Astonishingly, he emerged from the tangled metal, unhurt and completely undeterred. Ah, the exuberance of youth! Philip, however, wasn't alone in his argument with the Armco which runs the entire length of the 2.06 mile circuit.

The day's work was drawing to an end and Marti was sitting on the temporarily constructed pit wall when she saw Andrea, anxiously scanning the track. In the distance, Marti also spotted Jim and so bundled her camera equipment into her rucksack and set off in pursuit – not something she found easy with half a ton of gear slung around her neck and dozens of meandering fans bumping into her as they searched, eagle-eyed, in the hopes of catching a glimpse of their appointed heroes. Marti got within yelling distance and was just about to let rip when Andrea grabbed the unsuspecting Jim, dragging him behind the canvas make-shift garages.

"Oh shit!" The words didn't come out but her lips made the movements. "What's she up to?" Marti was annoyed that the girl was still intent on harassing Jimbo. Just when he seemed to be getting himself together, she pops up again. Marti knew Jim was still weak where Andrea was concerned, all the little madam had to do was click her fingers and Jim would go running.

As Marti got closer she could see them at the far end of a tyre truck. Deciding to be brazen, Marti marched straight up to them. Unfortunately her plan was foiled; they gabbled some hurried exchanges and Andrea shot off like a scalded kitten. Marti shook her head disapprovingly.

"Don't say it!" Jim boomed.

For whatever reason, Jimbo had become embroiled in this situation, and Marti could give him some credit for not shunning the responsibility. Too many of us hide, in the hope that life will not question our faith or the effects that we have upon each other. Sadly she feared that modern man was losing his consciousness. There is so much more, beyond the normal sense of physical awareness.

That evening Marti and Jim visited Rampoldi, a restaurant favoured by journalists, drivers and sponsors alike. They met up with the usual gang – Jack was there in fine reminiscent form and after ensuring that Marti was in the dubiously safe hands of Ossi, Jim made some egotistical excuse about the better man and left. Marti knew where he was going: "Take care!"

Jim acknowledged her concern with a knowing nod and went on his way. He had pre-arranged to meet Andrea elsewhere, in the old hilltop town and if possible away from prying eyes. It was a dodgy gambit for both parties; Sir James had been keeping his youngest daughter on a short leash all week.

Andrea was tearful on their meeting; her father was forcing her into marriage and she was at a loss for a reason.

Jim optimistically tried to explain that money wasn't everything: "Time and life, one and the same, are by far the most important gifts bestowed upon us," – Jim inhaled deeply before continuing with his sermon – "both of which can never be regained once lost or wasted." Jim must have got this from Marti – and she thought he didn't listen!

The whole concept was however, totally incomprehensible to Andrea. Jim tried again on a more simple level, "Nobody has to do anything they don't want to, at least past the age of 18. All you need is a little commitment and trust."

Andrea thoughtfully considered the compromise for a few seconds but decided that life without a Porsche, happy or otherwise, was unacceptable. The dear girl was in a terrible dilemma! Jim's attempts at counselling were floundering and in the past he might have given up at this stage – but a growing affinity compelled him to stay and comfort her in the secluded, local hostelry until everybody had left. Only then, and with deep deliberation, did he offer to take her back to his hotel room, as it had become blatantly obvious that she had no desire to return to her own shared accommodation. "Daddy or Stephanie will be waiting," she reflected squeamishly.

On Jim's bed, Andrea lay in his arms. Jim felt that she would have to make a decision on her immediate future, preferably by daybreak, and he employed a variety of conciliatory endearments in a desperate attempt to rekindle their romance. Jim was more than willing to take her away from this mess but had little more than his love to tempt her with. Andrea wasn't listening. She had become enthralled with the body she lay next to and enchantingly seduced it.

By sunrise, it had become apparent that Andrea had made her decision. Jim gazed lazily as she dressed in all her finery, convinced, after their night of passion that she would stay. She turned to collect her diamond-studded earrings from the bedside cabinet and Jim stretched out to take her hand. Her expression was strikingly cold. Jim was devastated; he felt his heart burst as a deep sigh deflated his chest. No words were needed to portray the gravity of her rejection and Andrea offered none, not even a last glance as she closed the hotel room door.

Jim couldn't believe he'd been so gullible and the hurt was

acutely embarrassing. At breakfast Marti could see his distress but daren't mention anything for fear of him bursting into tears.

Out on the busy streets, the weather and scenes were also beginning to steam. With so many of the drivers living here, it was only a short, Sunday morning walk down to the start line. Marti pictured Veridico, as he strolled along the tree lined Boulevard Albert. He was unperturbed as worshipping fans and well-wishers, in their hunt for autographed memorabilia, thrust programmes and hats under his nose, whilst others clicked away with instamatics. There were some jibes as to whether he would be racing next year and what he was going to do about Westwood's lead, to which he smiled politely and waved to the crowd before withdrawing to the security of the paddock. Here Marcus sought out his manager enquiring as to the receipt of any mail. He couldn't understand why the letters had stopped. Westwood was giving more interviews, firmly supported by Sir James and a couple of dubious-looking Italian sidekicks. Later, during lunch, Sir James was caught in serious debate with a number of other Italians. Marti managed to photograph the group without their knowledge.

The race was set to begin, red to green; everyone was confident that Westwood would take it, flag to flag. There is little opportunity for overtaking here and with his superior speed and reliability it was expected, nay a foregone conclusion that he would win comfortably. However, there's always someone with a different idea. With Westwood leading, the reigning Champion pressed hard for the first couple of laps but, was unable to sustain the attack and realising the extra power of the machine ahead, he appeared to settle and consolidate his second place. The race progressed and inevitably retirements began to mount – every gear shift of the thousands involved in negotiating this tight street circuit, forced more pressure on mounting hand blisters and strained neck muscles. One sad casualty being the German: he'd driven a magnificent race with barely a mistake, only to be let down by ineffective technology. The German's unfortunate demise seemed however, to be a signal for the race to really begin in earnest. Westwood had a problem and pitted; the car was stationery for some while, giving Veridico a chance to take the lead. He capitalised unrepentantly on the Briton's misfortune, holding out on ragged rubber and sheer determination just long enough to win!

Back at Sir James' hospitality rooms, the mood was one of utter disbelief. No one seemed to know the reason for Westwood's unannounced pit stop and the information was not forthcoming from the Javelin team's technical director. Sir James was sickeningly trying to appease his Italian buddies, offering surmised explanations. There was a lot of gesticulation on the part of the darkly clad gentlemen, who were seriously not amused by the lack of comment. Surely it wasn't that bad? Westwood did come a close second – and if the Championship was the problem, there were still plenty of races to contend.

Monaco's Grand Prix is traditionally run later in the day than most other European events and evening advanced as the sun ducked behind the imperious Alps. Celebrations in the Javelin camp were notably subdued and photographers were clearly discouraged. Andrea was behaving attentively toward David, who for his part was taking little notice of her efforts. He was still in discussions with his pit crew, as they tried to pinpoint a reason for their disappointing performance. The Italians were also in close proximity and still the truth of the mechanical failure that had caused Westwood to stop had not been established. Jim was 'God knows where' and Marti felt her attentions being distracted.

She was subconsciously drawn from the confusion to a celestial world of peace. Drifting quietly, there was no sense of danger, even though she was aware of not being in control. She found herself in an apartment block overlooking the harbour, the lift automatically took her to the ninth floor, whereupon a door opened, admitting her to a luxury suite. Serenity prevailed from within its butter-coloured spaces and she wandered from room to room until, in one, with a sunken central bay, she found a hammock, slung low from its ceiling moorings. It swayed gently to and fro and Marti could see one bare foot and blue jeaned leg swinging in time with the rhythm of its suspended retreat.

The evening light shone through an adjacent window, deflecting its rays in a fan as it passed through horizontal raffia blinds. As Marti approached the central figure, he turned his head to greet her. To his chest he clutched a thick book with well-thumbed pages and an engaging smile faintly traced his lips. Marti returned the welcome with a knowing nod of approval and his smile instantly widened to an enchantingly boyish grin. There was an acknowledgement of deep respect in his eyes as he reached up to her, swinging his legs round in a single movement to bring himself to his feet. Leaving the book behind on the swaying canvas nest he gave her a long, loving embrace, after which he proceeded to dance her round the flat in playful leaps and bounds as he conducted a fully audited tour of each and every room including the smallest! Both body and speech were perfectly synchronised and he treated Marti to a rare, graphically animated display of his somewhat saucy wit and wistful imagination. Eventually they came to rest in a jumbled heap in the wildly swinging hammock. As its motion gracefully diminished, his compelling laughter softened to a chuckle. He was tired again. His lips were slightly parted and the quiet, inner murmurings of the sort which precious, private dreams are made of were just audible.

Meanwhile, a lone Jimbo was quietly drinking himself under the table of some backstreet bar, and was belligerently mouthing off at any innocent soul who had the misfortune to come into contact with him. He was about to be forcibly ejected by the proprietor when two heavily built gentlemen, professing to be 'friends', took charge, carrying him bodily to a waiting vehicle. Jim put up some fierce opposition, but in his inebriated state was no match for the darkly suited heavies who easily avoided his mistimed punches. Jim was unceremoniously shoved into the boot of the car which then took off at high speed. Jim slid from side to side crashing against the metal interior of the luggage space. He banged his head several times before being able to sober up and brace himself for the next corner. It was pitch black but he could feel blood trickling from his brow. He was about to pass out when the car screeched to a halt and the boot lid flipped open.

Jim clambered over the tail-gate coughing from the petrol fumes he had inhaled; he was seriously disorientated and was just finding his balance when blazing headlamps struck him full in the face. Immediately raising both hands to shield his eyes he staggered towards the offending light, cursing demonstratively. He was barely able to define its three occupants. On reaching the bonnet, the beams were killed and he shouted to the men demanding that they reveal their identities. He needn't have bothered wasting his breath. Sir James was already getting out of the passenger side to greet him.

The two thugs who had originally accosted Jim, and whose faces were vaguely becoming familiar in his intoxicated and beaten bewilderment, were now standing either side of him. Stupidly he lunged at Sir James and they grabbed Jim, wrenched his arms behind his back and slammed him face first into the top of the long black bonnet. Sir James issued the orders and Jim sustained a crushing blow to his right midriff; a gasp of air was emitted and he tasted the blood from his facial wounds as it ran from his nose. Sir James nodded and another massive blow struck him; he nodded again Jim girded himself. This time, however, the grip was loosened enough, allowing him to stand, albeit bent in agony.

Sir James came towards Jim with that wagging finger and proceeded to give him a satirical ticking off, as if he were some naughty schoolboy being punished for some minor misdemeanour. Sir James warned of more serious consequences should he persist in seeing his daughter, implying that he would use 'any means' to stop him. The threats reverberated in Jim's head as the car reversed, swung a handbrake turn and disappeared into the darkness.

This still left Jim with his two bodyguards. He faced them and prepared for the worst. It came; his limbs were by now, powerless to offer resistance and could barely protect him from the torrent of kicks and blows that rained down. Jim lost consciousness and was left for dead in the dirt high above the glittering principality. He came too, shivering in a state of shock, and managed to crawl to the roadside. He must have staggered about a mile before a delivery wagon stopped, giving him a lift to Casino Square. From here it was only a short distance to the hotel and Marti who, like any other sane person, was sound asleep. Hence, she was somewhat startled by the tapping on her door; concluding that she wasn't dreaming, she apprehensively opened it. Jim fell through it, into her arms and she dragged him the last few steps to the bed where he collapsed, on the verge of hysteria.

He was in a dreadful mess; Marti wanted to call a doctor and the police. Jim went absolutely crazy at this idea, believing any intervention of this nature would only cause further aggravation, and so as not to upset him further, she reluctantly agreed to his wishes and tended his damage. "You really should go to hospital," she urged. Jim's chest, back and kidney area was just one mass of bruising and abrasions. "If there are any breaks you could be in serious trouble!"

Jim adamantly refused. Marti held her composure but feared that there may be internal damage; his head injury was also cause for concern. She watched over him till daybreak. Maybe after some rest he would see sense.

However, this was not to be. At breakfast it was abundantly clear that Jim's fear had now turned to anger! He was in no mood for conciliatory discussions – adding, "I'll sort it my way!"

Marti felt a shudder of pure terror run down her spine and remonstrated with him, but her words fell on deaf ears. In her opinion, for what little worth that had for Jim now, he was simply being ridiculous but on the drive back to Nice Airport he laid on the back seat pretending to be asleep, giving Marti no further opportunity to argue her case.

The return flight was endured in a similar manner, though Marti still knew he was faking it and it wasn't until they were driving down the M4 in a horrendous thunderstorm, that the silence was broken. He went off like a bomb, yelling and punching the dashboard. Marti couldn't see a bloody thing with all the spray from the road and traffic and having some nutter in the seat beside her didn't help, so she pulled onto the hard shoulder. Jim flew out before the wheels could stop and was pacing the grass verge in the rain. Marti draped herself wearily over the steering wheel.

"It must be the stormy weather that does this to him." She was trying to make light of the situation but was concerned for their safety – the hard shoulder of a motorway is no place for a tantrum.

Eventually Marti wound down the window and told Jim

firmly to "Get in!" It was a further five minutes before he obliged, but he was calm and the remainder of the journey was completed in relative safety, although there was now a large pool of water sloshing around in the passenger foot well.

Marti was exhausted by the time they reached home. It was always a relief for her to be back but never more so this time. "There's nowhere quite like it," she thought, though the pair were still not speaking.

The rain continued throughout the night and as she lay in her bed, she could hear water constantly dripping from the gutter, bouncing off the sill outside her window. Her worried mind was working overtime and she feared that she was not strong enough to cope with anyone else's emotional fall out. A silent tear slipped from the corner of her eye towards the pillow. It was cold and shivering; she pulled the duvet around her ears and curled up into a tight ball. Soon a warm glowing sensation overcame her; it began at the nape of her neck, flowed sweetly across her shoulders and down her back, engulfing her entire body with heat. Only the presence of another could induce such a sense of security. She knew his scent – like that of the sea on a humid evening, just as night falls. He reassured her with kind words and a generous scattering of soft kisses applied to her temple. Marti revelled in his tenderness as he pulled her close to his chest and abdomen. The fit was perfection, forming a single sensuous curve. She could still here the drip, dripping outside but as she drifted into sleep the sound became less and less. Soon it could be heard no more.

Marti awoke next morning with an incredible inner feeling of tranquillity. It was the first time he had come to her when she was in need and the beauty of his actions opened a whole new concept in their relationship. Marti's dreams were no longer her own, his level of consciousness had been raised to the point where he now possessed the ability to enter her world at will.

The closeness and spontaneity of both parties was too intense to be the creation of a single mind and Marti questioned the complexities of such a union. "Where does fantasy meet reality? Did he know what he was doing? Would he recognise her and, if so, would the intimate secrets shared in this other dimension, be known to him in this world? – Or was she simply obsessed with something she could never have?

Thoughts like these could drive a girl crazy, but Marti was resilient; she possessed a great deal of self-confidence and dedication and had the ability and desire, to channel these elements into achieving a single goal. Marti had already committed herself by making the gift but, for all her dreaming, the practical side of her nature never left her. In reality, her feet were always planted firmly on the ground, she expected no return and whatever the outcome of her adventure, she could never be deprived of the knowledge that she had tried to help and understand.

From the next room Marti could hear groans as Jimbo stirred, obviously still sore from his beating. He sounded quite pathetic and feeling mellower toward him she went to see if he was OK. Leaning over the bed in a motherly fashion, she whispered "good morning."

Jim was profusely apologetic for his behaviour, admitting that he was petrified on the night he took the beating and in truth feared for his life. Mournfully he asked if she had any more little white tablets.

Marti squeezed his hand. "I'll go and look." She said, switching the water heater on in the airing cupboard at the foot of Jim's bed. "I think you should have a hot bath!"

"We're getting pretty adept at this routine!" Jim laughed, but it hurt so much he had to hold his ribcage in an effort to counter the pain.

CHAPTER 11

It was now June and the circus was heading back across the Atlantic to Canada – Montreal to be precise, on the banks of the St. Lawrence River, and the Circuit Gilles Villeneuve, named after a famous Canadian driver who gave his life in 1982. It's a popular track built on the Isle Notre Dame and the city provides a diverse array of recreational facilities.

Marti and Jim arrived on Thursday evening and the customary rounds of pre-race practice and interviews ran their course. Westwood had not secured pole, but was nonetheless confident and indeed, appeared totally undaunted by the prospect of starting from third!

Marti took up her place on the inside of the circuit; about halfway down the start/finish straight. It was a short sprint into the Island hairpin. She was in situ, camera at the ready. The engines screamed as the lights turned green; tyres screeched and their combined might surged towards her at terrifying speed, almost stopping her heart as they passed.

Westwood was unable to improve on his starting position and, after a frantic battle for the first corner, had to settle in line. It was a race of tactics and durability rather than pure speed; those possessing the sharpest minds and not the fastest machinery took the lead. With nine laps completed, Westwood did not look comfortable. For the first time this season, he was being forced to drive in traffic and he was not a happy man, waving his fist at other competitors, his frustration finally got the better of him and he made an impatient attack on the leader Veridico, losing control on a dusty part of the track. The car pitched momentarily in a gravel trap, spun violently through 360 degrees and came to rest right on the racing line, its collapsed suspension made movement impossible. Marti watched in horror – 'not the best place to park!', as evasive action had to be quickly undertaken by the ensuing pack! There was a milliseconds' response time. Luckily due to his colleagues' skills Westwood suffered no impact. It was a somewhat unnecessary incident considering the early stages of the race; the safety car was deployed whilst the wrecked Javelin was removed to the sidelines and Westwood had to endure the humiliating walk of shame back to the pit lane. Marti's own opinion, however, was that there was another in David's vicinity, who appeared at times to possess an uncanny ability to entice the man into making ridiculous errors of judgement. But what did she know?

The race reached half-distance and there were barely a few seconds covering the first six places, which made for an exciting change from a spectator's point of view! Suddenly, the leader and defending Champion slowed. He had not had a happy season. The following parade passed him by as he taxied to a halt near the catch fencing. Marti was in close proximity, with camera focused, along with a dozen or so other eager wolves, all hungry for the 'best' shot. A picture holds a thousand words.

Marcus hopped out of his car and was climbing over the boundary wall when he first saw the advancing flock of vultures. Marti was one of them and as they drew nearer she could sense a fear in the man; he'd removed his helmet and was huddled against the concrete block wall for protection. The hovering media, cameras obscuring their identities and with fingers poised, were stopped by Veridico's hooded glares. They waited a while and after deciding that their prey was trapped, settled down to await the final shot. Marti had advanced this far with the rest of the hunting party but as the others stopped, she found herself still walking toward the victim. He couldn't get any closer to the catch fencing and was clutching his helmet and gloves to his chest as if to shield that tender, most vulnerable part of his being. His face was pale and drained of life and his body language resembled that of a caged animal resolved on defeat.

Marti stood beside him and slipped the strap of her camera over her head, placing it on the wall in front of him. A few minutes before the incident, she'd bought a can of fizzy drink, which in all the excitement she had pushed into her bag. She took it out, pulled the tab to open it and asked, "Are you thirsty?"

He turned, raising only his darkened eyes. It was a hot, humid afternoon; the heat in those cars must be extreme. Marcus however, had resumed his inspection of the on-going race so she asked him again. "Are you thirsty? You can take the can if you want to."

He turned to her again, nervously glancing over her shoulder at the rest of the press still gathered. She positioned herself between him and them, obscuring any chance of a decent photograph and suddenly felt an over-powering urge to embrace him. She offered the can again "It's good and cold!"

This time Marcus accepted and as he drank, she watched the sweat trickle from his brow onto his thick lashes. The salt must have stung and he rubbed his eyes. Returning the half-empty can he gestured at her camera, "Aren't you going to snap my identity with that thing?"

Marti was instantly ashamed of herself and of her profession. "No," she said, "I'm on a tea break!" Jokingly she referred to the time and how Brits love their tea, which seemed to cause him some amusement; for a fleeting moment she caught the faintest glimmer of a smile.

Marti sensed some agitation in her colleagues; she was still hogging the frame but thought to herself, "Tough, the bloke suffers enough judgemental press coverage," and concerned that much of his natural self-confidence was lacking, she continued to protect him from ridicule.

Like the fox, Marcus seemed to grow a little more used to her proximity and she tried to lift his spirits. "It was a shame the car stopping like that, I thought you had a good chance today."

He tried a response, but again his lips quivered and curled, as if the words were there, on the end of his tongue, but when he opened his mouth, nothing happened. Marti stumbled on the rough surface and momentarily lost her footing. The ever present photographers fired. Marcus immediately withdrew to the safety of his fence; he was clasping his helmet so tightly his knuckles were turning white.

"Would you like to get away from here?" she asked quietly,

163

but he continued to hide. She took him by the arm and asked again, stooping slightly to get his attention. Swiftly, he raised a hand to his face to conceal his grief. His breathing became erratic; Marti could sense the beginnings of panic. He was shaking and sobbing, she put her arm around him – "Come on," she insisted. Forming a cloak with her body to deflect the volley of shots unleashed by her counterparts, Marcus willingly allowed her to guide him.

It was a fair distance to the pit lane, which allowed Marcus time to collect his thoughts. He shrugged Marti off, coughed to clear his throat and managed to emit a few short syllables. "I'm OK, everything is fine," he informed her but Marti knew that all was not 'fine' inside this individual; his voice lacked conviction. They stopped by the pit entrance. He thanked her politely for the refreshment and, pulling himself to his full height, walked away with a characteristically bandy gait. The Centaura team must have wondered what had happened to their star player during this time lapse, but Marcus offered no explanation and headed straight for the showers.

"Oh shit!" Marti screamed, "The camera!" In all the commotion she'd forgotten it. In a flap, she ran, full pelt, back to the spot where she had left it on the wall but, of course, it had gone and so had all her other personal belongings.

"Shit!" she stormed, "shit!" The race was coming to its conclusion and not only was she without her tools or purse or passport; she was also miles from the finish line. It was impossible to run any further, and anyway what was the point?

Marti ambled back to the paddock and went, ever hopeful, to the lost property office. She gave the attendant a detailed description of her rucksack and to her utter amazement was promptly re-united with her gear, fully intact, complete with film. Apparently a marshal had found it and handed it in only ten minutes before she turned up. Marti was eternally indebted to this unknown saint and insisted that her sincerest thanks be passed on. If she hurried, it might still be possible to get some photographs of the victorious trio at the press conference.

CHAPTER 12

From Canada the show rolled on to Spain to begin its second series of European dates. France would follow and then, of course, the British Grand Prix, which, by all accounts, was poised to be a spectacularly patriotic occasion.

The trip to Spain's Jerez Circuit however, developed into an unhappy, rain-soaked weekend, provoking many accidents and although the sun intermittently broke through during qualifying, fortune did not shine on all on this particular Saturday afternoon. Tragedy struck one gladiator as his machine crashed at 180 miles an hour into the barrier – with such force that its torn and twisted metal remains were savagely spewed across the circuit, forsaking their occupant and discarding him, motionless, onto the tarmac. Doctors and officials were swift to reach the horrific scene but it was another nail-biting, twenty minutes before it was considered safe to move the man. The entire pit lane was in silence as drivers, technicians and tea boys alike held their breath in anticipation of news of their colleague's fate. His injuries were extensive and, though not fatal, surely the memory of any witness to the imminent possibility of a fatality in this sport would never die.

Marti held her own hushed vigil close to a TV monitor in the press room whilst she sipped coffee. She had firsthand experience of an actual, life-taking accident that had occurred at her local circuit, Thruxton. Her memory of this event was heightened by the fact that it happened on her birthday. A total stranger had lost his life on that occasion, right before her very eyes and although, until that point, he had been no more than another transient figure in her life, in death he painted an image that she would never be able to delete. She would never be allowed to forget his name. Death didn't frighten Marti, however; in fact she took comfort in the knowledge that it was inevitable and therefore she knew her final destiny.

Later that evening, after most people had left the track, Marti noticed a lone silhouette; Marcus was standing on the exact spot at which the crash had occurred. She made no approach, sensing the presence of fear, which in itself provides the lifeline and Marti felt that this solitary figure needed to strengthen this line.

The weather conditions on Sunday were atrocious and many officials pondered the virtues of allowing the race to continue at all. In the earlier drivers' conference many safety issues were fervently voiced. However, the governing mechanisms were already in place on the grid. The track was cleared and the parade lap commenced. The front line pairing of Westwood and Pasccari made a tentative start, providing Veridico, in fourth position, with the perfect opportunity. To everyone's amazement, including that of his team-mate Ericson who was beside him, Marcus aggressively thrust the nose of his car between Westwood and Pasccari and was charging for the inside line at the first bend. Westwood retaliated and there was a clash of wheels as he tried to bundle Veridico over the curbs. But Marcus was not the type to be intimidated, and despite collecting a vast amount of mud and gravel, he still forced his way into the lead and tore away from the rest of the pack like a bat out of hell! He continued to extend his lead – lap after lap by recklessly, sliding into every corner before blipping and stamping the accelerator to the floor, as he exited in the wake of dramatic plumes of silver spray thrown up from the track surface, the engine's turbo popped and crackled, whilst the back end of his machine swerved violently from side to side, under pressure to keep up. He won, but as Marcus stepped unsteadily from the cockpit in parc fermé, returning his feet to earth, the tremors began. His entire body shook with vivid recognition of the dangerous nature of his sport; his elevated blood pressure pulsated through the veins in his temples, throbbing mercilessly in his brain; the relentless thumping made his eyes bulge white. His hands quivered, his knees trembled and his manager, who must have thought his prodigal son had gone completely mad to have driven in such an aggressive manner in such atrocious weather conditions, looked on anxiously as the jittering wreck headed for the confines of his motor home. Marcus refused to be interviewed, on account of exhaustion. In truth he longed for the days before politics and such vast amounts of money were introduced. But did the column writers of fact or fiction understand his reasons for solitude at this precise moment? Would they ever understand?

As a respite after the drama of the past few days, Ossi invited Marti to a post-race, unofficial gathering. They were at the bar when Paul Ericson bounded up, asking Marti to dance. After a quick spin around the floor, Paul led her to a table where a sullen-faced Marcus was seated. Paul took Marcus' empty glass and asked Marti what she would like to drink.

"G and T please."

He nipped off jauntily, leaving her with an apparently deaf and dumb Marcus who was biting his bottom lip. He didn't appear to recognise Marti in posh frock and make-up, and she was about to make her introduction when suddenly, he spoke.

"Would you like me to fuck you now, or later?"

Marti was disgusted with him. Stunned rigid, she forced a response through clenched teeth.

"Neither," she said sternly, "but I would like to slap you!" Marti raged inside. "Who the hell does he think he's talking to?"

The man had not been drinking so Marti, unable to even use this as an excuse for his crude behaviour, promptly left.

A returning Ericson, who caught the end of their conversation, couldn't believe his ears: "I don't believe you said that – and to a journalist!"

Marcus scowled at the bottled water in front of him. Picking it up to examine the label, he cringed at the sickening prospect of seeing his words in print.

"You better hope she likes you!"

But Ericson's irony in the height of his friend's unwitting misuse of language was lost on Marcus as he left for home.

Thankfully, France provided lighter entertainment. The two-week holiday gave everyone time to re-adjust and assess their personal perspectives on chosen professions. After yet another win, Westwood was looking more and more the heir apparent and, as each race was completed, the mathematical possibilities of another driver catching him were being systematically eroded. Secure in this knowledge the circus sailed to England.

CHAPTER 13

This year's home Grand Prix was primed to be a major attraction, reinforced by the growing probability of a British World Champion, one who undoubtedly wished to please his adoring fans.

The intervening week, proved hectic in getting the massive transporters and equipment, back across the channel in time to set up shop once more at Silverstone, the historical home of motor racing. Fortunately all the teams made it and the whole rigmarole of practice and qualifying began again. The authorities, Silverstone Circuits Limited, were preparing for record crowds, in view of the standings in the Championship table plus the prospect of fine weather, with estimates of attendance in excess of 150,000 spectators for the main day's programme.

Marti wished to take Morris for the weekend, but Jim was not enamoured with her idea, preferring instead to hire a 'more appropriate vehicle'. With Marti vehemently defending Morris, they almost got to the point of travelling in separate cars. However, by Thursday Jim in his laziness hadn't bothered to do anything about finding alternative transport, so Marti got her way and together, they began to load their personal belongings into Morris' limited boot space.

"The back seat would be better." Marti suggested in horror, as Jim put his foot on the lid in an effort to close it against his oversized kit-bag.

It's not far to Silverstone –about 140 miles from Marti's cottage. They planned to leave at 3.00 am to avoid as much congestion as possible. The die-hard fans would already be in situ, bedded in with amateur bands rocking and beer flowing. Marti was excited by the prospect of the night's drive. The thought of starting in the dark and finishing in daylight appealed to her greatly, "It's kind of back to front really!"

The air was still and cool and Morris' old engine sucked it in with revelry, it was pure bliss to watch the dawn break on a clear horizon. Marti's imagination was running riot with a jumbled abundance of dreams and schemes. So whilst Jim dozed in oblivion she positioned the car on the road so that the white lines zipped under the bonnet, directly aligned with Morris' chrome bonnet badge, dead centre, a perfect balance. This fascinating aspect created an impression of speed far in excess of reality, and a fantastic sense of freedom – you could go on and on and on and on, if you wanted to. The mere knowledge of this possibility of endless space was usually sufficient to quell the commitment of such an act – and they arrived at the gates at 5.35 am. Jim had regained consciousness and was hungry!

Marti couldn't get over the difference in the place since her earlier, more regular visits, albeit that 90 per cent of the buildings were of temporary construction. Portacabins, tents and trade stands stretched for miles in every direction, encompassing the entire track. When she was last here in 1982 she had parked Morris on the grass behind the main start-line grandstand, walked straight in and picked out whichever seat she fancied. And while she appreciated that those events were of minor league racing, Formula One was definitely a different ball game, even from what it was in those days.

The gates officially opened at 6.00 am but even at this hour, on the first day, plenty of support was evident. Work began at eight, with an hour of timed pre-qualifying, followed by untimed practice between 10.00 and 11.30.

Marti went walkabout in search of some remnants of the past. Sadly, she discovered that the rickety wooden podium, which used to be in front of the main stand had gone. As she recalled a proud moment from a decade ago, when she had sat in that very same stand with a handful of others, applauding a young, laughing victor, her eyes filled with the beginnings of tears. She truly had to force herself to leave this sacred spot and then, she only got as far as the pole position markings on the track. She stood between them, so that she would know exactly what he saw when the green lights shone and he dropped the clutch. This state of reminiscence would recur often during the course of the weekend, as faces presented themselves, stirring deeply guarded sentiments. Marti was a mass of mixed emotions, and she dearly wished for the return of her 'Racer.' Unfortunately, walls and fences still provided defences, which were exhaustingly unbreachable.

On returning to the business side of the track, which caused a slight hitch, as Marti's press pass had decided to detach itself from its cord and was now floating freely somewhere inside her jacket, she joined Jim, Ossi and a few other colleagues for a liquid lunch and gossip session.

First qualifying began at one o'clock and lasted an hour. Prior to this, a brief public pit walkabout was scheduled for those die-hard fans that had paid the considerable extra fee for the privilege. Dads and kids clutching programmes with their favourite superstars' pictures in, complete with spaces for autographs, pushed and scurried to the entrance of every garage but, few were lucky enough to glimpse their idol or secure such a treasured piece of memorabilia, as the drivers' conference was also in progress in the main meeting room above the said garages.

Marti had taken up a seated position on the pit wall, close to the Centaura team's race data gathering pitch along the start/finish straight. She watched the crowds scuttle from one garage to another, anxiously surveying the area in search of a recognised figure. As the rumour of a possible sighting filtered through the gathering throngs, the whole flock surged as one towards the source, only to be disappointed on arrival to find that their hero had just left. Looking up at the glass-enclosed conference rooms, she noticed Marcus watching the same scenes unfolding, their eyes met briefly and they exchanged an acknowledgment. Momentarily, Marti recalled the conflict of their previous meeting in Spain. He recognised her; she was sure of it but did his expression offer any remorse?

From here, henceforth to the Javelin camp! Sir James was in the chair; he appeared edgy, snapping at reporters as they tried to force answers, based on rumour, as to Westwood's future plans. Many of these rumours suggested Westwood's abduction by Italian giants, Ferrari: an odd notion as the reds were currently underperforming and he was already with the best team and winning everything in sight. There was no tangible evidence of discord in Westwood's team and indeed, the team principle was both bemused and enraged by the allegations. Westwood, however, was wavering under considerable pressure from personal and professional angles. Jim was deterred from interrogating Westwood by the presence of his two friendly gorillas from Monaco. He was ill at ease and from the back of the room was unable to collect his best material. Sir James never left Westwood's side for the entire meeting. If he could have found a way, he would have been in the car with him.

Events progressed to Saturday afternoon and the final qualifying round where time really counts. Marcus had a quality of quiet determination about him, although on the long, fast Silverstone circuit, his machine was considerably underpowered in comparison to Westwood's. Eventually, in the last seconds of the session he managed to rag an admirable third on the grid; Westwood was first, and they were split by the effervescent Italian, Roberto Pasccari.

During this final battle for position, Marti had been on the far side of the circuit watching through the wire fence as the slender, fragile machines darted past. Standing at Becketts, on top of a dirty tarmac slag heap, there was no way of denying the fact that there were two worlds, no matter how much she wished otherwise.

Jimbo in the meantime had found a "tidy bit of trim" and was intent on a rapid return to the hotel. Marti offered them a lift but this was met with a stony glare from Jim, daring her to mention Morris! She returned his compliment with a smug grin as Jim's leggy companion folded herself into yet another conveniently parked Porsche 911 which Jim hastily took control of.

"Have a nice time!" Marti called out as he screeched off towards the exit, crossing the track in a cloud of dust. Her comment was intentionally demeaning, though not because of Jim's scorn for Morris. Marti would have what she wanted and was not a sufferer of materialistic insecurity.

Jim's new lady friend was a bit 'up market', and expected lavish entertainment. Halfway through the evening, Marti, relaxing in her room, was therefore paid an unexpected flying visit from Jimbo as he flashed in and out in search of financial backing. His words "I'll pay you back when we get home!" rang down the corridor as he fled at speed. Jim's antics never failed to amuse Marti.

Marti was enjoying an evening alone. Well, she did have company, though he was deep in concentration or meditation; whichever, he didn't want to be disturbed. Marti was reading the newspaper whilst he lay still and quiet on his back beside her and although he didn't wish to speak, he did want to hold her hand, which made turning the pages somewhat difficult. Every so often his fingers would curl into a tight grip and Marti would turn to him, assuming he was going to say something – but no. The little grips were merely a product of his automotive system. In this peaceful limbo, it was relatively easy to mistake him for an angel. Marti stopped reading and studied the gentle rhythm of his breathing; her heart filled once more with pride, she was deeply honoured to have been entrusted with the knowledge of his multi-faceted personality but wondered if she would ever meet the whole of her desperado. She knew his need to be complete was great, but somehow he always managed to withdraw inwardly, creating deadlock. Marti's most worrying concern was that he'd thrown away the key. Her fear was faintly brushed with despair. He was safe with her for now, and for the time being this was as much as he could manage. Marti snuggled a little closer; he stirred, adjusting his position to more comfortably coincide with hers and sleep was soon upon them.

Marti's self-defence mechanism, however, was preparing her for the day when, her purpose served; he would no longer come to her. She hoped that it would never happen but just in case, she made sure to take time to enjoy every precious moment shared. Come what may, and right now she felt that fate had already chosen its path, she would always have her treasured memories. She'd still cry, no matter how prepared she was, but not in his presence; she would take her tears to a private place. It would be foolish to think otherwise of the relationship and Marti wasn't foolish.

Race day arrived and Marti and Jim set off for the circuit. It was seven o'clock by the time they arrived but already thousands of loyal, long-suffering fans had been queuing for hours in their cars and many more, bedraggled by overnight rain, stood in line at the entrance gates, to pay the fee for their trouble.

Marti parked Morris in the centre field, next to some rather more extravagant models, and carefully studied the car's position to be sure she would be OK, before leaving her. The sky was buzzing with a continuous stream of helicopters flying overhead, as they ferried participants and honoured guests, to and from the track. At one time Marti counted sixteen of the noisy, insect-like machines, either taking off or landing – and this didn't include those already in mid-air, circling the field, awaiting a space to drop their auspicious cargos.

There was a final, half-hour warm-up session at nine-thirty, before the day's schedule started at ten-fifteen with charity races and publicity stunts. Jimbo was in the pit lane discussing engine specifications with a stray Centaura mechanic; his lady of the night far from his mind. Jim seemed most at home in these more manual surroundings. Marti was just wandering; her camera dangled heavily from her neck, she wasn't feeling comfortable with things at all. The scenes were becoming familiar and even the script sounded pre-written with cautious, race-speak jargon that read like the list of additives on the side of a processed soup packet.

Suddenly she came face to face with a worried looking Andrea. "Oh, good morning," Marti blurted. Having almost knocked the girl over, she felt it was the least she could say. Andrea seemed afraid of their meeting and so she should. Marti gave her a piece of her mind about her shameful selfishness and her abysmal treatment of Jim and told her in no uncertain terms to "Leave him alone!" Andrea, unperturbed by this tongue lashing still had the cheek to ask Marti if she knew where he was. "Are you kidding?" shrieked Marti, who had no intention of giving him away this time.

As Marti turned on her heels in disgust she spotted her editor, Mr. Bennett, heading for the Power Play trade stand. He had been avoiding her for the last month and despite verbal and written requests, and an in-depth search of the offices, secretly undertaken by Andy, the receipt of Marti's manuscript had not been acknowledged, not even a feeble excuse of its possible loss in the post, or a denial of its existence had been offered by Mr. Bennett. Marti was not the most patient of people but having given him a fair chance, she decided that this was as good a place as any for a confrontation.

Andrea eventually found Jim with the use of her own initiative. The pair hid anxiously between the burger huts. Apparently, Andrea feared that her father was in some kind of financial trouble and was using herself and Westwood as security. Having discussed the matter, both she and David had decided they did not want any further involvement but neither could see a way out. There was a way of course, but they would have to make a massive sacrifice and heaven alone knew what Jim was supposed to do about the mess! So far, he was the one who had suffered the worst consequences for attempting to defy Daddy and his militia. After about five minutes the couple were joined by 'Speed King' Westwood and all three were now ensconced in serious debate.

Meanwhile, Marti, having exchanged formalities and theories with her unsympathetic boss concerning the whereabouts of her manuscript, was enduring a particularly deep bout of despondency.

It was now lunch-time, so she set herself apart from the crowds to eat her apple in peace. Watching the VIPs being attentively directed to their respective suites, Marti slipped into a trancelike state and was soon in the company of a jolly chap, dressed from head to toe in red. He was particularly chipper and cheekily stole her apple, taking a large bite out of it. He offered the return of the partially consumed fruit with a grin. Marti snatched it from him; the muscles of his face twitched nervously as he awaited her reaction. She smiled assurance and backed it with a wink; he chuckled with delight, and proceeded to poke her camera inquisitively, "Who's in the box today?" This jovial cynicism made them both laugh aloud and they rocked into each other, nudging shoulders in unison. He looked at his watch and sighed "I have to go now." Before leaving, however, he told her not to worry and that, "This one was for her."

Marti was a little puzzled by his parting statement and shook her head in bemusement.

It was getting on for one o'clock, and the flight of the Red Arrows was due to commence at five past. They arrived bang on time, and produced, as ever, a brilliant display of death-defying precision aerobatic manoeuvres, which brought silence, followed by gasps of admiration from the grounded onlookers. As the Arrows completed their act, the Formula 1 cars took to the stage, made a couple of practice laps, re-entered the pits for fine tuning and resumed their positions on the grid, in readiness for the parade lap.

Off they went, at a relatively slow speed. Marti awaited their return, photographing them as they lined up: Westwood first, Pasccari second and Veridico third. The red lights came on, the noise level increased and the tyres tore at the grey surface of the ex-RAF base as they powered away. Pasccari was flying down the straight and took the lead into Copse, closely followed by Veridico who also got the jump on Westwood as he tried to block the attacking Pasccari. Three laps in however, Westwood, regained one place by passing Veridico with relative ease on the Hanger straight; second and third exchanged positions as they went under the bridge. Westwood then set off in pursuit of Pasccari who, having had a clear road ahead, had built up a substantial cushion, but Westwood was rapidly reeling him in, generously aided by the awesome superiority of the back-pack that propelled him. Within four laps he'd caught and overtaken Pasccari; normality was thus resumed.

Now in the lead, Westwood proceeded to demonstrate the effectiveness of his machinery, by stretching the gap between first and second to forty-odd seconds. Meanwhile, with Westwood conducting this exhibition of power out on his own, Veridico was also catching Pasccari and there ensued a momentous dogfight as the pair battled to protect their ground. Marti found herself waiting, heart in mouth, for every return lap to see if the positions had changed; she was so enthralled by the duel that she completely forgot about the rest of the field. That was until, on lap 32, Veridico cruised past closely followed by a jet of blue smoke as his engine deposited oil all over the surface of the track. He was out, and Marti was bitterly disappointed.

Westwood won, and the track invasion commenced before

many of the other drivers had completed their final lap, causing absolute chaos as marshals hopelessly tried to deter the army of fans from advancing. The start/finish line was a quivering sea of Union Jacks, as jubilant supporters crushed together to catch a glimpse of their British hero. Westwood was raised aloft on the shoulders of his team-mates, and manhandled to the podium. He must have been black and blue from his rough carriage but was obviously not bothered by their exuberance. After the presentation of trophies and the playing of national anthems, he proceeded to shower champagne over the heads of his gathered worshippers as they mushroomed beneath his feet.

It was a long time before any kind of order could be reinstated and the final race of the day could begin. Even at the end of the day as darkness drew in, many thousands of fans were reluctant to leave the aftermath celebrations, as renditions of 'We are the Champions' rang out in the night sky performed by a collection of unlikely musicians.

Marti, yet again alone, had gone to a point on the airfield where two old runways crossed. She sat on the concrete; it was still warm, having taken the day's sun. A desperate feeling of emptiness and dare she suggest it, a slight sense of boredom engulfed her. With ten Grand Prix completed, a pattern had been established both on and off the track and the end result, she feared, had already been decided upon. The evening air was cooling and her face tingled from prolonged exposure to the sun and wind. A mixed odour of fuel and barbecue grills hung heavy; she placed her camera on the ground in front of her and whilst seated at this crossroads, pondered the virtues of selling one's soul in order to achieve what one desired. "It should be midnight," she thought, poking her camera away with her toe.

Helicopters were still busy overhead with their return trips. Marti got up hurriedly and went to find Jim; all she wanted to do was go home. To her surprise, he was already waiting for her with Morris. They jumped in; Marti gave the key a quick flick to which Morris instantly responded and after weaving their way through the traffic, they were soon on the open road heading west.

Throughout the journey, Jim babbled on excitedly about the race and Westwood, how he overtook, how he dominated, how close he had come to an accident on the first bend and so on, in excessive detail. Marti wasn't in the least interested in his commentary; she was intensely troubled by a tragic sobbing which was congesting all her worldly thoughts; but he wouldn't come out, not until he was sure they were alone, just the two of them.

The second Marti's head touched the pillow, he was there. "I tried so hard." He was mortified by his failure and repeated the sentence over and over. The disappointment and grief at being unable to deliver his promise was immeasurable and he became more distraught as he continued.

"I wanted it so badly and I've let you down!"

"No you haven't," she assured. "There will be other chances."

This brought little consolation; for some reason it had to be *this* time.

Again he cried, "I tried so hard!"

"I know you did babe, you did your best, and I don't need any more than that."

She was trying to take his hand but he was unwilling, shunning her contact in the old belief that he was not worthy.

"Come on," she encouraged, "we'll do it again, another day."

"I wanted it now!" he insisted.

Marti again tried to take his hand. She knew he needed a hug desperately, but was denying himself the luxury. However she persisted, explaining that true love was unconditional and eventually he came softly to her.

CHAPTER 14

July dragged on and on; the weather was abysmal and, for Marti, the thrill of attending foreign circuits was beginning to stagnate. Principally she felt her reasons for being there had altered dramatically, therefore she could no longer record events in a proper unbiased manner. Her feelings were confirmed in a telephone conversation with Andy from Power Play shortly after the British Grand Prix. The editor had been making ugly suggestions and Andy had been selected to deal with the unsavoury situation. He was very kind, although slightly embarrassed at having to deliver his boss' opinion, but the bottom line was that if her portfolio didn't improve at the forthcoming German event, then they would have to consider other sources. Marti put down the receiver; not in the least bit upset by the news.

Jim had been summoned by Marion and was gallivanting around the countryside in the Jag whilst Marti spent much of the intervening two weeks at home. In fact, she hardly stepped foot off the property and had become a prisoner of her own self-will. Her 'friend' was at her side constantly. Concerned for his future, he thought that his critics, recently, had been unnecessarily destructive in their assumptions of his attitude. Marti, together with the assistance of her translucent partner, made use of the time to catch up on a few jobs around the house and garden, weather permitting. Both had been neglected of late and the need to tidy her intimate surroundings was essential if she was to regenerate her persona. The two parties had reached a particularly low ebb, but between them they achieved some constructive progress and managed some fun and games in between work.

During this time, the national papers were full of speculation about driver team pairings for next season, with both forces demanding unassailable contractual terms. The media had narrowed this down to mean cash flow citing – that in a worldwide recession, even the big guns were starting to feel the pinch. As with any company, the quickest and easiest method of reducing expenditure is to cut the largest singular outgoing – i.e., the wage bill – this therefore pointed a figure directly at the drivers and their mega-buck remunerations. In terms of financial security, this fix probably wouldn't have hurt these individuals; but yet again, it's the manner in which employers conduct their dealings, which causes unrest and bitterness. Loyalty no longer counts for anything, which tends to make some people more defiant and more determined to take a stand against authority as a matter of principle. Business it appears is business at any level.

The travel tickets arrived for Germany and Marti and Jim were once more in the air en route for Hockenheim. On arrival Marti was hardly able to summon the enthusiasm to take her camera out of its case let alone remove the lens cap. Jim on the other hand was deadly keen to catch up on the gossip, immediately setting off to find the affiliated gang of reporters. Marti followed despondently and they found the group gathered around Westwood's pit area. Sir James was close at hand and although Andrea was not present at the meeting, Stephanie was. That took the wind out of Jim's sails for a moment to say the least; from her curt remarks, it was obvious that she was still smarting from the con job he'd pulled on her in London. All attentions were focused on Westwood to make a statement as to his future; after all a win this weekend would clinch the title and therefore, surely he should have the pick of the bunch as far as contractual negotiations were concerned. "No comment," was Westwood's only reply when probed by reporters, so the press would have to make its own headlines from what sparse information could be scavenged over the course of the next forty-eight hours.

During Saturday's final qualifying the regular line up of Westwood, Pasccari and Veridico was resumed on the grid and as the day's computations came to an end, Marti, Jim and the rest of the gang took up residence in the hotel bar. Marti's doubts about her occupation were growing by the hour and listening to the rubbishing of other people was doing little to inspire her otherwise. Ossi, ever the cavalier, realised her despondency and came to the rescue. He cheered her up no end with his sweet talk and they actually discussed topics other than motor racing, which brought great relief for Marti. He still made a few half-hearted romantic passes, but by now he understood the set up and generally kept the conversation lightly amicable. Jim meanwhile was well away chatting comfortably with a couple of mechanics. Fully aware of his technical ability, Marti couldn't help thinking that he should have stuck to the practical side of the business.

Westwood and Pasccari joined them for a short while and in their common interest and knowledge, a thread of respectful comradeship strung them all together, fusing their attentions for some time. Marti's 'friend' who had been clinging to her like some lost waif, having found his first mooring place since setting sail, was becoming fractious in his tiredness and so she thought it best to retire to her room. She bid Ossi goodnight with a kiss of thanks and after informing Jim of her intentions, was honoured likewise by him. On leaving, however, she noticed Stephanie's arrival.

For the lads in the bar sharing a good time, Stephanie now provided the main source of female diversion, and she soon took command of this status. An hour past filled with giggling innuendos before Westwood, Pasccari and the 'grease monkeys' left on the pretext of requiring an early night in view of the following day's workload, which left Jimbo with Stephanie. Needless to say, with both parties out for what they could get and liquor fuelled, they also soon made an exit.

They were in Stephanie's room where, unusually, she played for time, faffing around in the bathroom with her make-up and hair. Jim was suspicious, though made no mention of the fact but after he had clattered his glass on the coffee table and rustled the daily paper vigorously to draw her attention she finally emerged in towelling robe and made a lunge for him. She was tugging at his shirt, which was stuck fast in his tight, Levi jeans, when a knock came at the door. Stephanie answered it swiftly, leaving Jim stretched out on a large, puffy golden sofa half naked. It was Westwood! She welcomed her guest, anxiously encouraging him to enter. The two men came face to face and simultaneously realised the deception of the woman! Westwood dashed back to the door and was able to make good his escape; Jim unfortunately, being further from the opening, was stopped by a furious Stephanie.

"You know what I could have done to you, don't you?"

Oh God the threat of Daddy loomed all over again!

Jim felt a little intimidated but nevertheless, not wanting to miss the opportunity of a chance copulation, returned to the sofa, once more taking up a submissive posture. Stephanie disrobed and straddled his hips. He took each breast in hand fondling the nipples, pinching them as she leant over him. Her soft flesh pushed against his face as he kissed the dark brown skin. Stephanie raised herself then slowly lowered, encasing him with her warm, moist inner tissues. The massaging motion of her interior muscles contracted and released bringing rhythmical pleasure. This role was reversed several times before they came together producing moans of ecstasy.

This night Marti's hours were severely disrupted as her young man fought pain and anger, inflicted by his colleagues' insinuations as to his lack of care for others and a lunatic approach to his profession. He was deeply hurt by the untruthful misinterpretations and desperately disappointed by his contemporaries' inability to understand or tolerate an individual's character and needs. Safety was at the forefront of his outspoken theories, and was backed by personally collected medical knowledge and historical information. The unjustifiable comments didn't end there; and indeed they incorporated his personal life style and beliefs, suggesting that he thought he was immortal, which scarred even deeper. He sincerely thought that he should not need to endure such ridicule from his own kind and though a brave face was always portrayed in public, the terrible injustice of it all burned eternally inside him. Marti consoled the beautiful man within, calming him by gently running her fingers through his plentiful dark waves of hair. He was to cry a lot that weekend and channelled his aggression into his work, to produce the results he desired and hopefully quash any further rumours of his fading ability. Marti also vowed to do better, though whether this was down to her or "The Racer" was unclear.

The race began at two o'clock and again, Pasccari got the jump on his ex team-mate but at the end of the fourth lap he was forced to relinquish his lead to the hard-chasing Westwood. With Veridico poised in third, these positions were maintained for a further 28 laps. The leading cars were closing on back markers and began picking their way with trepidation, through the traffic; it is usual for the drivers of these slower machines to operate with etiquette in such situations and allow the leaders a clear path, as was the case when Westwood overtook Paul Ericson at the exit of Ostkurve. Unfortunately, Ericson was unaware of the proximity of Pasccari who was hot on Westwood's tail and, in re-taking the race line, Ericson left an already committed Pasccari little room for manoeuvre, forcing him onto the grass where he lost control and hit the barrier. Veridico who managed to avoid the mix-up was now second, though some 25 seconds adrift of Westwood who was literally flying. With this comfortable cushion, Westwood came in for tyres on the next lap. The pit stop was a disaster due to a malfunctioning wheel nut gun – the change over took far longer than anyone dared to imagine. By the time he rejoined the race from the slow lane, Veridico had 10 seconds on him, but of course he was on worn rubber. Westwood was soon up behind him, and made several challenges but was almost dumped on the 45th and final lap by the still World Champion at Bremskurve 1 when he attempted a ridiculously timed, overtaking manoeuvre. Westwood had to settle for second, failing to secure sufficient points to clinch the title.

In the meantime, the relatively petit Italian figure of Pasccari had arrived back in the pit lane on the back of a scooter, and was heading directly for Paul Ericson's garage with a face like thunder. He grabbed Ericson by the throat, lifting him bodily off the ground and pinned him to the wall.

"You could have fucking killed me!" he yelled at the shaken Austrian, who admitted, up front to not seeing Pasccari after he had let Westwood through.

"What's wrong with you, don't you have mirrors?"

Ericson was gutted by his error of judgement, and his furrowed brow depicted his sorrow and fatigue.

Temperatures were rising and the swearing continued in front of several journalists attracted by the commotion, until the two were physically pulled apart by a couple of mechanics who ushered the fuming Italian and the press out of the garage, rolling down the steel doors after them and slamming them shut, tight against the concrete.

Pasccari was livid. Although well able to match many a practical joke off the circuit and who was normally one of the more easy-going of the bunch, once on the track, he knew only too well the serious consequences of any lapses in concentration. It was dangerous out there and at some stage or another you had to rely on another driver knowing and performing his duties with the utmost care and dedication.

As Westwood only received 6 points for his second place, he would have to wait at least another two weeks before being afforded a further crack at the title. He was neatly shielded from the glare and formalities of the post-race conference and was hurried to a waiting helicopter which flew him directly to the airport. The plane's destination, however, was not to be England.

It was gone midnight when Marti and Jim got back to Roebuck and on that Monday morning they posted the details of their completed assignment to Power Play.

That night, Marti woke with a start. "Marti! Help me!" She heard the call loud and clear. There was fear in his voice and she found herself in a high-rise apartment block. There was an open door through which she entered; she called out but there was no response. A deathly silence hung in the air as she frantically searched the rooms. The hammock was empty; beside it on the wooden floor lay an open book, its pages untidily scrunched under the weight of its cover where it had been hastily discarded and the blinds fluttered at the open window. She kept calling but still there was no reply. Finally a trail of clothing and scattered, broken objects led her to the bathroom, outside of which, on a white glazed cabinet stood a partially emptied bottle of vodka. Inside the room, flat on his back, was her man's semi-naked body.

He was unconscious, a stool lay, upturned, on the ground behind him and there was a two-inch gash to the side of his head, where he had made contact with the sink. The cut was bleeding profusely but suddenly, a horrible, guttural choking sound in his throat distracted her from the wound.

"Oh God – no!"

Marti tried to lift his upper body, turning him to one side but for a smallish individual, his solid build presented a considerable weight and she had to wedge herself between him and the wall, to form a cradle. Marti freed the blocked air passage and he was promptly sick, the stench made her retch but at least this brought him round. To a mineral water drinker, half a bottle of vodka could do a serious amount of damage. His eyes rolled back in his head, he really didn't know what was happening. Slumped against her, trembling, he clung tightly with both hands to the arms that secured him.

He was violently sick again and again, and even when Marti was sure there could be nothing left to bring up, he still urged. She struggled to drag him back against the wall, easing herself out of the way in the process and propped him against the side of the bath. He was frightened and embarrassed and didn't want to let go of her hand.

"Please don't leave me, please – I'm sorry."

"Hush, hush, don't worry, I'm not going anywhere." Marti assured him she would not leave, but as she ran the bath water he was still reaching for her and apologising.

"I've never done anything like this before – it frightens me that I do it now, I'm so sorry."

"It's OK, it's OK," Marti repeated whilst tending to his injury. She touched the broken skin, the pressure, though light, caused no reaction; there was no sensation of physical pain at this particular point in his life. Marti took a flannel, dipping it the warm bath water to bathe the gash; it was not as bad as first feared, but was still bleeding. With Marti's assistance he managed to get the rest of his clothes off and clamber into the bath. He was acutely shy and was pleased that there were bubbles on the surface, though he couldn't for the life of him work out where they had come from. But then, he was like that about a lot of things right now.

On inspection of the disgustingly stained jeans, Marti suggested that they burned them, which comment produced the faint glimmer of a smile. Stuffing them into a plastic bin liner, she tied the top and took it out to the kitchen; the door to the balcony was locked. Marti took a key from a coffee pot on the sink drainer to her left, opened the door and dropped the bag onto the tiled floor. It made a loud thud on landing

"Marti! Marti!" She returned quickly to find him shivering and dripping in the hallway. "I heard the door..."

"Hey – come on, you know you can trust me." She said, ushering him back into the bathroom. His steps were faltering and as Marti took a large towel from the airing cupboard behind her, a strange notion occurred. She knew exactly where everything in the apartment was!

His head was beginning to pound, but it wasn't from the bashing it had received.

He bent down to dry his feet, "Ouch!" looking to Marti for an explanation; for the sensation of a serious hangover was something of a new experience.

"You'll get over it," she giggled, kneeling before him to complete the task. He blushed, a delicate shade of pink. Marti helped him to the bed and he scrambled in still holding a damp flannel to his head.

"It feels better lying down." This naive statement brought a wry smile to Marti's face as she dimmed the lights and went to fetch a plaster.

Having applied the patch she sat on the edge of the bed. "What was the vodka for?"

He turned to her; there were tears in his eyes as he laid himself across her lap, nuzzling against her belly, safe in the knowledge that she could brush away his fears with gentle strokes to his temple, a touch which he had grown exceedingly fond of.

Relaxed and reasonably comfortable given the circumstances, he told her of his unhappiness. He was fed up with taunts about his sexuality and the never ending enquiries as to why he was so frequently without a girlfriend. Of course, he had been associated with several very attractive women, 'who hadn't been in this game?' But none lasted the course or they were poached by the opposition. His critics had also provided their own assumptions and answers to his bachelor status, which do not need to be quoted.

What had started as a joke, which he could handle, had become increasingly and more frequently, personal and spiteful.

"I'm tired of it! There's nothing wrong with me."

"I know that – people like to gossip, either about something or somebody and in this current moment, you just happen to provide a convenient vehicle for their ridiculous headline cravings."

"Why can't they accept me?" he pleaded. "They think I'm some kind of monster, but they don't know me."

Marti hugged him and tried to lighten his thoughts. "I know you're not a monster, the bolt in your neck is hardly noticeable! Don't let them intimidate you"

He pondered her joke – "I try not to, but with everything else going on I couldn't cope any longer." There was a large intake of breath before he finished his sentence. "People don't like me, they don't understand." This point had never bothered him in the past, he wasn't here to be liked, but just in case he needed to hear the words, Marti told him that she liked him – very much.

A damp patch was beginning to form on the front of her shirt as she continued to comfort this lonely soul until he was able to fall asleep. She was deeply saddened by the fact that he felt compelled to drink alone in order to ease his misery. He was quite poorly for several days following his 'bender' and stuck close to Marti at all times.

CHAPTER 15

On Friday morning; the 'phone rang and Jim answered it! It was Andy. Jim handed him over to Marti who was sat halfway up the stairs. The cable wouldn't quite reach her; but with Jim's firm hand of insistence around her wrist; unwillingly she moved closer.

"Hello."

Andy's Essex dialect wafted cheerfully down the line like a tweeting budgie, the big white chief had pronounced her fit to work, albeit on a race to race basis. The news of keeping her job didn't seem to stimulate much enthusiasm, but at least it meant she would be attending the next meeting in Hungary, where she knew she was needed for far more important reasons than taking pleasingly evocative photographs.

The Hungaroring is 12 miles from the city of Budapest and became Eastern Europe's first Grand Prix venue in 1986; since when, there have been four winners. Westwood was hoping to be the fifth and in so doing, lay claim to the World Crown.

Marti and Jim arrived at the circuit to be greeted by Jack Brenner with the news that Andrea was in town. Whether this was a wind up or not, who knew but Jim appeared to take the information lightly. After Jack had gone Marti asked what, exactly, the situation was with him and Andrea. Jim simply shrugged.

"Oh, come on, I saw you with her and Westwood at Silverstone, and you've been pretty amiable with David since then. What's going on?"

He insisted that there was nothing, and pursued another course of conversation. He was so good at changing the subject! Cheekily, he asked if she had a film in her camera.

"Umm," she grumbled. "You're as funny as fuck sometimes."

"OK, let's get a coffee and I'll tell you. Andrea and David are going along with Daddy's plans for the time being; neither intend to marry – not each other anyway – they're just keeping the old man happy for the sake of family peace as much as anything until they can find out precisely what he's up to."

Jim's divulgence didn't really throw much light on the subject but at least Marti felt better for being included.

"What have you been up to?" Jim enquired. "You were in a right old state the other night, you woke me up and I almost came to see if you were alright. Are you worried about the job?"

Hardly she thought to herself but was conservative in her reply. "It was just a dream, nothing more."

"Oh that's OK then." Jim accepted her explanation with little fuss and they set off on their hunt for verbal and visual portraits of suitably inspiring candidates.

The main line of gossip centred on the merry-go-round of gaining employment for the following season, and it appeared that many of the sport's top guns were being forced down the ladder or, indeed, right off the bottom rung as the trend leaned towards retirements, however temporary their perception. Leverage of experience was pitted against new bravado and sponsorship funds from a multitude of modernistic, international technology businesses, all keen to have their logos emblazoned down the side of a super-tech race car. It would seem that life revolves in the same spiral for all; no matter how much effort and time is invested, there's always someone of little moral capacity willing to push in and make demands, regardless of others. The real annoyance of all this is that they are usually the ones listened to most; or perhaps they just cry loudest. Still it rattles a few cages and makes good literature. Sadly, though, the significance of our endeavours is lost with it, and possibly also our will to participate, until, in the end, we all wonder what the hell we are doing out here. This type of behaviour should be discouraged, the phrase 'heading for a fall' springs to mind but, unfortunately, the opposite occurs and we are forced into undesirable agreements by the ever present pressure from above. Only time will tell.

Having spoken with him earlier in the day, Jim had arranged to have dinner with Westwood and Andrea.

"What about me?" Marti pleaded dejectedly.

"Ossi's about."

"Oh thanks, Ossi's about," she repeated, sarcastically, and turned to go upstairs.

Who should be standing there but Ossi! He was grinning from ear to ear; Marti felt a hot flush of embarrassment, enhanced by his invitation to accompany him for the evening. She accepted his offer as she fled up the stairs to her room. Ossi called after her leaning on the bottom banister post "I'll see you at eight – in the bar!"

"Fine!" Came the distant reply.

Marti had an hour. Deciding to make a bit of an effort, she rummaged through her suitcase for some appropriate attire.

"Marti." The call was quiet. "Do you have to go?"

"Well – I said I would, and he's a nice bloke."

"Oh, then I suppose you must."

There was a long silence as she sat on the edge of the bed, dithering over the red or black home-made dresses which she had retrieved from her case.

"Wear the black one." The voice prompted.

"Hum." She smiled and asked him why he thought that dress was best.

"It's not – I like red and I want you to wear the red one for me."

She was quite taken aback by the seriousness of his request, and indeed, by the fact that he'd never made such a demand of her before. Marti wasn't sure she liked it either.

"You're not jealous are you?" There was further silence as she began to get washed and changed.

Although their arrangement was to meet in the bar, Ossi called at her door just before eight and as she let him in, she felt someone tugging at her sleeve.

"Will you hang on a minute, I'm not quite ready," she said, nipping back to the bathroom.

From the front Marti's black dress was high necked and slightly austere but from the back, cut low to the base of her spine the sinuous structure of her form was highly visible to Ossi.

"Mamma!" he gasped with a husky breath.

In the bathroom Marti asked her 'friend' what his problem was.

"I didn't mean to tell you what to do." His head was bowed, "I feel ashamed of my conduct, but I would dearly love to take you to dinner, or somewhere – maybe." His words drifted off at the ends.

Marti felt a guilt complex coming on. "I promise not to be long, but you can come with me if you want." She tried to reassure him that Ossi was simply a colleague and her 'friend' said he was okay with this situation, but she could tell he wasn't happy.

Ossi, who had been waiting patiently, meanwhile was becoming agitated. "How long you going to be in there?" Marti promptly emerged and they left for the dining-room.

The meal was extremely enjoyable but Marti was becoming confused by the conversation. In one ear she was receiving sweet talk from Ossi, whilst in her head, she was getting snide comments such as "He's not your type," or "he's not sincere, don't listen to him." Eventually she found her 'pal' answering Ossi, before even she could do so and was reduced to a fit of tearful blubbering. Ossi sat back in dismay; he was more than put out by her disjointed responses. He had been being serious in his affections and her weird reactions were disconcerting and disrespectful. Marti held her head in her hands, apologising to Ossi, she tried to explain that whilst his company was appreciated and wanted, she was not available for a relationship. 'God what was she doing here?'

"I'm so sorry Os, it's not you, really – I have to go."

Once back in her room, her 'friend' came out to play. Bouncing on her bed, on all fours, he grinned wickedly, overjoyed with the results of his prank. Marti wagged a finger at him.

"You're a little devil at times!"

He was sitting on his haunches; Marti pushed him off balance and he rolled from side to side, chuckling in delight at having got his own way. They romped, playfully, until, out of breath, he laid his head on her breast. A sudden seriousness came upon him and he held onto Marti for all he was worth.

"I don't want to lose you, Marti."

She made him lift his head to make eye contact.

"I'll always be here for you."

He understood the sincerity in her words; the tension of his grip lessened as he relaxed into slumber. He was still there at daybreak and didn't want to go to work, but it was Marti's turn to be boss and she told him in no uncertain terms that he had to; reluctantly he left.

"Will you come and see me later?"

Marti promised on oath.

Saturday's practice sessions were fraught. The apparent reason, according to Jim, was a difficulty in being able to combine the set up of the cars' suspensions, so that they would handle well through the corners, without jeopardising too much speed on the short straights.

"That's good." Marti said vaguely, she was generally interested but not at this particular moment in time. Jim flashed a look of bemusement.

Leaving him on the pretext of sorting out her camera angles, she walked from pole position to the end of the Start/Finish straight. Sitting on the grass beside the track she studied the scene through the view finder. There he was, hands in pockets, head bowed, slouching across the tarmac toward her. He plonked himself down, slightly behind her, just out of her view finder's radius.

"I don't feel good today, it's just not right." They talked through his troubles for a while; he felt he was being persecuted for his beliefs and couldn't concentrate on the job in hand. "It's not nice," he said, "it's not nice at all." He was very negative in his outlook; Marti asked that he take care of himself first. Heroics were not necessary to prove his point or impress, particularly where she was concerned and she assured him he would have another day. Alas his spirit appeared drained of all drive.

During the actual race, Veridico was taken out on the first bend by an over-exuberant Philip Rheutemanne who, after pitting for a new nose cone, was able to continue on his way.

Meantime, Marcus had parked his car neatly against the tyre barrier, so as not to interrupt the on-going race and was signing autographs for a group of excited young fans, seemingly undeterred by his earlier up-ending, he revelled in the children's delight of his company.

Westwood went on to take the chequered flag and in so doing picked up that elusive title of World Champion. His team, family and fans went absolutely crazy. There was a strong contingent of British supporters and it was ages before Westwood emerged above the heads of the crowd to be photographed. At the post-race conference David was highly emotional and had difficulty in expressing his feelings of satisfaction, joy and relief. Jim was right up there with him, he'd become Number One Fan.

On the flight home, Marti was joined by a rather solemn little lad, who sat on her lap, quietly gazing out of the window. It was night-time and together they counted the stars. Marti asked if he had a special one, sadly the answer was 'No', so she encouraged him to choose a light and told him the story of 'The Little Prince'.

CHAPTER 16

Two weeks later, and our journalistic duo were again in flight, on course for Milan, Italy, and the national home of motor racing, Autodromo Nazionale di Monza. Prior to boarding, Marti had been nosing through the magazine racks in the departure lounge at Heathrow. She picked up the current issue of Power Play and, flicking through its pages, to her dismay, discovered that the editorial team had printed her secretly-taken photograph of Sir James and his suspicious Italian heavies. The picture was supported by the slightly ambiguous headline; 'West-wood Liras East for Serious Gains', whilst the opposing page carried an advertisement for a recently-released novel which read "HIGH SPEED SEX: BEST SELLER!"

The last call for passengers boarding rang in Marti's ears. She stuffed the book back in the stand and stormed off to find Jimbo, who had already taken his place in the queue. Marti barged him out of line, away from any radar contact, and told him of her revelations. She was ranting furiously while Jim was plunged into silence; he didn't know what to think and knew nothing of the photograph.

"Why did you take it?"

"It seemed like a good idea at the time." The queue was fast diminishing and a seething, edgy couple rejoined its tail end.

Loaded with reporters, the fuselage hummed as it hurtled along the runway. The second the sign lit up informing its occupants that seat belts were no longer necessary, Marti and Jim were swamped by their colleagues, bombarding them with questions to the point of suffocation. Neither was responsible for the text nor indeed had they read it, but obviously everybody else had, and their assumptions had already been defined. Apparently it suggested that Westwood had already signed for an Italian team, citing Sir James – Javelin's main sponsor, as his mentor and instigator of the plot subsequently, 'selling' David to Italy.

Marti and Jim were rescued when a stewardess asked the howling hacks to be reseated in order that the staff could serve their meals.

"Jesus!" Marti drew breath, "if it's like this now, what the hell's going to happen when we get to the circuit?"

Jim was even more perturbed; "You only took a picture, I slept with his daughter!"

"That should be plural, I think." Marti, even in her aggrieved state, still couldn't resist a dig.

"Oh smart ass, trust you to pick bones at a time like this. Anyway it's your fault."

"Oh yeah?" She was about to retaliate but suddenly realised it was not each other that they should be arguing with. Pointing this out to Jim, she added that it might be a good idea to stick together during the course of the weekend. "Shit!"

Jim waited in anticipation of her next word as she stared glumly through the porthole.

"Is that all you're gonna say?"

Marti turned to him. "Hum – I just remembered what I hate most about being on an aircraft – you can't turn the damn thing around."

Their packet food was delivered with its customary smile; Marti didn't fancy it so dustbin Jim, after devouring his own, tucked merrily into hers, whilst she sat in silence meticulously scanning the sky for her star. Oh how she wished for it to sweep down and carry her far away from all this nonsense. As the great metal bird's wheels touched down on foreign soil, the couple anxiously glanced at each other. Having cleared customs, they encountered a certain amount of hostility from the local press and TV stations, but battled their way through to secure a taxi to take them to their hotel, they thought they were safe but the driver constantly bickered about newspaper releases and insinuation of unlawful infiltration into team management.

"What the hell was he on?"

Once at the hotel they bolted themselves into their respective rooms to await the hours of daylight, though they were both startled by several knocks on their doors and abusive shouts from the corridor.

Marti's star also showed itself that night, though its brightness was overshadowed by confusion, born out of political wrangling which obstructed its future order and progress.

It would defend passionately its personal dream to be P1 but could not tolerate indiscriminate interference from others, whose knowledge was prejudicially limited, and whose gains were achieved through deceit. Marti understood exactly what he meant. No preferential treatment was sought or indeed wanted, just an equal opportunity on which to capitalise a skill. If the odds were not even and just, it was prepared to sacrifice itself for its beliefs, thus depriving the world of its beautiful mystery and possibly, also the opportunity to learn about something less restrictively formulated. (It would play any game if the rules were fair and unwavering.) Too many unique innovations are lost in this way, through fear or finance by both the famine and glut of these commodities, or through sheer abstinence. The abuse of power and insatiable greed was ever present. Passion and compassion are far finer qualities to be guided through this life by but, sadly our planet appears to be losing both. There is little self-respect, let alone regard for others. And if we are unable to love ourselves, how can we be expected to love others?

Marti and Jim arrived at the Monza merry-go-round at eight o'clock. The Tifosi was already in force availed of anything red, yellow or sporting the rampant horse. Approaching the entrance to the pit lane they saw Ossi; Marti waved and was about to shout to him when he darted for cover behind a stack of tyres. "Perhaps he didn't see us." Marti defended his actions but Jim was not so forbearing.

"He saw us."

The Javelin garage was crawling with bodies; heaven knows how the mechanics were supposed to carry out their duties and the atmospheric tension could be cut with a blunt knife. Ossi was in discussion with one of Westwood's bodyguards. In this light, the smooth talking Italian took on a sinister appearance and neither Marti nor Jim felt at home in this environment.

Promptly they left, instinctively making for the more public arena of the paddock. From here they watched with yet more unease as a long black limo, drew up in front of the Javelin motor homes. The all-conquering figure of Sir James emerged from the rear of the vehicle, clad in a black tailcoat and bootlace tie. He was closely followed by Andrea, in her finery, whom he escorted to the hospitality suite and the waiting staff. Marti could feel Jim's agitation without the need to look at his face.

"Just stay away, don't go near her, please!" Marti begged him to steer clear.

"I will."

She gave him a disbelieving frown.

"I promise," he vowed; but this did nothing to convince her and Marti made a conscious decision not to let him out of her sight.

"Let's take a walk around the circuit."

Wandering as far as the exit to the Parabolica curve, they squatted behind the crash barrier to consider their strategy.

"We're never gonna get near Westwood this weekend." Jim huffed despondently.

"Never mind him; I think we should concentrate of getting ourselves through the weekend!" Marti felt particularly vulnerable.

The cars were due to take to the track shortly and a marshal prompted the dejected pair to assume a safer viewing position. Jointly, Marti and Jim selected the main grandstand, a high profile vantage point, yes, but with plenty of spectators for cover. From here it was possible to keep an eye on the situation without them being placed in any undesirable scenarios.

Marti managed a few unimaginative shots at the drivers in practice and by lunch-time, they plucked up enough courage to venture back onto the business side of the track. Sitting outside one of the snack bars, an apparent air of normality prevailed and indeed they were soon joined by Jack Brenner; the only 'colleague' brave enough to be seen to be acquainted with them. He was his usual Cockney self and of course full of chat about the scandal surrounding the articles published in Power Play that month. As if Marti needed to be reminded. Jack warned of an acute degree of animosity filtering through the home camp nets. Meaning, they presumed, Italy and about the identities of the two gentlemen accompanying Sir James to the point of suffocation. Nobody really knew, or if they did, they were not letting on, who these guys were, but strong suspicions of Mafia interventions were implied. Marti was curious and flabbergasted. "What is this – James Bond? – why would Sir James risk involvement with them?"

Jack raised his shoulders. "You tell me, luv."

Marti didn't like the way he said this. He suggested they think about it carefully. Marti didn't like this suggestion either and sought Jack's opinion of Ossi's status in all of this mess.

"He's a nice bloke, I like him, damn good journalist as a fellow professional but, he is on home turf, so I'd watch him like a hawk."

Jack strongly advised Marti and Jim to take heed of his words – he was taking a risk being seen in their company and made it clear that he may not always be able to acknowledge their existence.

Although they were kept under close scrutiny throughout the day Marti and Jim were allowed to proceed with their work, more or less un-apprehended. The only objections came from the Javelin Pit, where the steel roller doors of the sterile garage were slammed in their faces. When not driving, Westwood was kept like a prisoner in his own motor home; not a single reporter could get near him, which caused greater interest for the blood hounds of the tabloids who had no bounds to their dissection of a subject, as the scent grew more pungent with every snippet of gossip. It was like a fox-hunt or badger cull, the imminence of a fatality hung in the air. They could be spotted in packs, heads buried together in deep debate. With so much attention being focused on Westwood, his team and Sir James, it seemed that many other competitors, however famous, had been forsaken. (Both press and public have such short memories.)

Throughout the day, Marti was also closely attended by her 'friend': he appeared worried and pre-occupied but would not express his concerns openly. The constant proximity of Jimbo was inhibiting him; she apologised for this but explained it was not possible for it to be any other way at the moment. His eyes hooded over and although he said he understood, he withdrew himself to a private planet, the geography of which only he knew.

At the end of the day Marti and Jim returned to the hotel; they were still being followed, aware that every move they made was being monitored. After dinner, they retired to the bar. Their colleagues were divided; fifty-fifty, half were inquisitive as to where they had got their information for the write-up, and half wanted nothing at all to do with them. The nationalities of the two divisions were surprisingly diverse.

Ossi entered the room, and Marti greeted him in her normal manner with a wink and a smile; nervously, he acknowledged her but kept his distance and obviously didn't want to speak to either her or Jim. Both had become tired of the intense questioning and made excuses to retire.

As Marti unlocked the door to her room, with Jim hovering beside her, Andrea appeared.

"Quick! Quick! Get inside." All three bundled through the opening at once.

"What's going on?" demanded Jim.

Andrea went on to tell how she'd sneaked away from her father by saying she felt ill and that Stephanie was here, somewhere, but she didn't know where. She was particularly worried by this fact but was more perplexed by the behaviour of her father. Apparently Sir James had arranged a meeting in the city that night and had in his possession, according to Andrea, a vast amount of cash.

"I've seen it," she said wide-eyed; "he's going alone, tonight at 2.00 am." Her voice was strained.

Jim asked what Sir James' room number was. Marti glared at him in utter shock and horror.

"127," was the figure that came from Andrea's pink painted lips.

"Don't worry." Jim told her to go back to her suite and stay there. "Don't answer the door or the telephone to anyone, and I mean anyone." He checked that the corridor was clear before shoving the reluctant young lady out.

Jim pushed the bolt across and paused before turning to Marti who was by the window, open-mouthed.

"I can't believe..."

"Don't start," he warned, drawing the curtains in front of her. There was a defiant seriousness to his tone and Marti knew him well enough by now to realise that to argue would only serve to make him more determined and less forthcoming.

Jim sat on the edge of Marti's bed, head in hands, contemplating the ensuing nightmare.

"I'm gonna follow him – but you knew that already!" Jim looked up. "I want you to do the same as Andrea; stay here, bolt the door and do not open it for any reason!" Jim waved a finger in Marti's face; he was preparing to leave. "I'll see you at breakfast." Marti forced a smile but he'd gone before she could utter any objections.

Marti glanced at her watch; it was 11.30 pm, so she stretched out on the bed waiting for the appointed hour. She didn't get undressed, and even kept her shoes on.

"Marti!"

Her eyes immediately opened.

"Please, I don't want you to follow him, I am afraid for you."

He was close to her, shy and timid, but nonetheless emphatic in his request. Marti felt her heart torn; this most beautiful little boy was gazing up at her with large pleading, tearful eyes and frantically trying to smother her with his frail body in an effort to keep her from rising.

"What will I do if something awful should happen to you?"

He was terribly frightened and she tried desperately to convince him that no harm would come to either of them.

"I'll be here to look after you for as long as you want." On speaking these words she remembered a story, which she had read on many occasions, about the taming of a fox and the inevitable sorrow and grief which struck one's heart on the departure of such a valued friend. Having invested so much time in obtaining the right to true friendship and trust, she wondered if the effort put in was worth all the pain and the pressure of delivering her promise was suffocating but, looking down on the sobbing infant, so tightly tucked into her side, any doubts experienced as to her abilities, quickly had to be dispelled. These matters of which she thought were of no consequence. Right now, a frightened little boy needed her and she could not turn him away. Forgetting her personal worries she hugged him close to quieten his nerves. In their time together, she had discovered that he had a soft spot, just above the point where his eyebrows met and when she kissed it, a sweet angelic smile of contentment would light up his features. This reaction brought much pleasure and an immense sensation of satisfaction. From this single kiss, a whole routine had been established which had to be strictly adhered to before sleep would even vaguely be contemplated. Marti had to start at the top, with the soft spot, follow it with a kiss to each temple. Left for love; right for luck. Then one to the middle, his nose, just because it was there and finally, one to the lips. This act completed, she rocked him gently to induce drowsiness and although his breathing was somewhat choked on this night, a form of peace prevailed.

Marti rested though could not sleep herself. On next looking at her watch, it was 12.30 am. She would have to leave her little man soon and the dilemma played agonising games with her mind. He was warm and calm, hardly stirring as she pulled the covers over him and replaced her body with a pillow at his side for comfort, although he had over the years developed his own form of self-consolation. In times of distress, he would suck the little finger of his right hand, whilst hiding his face from view with the others. He snuggled into the soft feather cushion and Marti wiped a tear from her cheek, as she hoped that he would not wake to this deception, before her return.

The hotel was in absolute silence; she opened the door just sufficiently to peer round its frame with one eye; the passageway was empty and appeared to go on indefinitely in both directions and indeed ahead of her, forming a cross. Marti waited, squatted on the floor with her back to the wall with baited breath for Jim to make his move from the neighbouring room. As soon as she heard him, she turned to the sleeping babe for one last check and as Jimbo disappeared from view, she tip-toed swiftly after him, catching him as he began to climb the fire escape. Jim didn't say a word and simply shook his head disapprovingly at her inability to obey his instructions.

They reached the floor on which Sir James' suite was located just in time to see the back of his large figure disappearing into the lift. Jim turned on his heels, taking flight, with Marti close behind. Clearing half a dozen steps with each bound by use of the slippery handrail, they crashed into the lobby to be greeted by a seriously concerned night porter.

Jim pushed him to the ground; rushing to the car park, they saw a sleek sedan slip through the gates. Jim made a dash for their hire-car, fully intending to leave Marti behind, but he had forgotten one vital thing: the keys! Marti had them and was already in the driving seat, engine running.

Jim scrambled in, grumbling something about her organisational skills while Marti floored the accelerator. in pursuit. Jim frantically issued orders.

"Don't lose him – don't get too close!"

"Shut the fuck up!" Marti was scared, but these inane comments were turning the whole event into something of a comedic satire, although her laughter was more an outlet for nerves than a reaction to anything remotely funny.

They trailed Sir James through the run-down backstreets of Milan. The alley-ways were darkly foreboding and empty of souls and it was difficult not to be noticed when they were one of only two vehicles on the road. Marti stopped at each corner to wait for the limo to slither around the next before pursuing further. Eventually it came to a stop and Sir James got out, carrying a large black briefcase.

He went into a derelict tenement building. Jim followed stealthily whilst Marti waited, concealed, near the side entrance. It was extremely dark and quiet progress was hampered by the lack of light. Once or twice Jim stopped, cowering in the shadows after stumbling over waste products and debris. Hearing voices coming from within one of the dusty cobweb filled tenements it was easy for Jim to make out Sir James' grunts and he thought that there were at least two others present. Jim was laying flat on his stomach on the ground; through a hole in the wall where the door frame had come away from the brickwork, he could see approximately half of the room. Sir James put the briefcase on a dusty table and one of his accomplices opened it.

"Shit!"

The thing was stuffed full of crisp notes: Andrea was right!

The dark gentlemen seemed happy with the contents and closed the lid, setting the box on the floor, temptingly close to where Jim was hiding; he could have touched it with his finger tips.

A million and one thoughts rushed through his brain at the prospect of being in possession of such a large amount of dosh. He was abruptly brought back from his dreams however, by voices raised in anger. Apparently the money wasn't enough, Sir James was expected to produce a signed contract from Westwood and when this was not forthcoming, the foreign gentlemen grew agitated, hurling uninterpretable expletives and exaggerated gestures of disbelief. It was a strange experience for Jimbo to watch the old man take some of his own medicine and with retrospect felt his fear. Sir James insisted sheepishly, that he would have the document in his possession after the race on Sunday. One of the assailants seemed prepared to accept this but the other was more persistently aggressive, arguing that they should finish him here and now. Jim was deeply concerned by the gravity of this guy's insinuations.

"Get the girl!"

At this, Jim tried to get down lower; his cheek was rubbing in the dirt but he still couldn't see the faces clearly, it was like watching the bottom half of a television screen.

'The girl' was brought into the room. Jim immediately recognised the legs. It was Stephanie; her hands tightly bound behind her back. She was cut free and shoved towards her father; then another, identical briefcase was produced, thrust at Sir James and they were ordered to vacate the premises with a threatening reminder that they would not be alone and that serious consequences would follow, should the contract not be in evidence by six o'clock on Sunday evening. Jim by now was already part-way out of the building but on finding himself on the street, there was no sign of Marti.

"Jesus Christ – where the hell is she?"

He was panicking as he ran to the street corner; the hire-car was still there, but no Marti. He heard the engine of the limo turn over and on finding the doors unsecured on the hire-car, dived behind the front seats. Sir James passed, unaware of Jimbo, who could feel his heart pounding against the floor of the vehicle; rigid with fear, he was unable to move. When he did eventually venture above the back seat, another set of headlamps swung into view and he again darted for cover. Sure now that the coast was clear, he resurfaced to search for Marti.

The setting reminded him of when he was in London and his imagination of the state in which he would find her terrified the life out of him. Jim re-entered the tenement block and heard scrabbling noises coming from the derelict lift shaft. Hesitating, he took cover in the shadows, straining his eyes to identify the figure.

"*Ouch*!"

His whole body rose with relief; it was Marti, covered in dirt and dust. "Where were you?"

If he hadn't been so relieved to find her unharmed, he could have smacked her one there and then, but instead gave her a generous embrace. "Let's go home."

On the way back to the hotel Marti offered an explanation for her disappearance, saying that she had heard voices and gone to investigate. She discovered a vehicle parked in an alley-way at the rear of the property; she wasn't able to make out its occupants but could see that they were using radios. This set Jim to thinking about the second vehicle, from which he had earlier ducked.

"Perhaps they're not all on the same side," he muttered.

By the time they reached their hotel rooms, it was 4.10 am. Jim put his arms around Marti in an attempt at reassurance and they parted in the hall. Marti, not wanting to disturb her kindred spirit, quietly turned the key in the lock and tentatively entered. Thankfully he was still there and still sleeping. She closed her eyes momentarily, letting out a huge sigh of relief. The pure beauty and innocence captured in his image brought all Marti's, latent, maternal instincts rushing forth like a great flood following a storm, creating a sensation of effervescent fear, pride and joy in which she indulged herself as she watched over him. Marti soon dozed off, exhausted by her nocturnal escapades and when she did again wake, he had gone and the brilliant sunshine of a new day poured through the open blinds, though it was not she who had opened them.

Marti freshened up and called for Jim. She knocked on his door and when there was no response she smiled to herself, knowing his tendency to oversleep.

She knocked again. "Jim," she called quietly. No reply. "He'll be hungry," she thought. "He's probably already gone to the dining-room." Not unduly concerned, she rode the lift to the ground floor but, when Jim could still not be found, her heart began to race. She could feel its palpitations thumping against the walls of her chest and a hot flush burned her neck and cheeks.

Marti enquired at Reception asking if any messages had been left but the response was negative. Just then she spotted Jack Brenner in the exit with his trilby tilted lower than ever and dashed after him. Catching hold of his arm she spun him round to face her.

"Have you seen Jim?"

Jack was a little perplexed.

"No!"

"I suggest you ask your mate Ossi."

He pointed across the car park to the man in question, who was about to drive away. Marti ran towards him but it was a futile excursion, because the minute he saw her, Ossi stepped on the gas.

Dejectedly she returned to the reception desk, at a loss as to what to do next. Initially she thought of 'phoning Andy back at HQ, but he could do little for her from London. "Andrea, that's it, find Andrea!" She asked the concierge for Miss Fairbrother's suite number but no amount of lies or bartering could persuade the divulgence of this information from the desk clerk, who was admirably carrying out his duties to a 'T'. Marti then told him that Jim was missing and asked if it was possible to check his room. This request was granted as their booking was jointly registered. Under instruction, a rather small bellboy appeared and he was handed a set of master keys. Together they checked out Jim's room. It was empty, as she had suspected; the bed had not been disturbed. Turning to the young boy she was half tempted to bribe him to lead her to Andrea's suite but on checking the time it was hardly likely that she would be in and anyway Marti had to make an appearance at the track. She thanked the kid, slipped him a tip and let him go. Returning to her own room, she collected her camera equipment and bags. Marti set off alone, heading for the circuit where she hoped someone or something would materialise.

Practice had already begun and her late arrival was well noted by several ominous characters. She took a deep breath and ventured towards the paddock. There didn't appear to be any sign of Sir James or Andrea or Jim but the heavy mob was particularly in evidence in their surveillance and protection of the Javelin ensemble. On the fringes of this pow-wow, Marti caught a glimpse of Ossi; he hadn't seen her, so she decided at an opportune moment to make a surprise attack. He was startled by her forthright boldness and obviously, by his jittering reaction was none too enamoured with the thought of being seen in her company. He twitched nervously when she asked if he knew where Jim was, and indeed the question drew the attention of others. With such a varied audience, Marti felt somewhat safer and continued her interrogation.

"He's missing, you know!"

Surely he was aware of this fact but adamantly rejected her claims that he had knowledge of Jim's plight. "You're a native boy, should I report him missing to the police?"

Ossi was moving slowly away from the congregation, trying to draw her with him but Marti sensed this and believing in the old saying of safety in numbers, at this point in her life at least, stopped short.

Bravely Marti endeavoured to continue her work. At lunchtime she made sure again to be as near to as many people as possible. A little voice was telling her to go to the police, but remembering Jim's unwillingness to involve such authorities, she refrained from doing so. If she could just find Sir James or Andrea or simply get near Westwood, perhaps a little more light could be thrown on the situation. As she was finishing lunch, much of which was picked over and rejected, she noticed Westwood, accompanied by Veridico, crossing the paddock toward the Centaura Camp, the couple made a vaguely odd pairing but something urged her to follow them. She was shaking, the two men entered Veridico's travelling abode.

Marti was bemused: they were not the best of buddies on or off the track but she could hear herself being invited to join them. In the hope that this temporary shelter would provide neutral ground, she ventured after them. Her access was not obstructed. Once inside, her eyes flitted round the interior. Westwood was alone, and from his wordless reaction was not expecting her. He attempted to leave but Marti clung to him, desperately pleading that if he knew anything of Jim's whereabouts, he should help her. He was not at all keen until she implied the instigation of police assistance. This seemed to make him take note.

"I don't know where he is, but I do know that it's not Sir James who's holding him."

"Oh thank God!" At last she had some information. She was almost in tears. Westwood recognised her anguish and sympathetically summoned the decency to refrain from leaving.

"I don't know what I can do to help; they're watching my every move."

He did however, mention that Andrea and Sir James were expected at the track that afternoon and that, maybe, if she could get to either one of them, she could find out more. Westwood then prepared to leave, but not before strongly advising once more against the involvement of any authorities.

This left Marti on her own in the motor home where she sat for awhile, staring through the convex windows, pondering the predicament. The funny thing was, she never felt entirely alone these days, and despite the fact that Jimbo was missing, the level of her resilience and optimism seemed as high as ever. Outside, a motley assortment of journalists were beginning to gather; all had twitchy fingers and some were peering though the blackened glass, endeavouring to spy on the occupants. Safe in the knowledge that she could not be seen, Marti pulled faces at them.

"Now I know what it's like to be a goldfish," she thought. Rising to greet them, she tucked in her shirt and straightened the legs of her torn jeans. On hearing movement from within, the eagerly awaiting posse jockeyed for position; a rumble of disgruntled groans reverberated through the pack on discovering that it was only their fellow hack, Marti. The insignificance of it all was too much and she wondered off toward the conference centre, where she was invited to a one to one interview with Veridico who systematically, updated all the days testing results and outlined his hopes for the future.

As Marcus scooped up the numerous, sheets of computations and several coloured, flimsy handwritten notes, from the desk, to bring the meeting to a close, he looked Marti right in the eyes. "I owe you an apology."

Marti returned his stare and nodded in acknowledgement.

Marcus continued. "I am, truly, sorry for my behaviour in France, it was totally inexcusable, and I hope that you will be able to forgive me someday."

Marti nodded again.

"If I can help you in any way – I will."

Marcus' parting comment lingered in Marti's thoughts.

A short while later, when final qualifying had been completed with Westwood on Pole, there was still no sign of Sir James, and Marti was beginning to wonder what she would do if he didn't show. Marti was en route to the Press Office when she noticed a group of female fans, clucking round a well-fancied driver, who for his part seemed to be enjoying the attentions of the leggy Italian beauties. Marti stopped to observe as he put his well-oiled tactics into operation. He produced a scrap of note-paper, picked out a particularly attractive blonde and handed it to her asking that she jot down some useful details. Of course, she was keen to oblige such an eligible young man. On the return of the slip a broad grin crossed his face; he neatly folded it in half and popped it into his back pocket. Marti wondered how many more he had in there. She caught his eye and raised her camera; clicked off a few frames and with a wink, moved on as did he. The girl in question was promptly mobbed by her jealous companions, after which she was probably never spoken to again. Marti giggled at the wickedly provocative goings on. She took a deep breath before continuing with her work.

At the Press Office reporters were being handed the days' computer readings and stock driver comments, which were dished out after most qualifying sessions by the teams' media management personnel. The technical wizardry of the Monza Press organisation was staggeringly comprehensive; it was probably quite possible to follow the entire weekend's events, without setting foot outside the building – which seems a bit of a waste, but then some prefer to work this way.

Listening to the bleeping fax machines as they transmitted their data around the globe, Marti took a piece of paper and addressed a note to Andy. She placed it on the machine, tapped in half of the digits and then changed her mind; bashing the reject button, she snatched up the paper, ripped it into shreds and threw it in the bin. This was a place where much of her work ended its life – either in the bin or filed under 'W' for waste paper!

As pole sitter, rather than be chased, it was Westwood's duty to come to the journalists, so in Jim's absence Marti took up his seat. Westwood assumed his customary stance and to Marti's relief was accompanied by Sir James. Her insides tied themselves in knots and in her impatience to get hold of 'Daddy' she hardly noted a word of David's wittering. Indeed, she left before he had finished his techno-speech, which was a little rude but understandable in the circumstances, as she could ill afford to miss the opportunity. She waited outside the back door and immediately pounced on Sir James as he emerged into the open, demanding in a loud voice to know where Jim was.

Sir James tried to hush her, pushing her aside, but Marti persisted and with so many witnesses in attendance he was forced to restrain his aggression, instead carting her and his following lamb – Westwood – off to his site accommodation. Once inside the air turned blue; both parties were furious at the other's intervention. David, meanwhile, sat glumly in the corner, for once wanting no part of the action. Sir James even had the gall to accuse Marti of being the instigator of the trouble, addressing her as 'the stupid bitch who took the photograph'. Marti was incensed by this and was fighting tears of anger in an effort not to be undermined. Swallowing hard, she continued her demands concerning Jim's health and whereabouts. The evil patriarch insisted no harm had come to him, saying he would be released after the race. It wasn't enough.

"How can you expect me to believe that?" Marti required solid evidence and if it was not produced she'd have no option but to go to the police and report Jim as a missing person. Sir James almost exploded on hearing her intentions and launched into a savage physical attack.

At this stage David stepped in to dissuade the old man's volatile temper, stopping his arm above her head.

"Jesus Christ! This is ridiculous, why don't you just let the guy go?"

Marti was surprised by what David had said. Considering his earlier denial of any knowledge of Jim's fate, it raised grave doubts as to his integrity and indeed his innocence. The brief interlude brought about by Mr. Westwood's bravado allowed everybody to calm down. Sir James agreed to Marti meeting Jim – in the hotel bar at eight thirty that evening. Marti was by the door, making ready her escape route.

"It's your last chance!" she threatened, before making a run for it.

In her hurry to get away, she bumped straight into Marcus Veridico. He steadied her.

"What's the rush?"

Marti was embarrassed and blushed profusely; unable to speak, she veered from his arms. He stopped her.

"What are you afraid of?" he asked.

Marti gazed, longingly into his deep dark eyes for what seemed like an eternity; they held a look that no amount of time could ever erase and the simplicity of his question touched her heart.

"If only you knew," she thought but was unable to answer, instead lowering her head to break the spell. He released his grip and Marti ran off to the safety of her car, where she threw herself onto the seat, head back, struggling for breath and again fighting tears.

Marti returned to her hotel room and waited. She seemed to spend half her days watching the clock: a sad, not to mention ironic, reminder of her days in the office. Her emotions were in complete and utter turmoil. "What do I want?" Silent tears streamed from the closed corners of her eyelids. There was so little time to consider her own needs, softly – quietly a familiar, gentle warmth engulfed her; this sanctuary allowed and encouraged her inhibited sobs as she hid herself in his celestial body.

At ten to eight Marti was in the bar anticipating the arrival of Sir James and hopefully Jim. She was scared, already starting to panic at the thought of again misplacing her trust. Many of her colleagues were present but few were inclined to make conversation, even out of politeness. Suddenly she noticed Ossi; he was making his way towards her. Apprehensive of his approach, she turned away but he was now stood beside her.

"If you want to see Jim I suggest that you come with me now."

Marti looked him straight in the face. His features were coldly unfaltering, the fire and flare had been totally extinguished. Without uttering a single word in response, she followed him out of the hotel to a waiting car.

Marti was unable to identify the driver, he wore a cap and had a scarf wrapped over half of his face but she got the impression, that he was most likely to be one of Jim's abductors from Monaco. The journey was extremely tense; every corner turned provided fresh insight as to the seedier, more unscrupulous inhabitants of a major city, the prospectors and gutter scavengers of which stalked its streets by night. Young children, not even in their teens, gathered in darkened alleys around oil-drum fires, forgotten wretches of the faithfully impoverished society into which they had been involuntarily born. Marti was sickened by their pitiful plight and seriously questioned the possibility of surviving such conditions, with any level of respect for mankind intact.

The vehicle drew up outside the same derelict tenement which Marti and Jim had visited the previous evening. She was ordered out of the car by Ossi who had taken to using sign language, and led up the dilapidated stairs to a door on the third-floor landing, the smell of urine exuded from a pile of old carpets and rags in one corner, and a cracked mirror hung to the left-hand side, in which she caught the image of her vulnerability. She couldn't see that there was any light in the room and prayed in her heart that Jim would be in there. Ossi unlocked the door and pulled it open just enough to shove Marti through the gap. Stumbling half to her knees with the force of Ossi's helping hand; she heard it bang shut behind her. She tripped again in the gloom.

"Ouch!" the cry came from her stumbling block. Well, at least she had found Jim.

As her vision became accustomed to the lack of light, she could make out Jim's shape sprawled on the floor, bound, wrists to ankles behind his back, gagged and blind-folded. Marti removed his shackles. "Careful!" he winced. Marti felt his lip bleeding and even in this poor light could see that there was dirt in the wound, deposited there from the rag that had been stuffed into his mouth.

212

Once Jim was sitting upright he remonstrated with her: she should not have come looking for him and he was possibly right but she had made contingency plans, leaving a note at the hotel reception desk, with instructions for it to be delivered to Jack Brenner first thing in the morning – provided, that is, if Marti had not returned to collect the same herself by that time. This knowledge seemed to give Jimbo a little more confidence in their eventual ability to escape. Meanwhile, Marti was already fumbling around the room searching for any available means of getting out.

"I don't like being shut in," she said.

"Who does?" Jim answered despondently.

"No. I mean I really don't like it!"

Jim was sceptical of her insistence. "You telling me you're claustrophobic?" he sniggered.

"Yep! So if you don't help me find a way out of here soon, I might just start tearing you apart!"

Jim got to his feet. He managed to prize a couple of boards off the shuttered window frame but they were three floors high and there was nothing to climb down. Marti peered out, "It's too far to jump – yet!"

Jim looked at her nervously and tried both doors, neither would budge. In a rage he kicked the bottom of their original entrance; its posts shifted and cracked under the force. Remembering the hole through which he had spied on Sir James the night before, Jim eagerly reached for one of the boards. The bricks and rotten woodwork crumbled easily as he furiously hammered away, until he had made an opening big enough for them both to crawl through. Marti was first out.

On the street voices could be heard; they were young, defiant and vengeful. Marti and Jim remained closeted as two warring tribes prepared to do battle. Verbal, recriminating, condescension echoed off the blackened walls of the tainted, hovels from whence these youths had germinated. Missiles of stones and rotten timber were hurled with bitter venom from one end of the street to the other. With such an unlimited supply of ammunition, the fight was set to continue long into the night with the result, if there could be one, being decided on endurance. Fire bombs were added to the attacks, lighting the sky before exploding on impact with their random targets and setting the damp pavements aglow – as if to emphasise the burning desperation and desires which had been kindled in the bellies of these feuding urchins. One of the burning cocktails landed frighteningly close to Marti, bursting on impact. Jim frantically extinguished the flames but not before the flimsy, lightweight material of Marti's jacket had caught and begun to smoulder. She tore the garment off; dousing it in the dust.

Suddenly, unannounced the police arrived. It was only when they turned the corner onto the battle field, that they raised their sirens and flashed their ominous strobes. It was more like the army arriving, with each officer toting a gun of one sort or another; some even sported semi-automatic rifles which they let rip high into the smoke-filled sky over the housing blocks. This sudden shrill volley of gunfire abruptly killed all other sounds and the street now took on an even more sinister atmosphere, as it flashed black and blue in silence. The search was on for the kids who had now fled these derelict homes which had been stained by the human occupation of the generations who had preceded them. Our reporters endeavoured to do likewise, making a run for the spurious safety of the alley-ways and dens. Eventually they emerged at the back of the railway station, a weird environment in itself with its transvestite population conducting business by cover of darkness. A city never sleeps. The stunned, dishevelled bystanders took refuge in a depressingly dingy cafe, where they waited for several hours until calm was restored.

As dawn was breaking they returned to the hotel, gaining access through the service entrance at the rear. They scuttled across the deserted foyer, using the fire escape. Marti then went to each of their rooms to collect the camera and recording equipment whilst Jim kept watch from the stairwell. On her return they descended to the ground floor and waited in the stuffy concrete shaft until they were sure that all personnel concerned with the day's events had left.

Whilst driving to the circuit, it was decided that they would leave the car some distance from the track and go in through the public entrance gates. If they remained undetected then they would not raise alarm for the captors. Once inside the Monza

214

motor sport arena, they took up a couple of seats in the main stand, right opposite the pit lane. Through a 1000mm lens at this distance it was possible to view anything they wanted – and probably a darn sight more than if they were actually in the middle of the circus; and again there was the added advantage of not being seen themselves. Marti wished she had thought of this earlier in the season.

Each garage with its mechanics and technicians was an industrial hive of activity. Marti focused on the ex-world champion, drawing him ever nearer into her viewfinder as he meticulously checked the finer details of his machinery in person.

Jim nudged her vigorously, causing a temporary loss of vision. "What's going on?"

Marti, shaken from her dream, jerked the viewfinder along the busy line of teams until she came to Javelin's set-up.

Jim was getting impatient. "Let me see!" he snapped, ripping the camera from her neck. She gave him a disconsolate glare as he fiddled with the lens to produce a true picture. With Jimbo ensconced in his spying activities, her attentions were drawn back to their original train of thought and vision. Marti gazed, adoringly, at the man who had grown from the boy. A real man – one not afraid to make a stand, alone if necessary – the one who says what others only think... "Ooouch!"

"There he is!"

Marti, in her daydream, was caught totally unawares by Jim's boorish interruption. Picking herself up from the floor, she said calmly: "I presume you mean Sir James?"

Jim apologised for the excessive force of his shove and brushed the dirt from her jeans. "Yeah – they're all here – Oh shit!" Suddenly he became quiet and still.

Marti waited in anticipation, prompting a response from the slumped figure in the seat next to her; Jim lowered the camera and handed it to her, suggesting she take a look for herself. Marion, Jimbo's mentor and the lady who supposedly was totally unassociated with motor-racing, was acting in close attendance of Andrea.

Jim became sullen; Marti let him wallow while she urgently scanned the other stands and enclosures. There was an unusually high level of security in operation at all gates and concessions and indeed, the general public had been restrained from entering the paddock and pit areas. Marti asked Jim for his ideas on the prolific policing. He just shrugged nonchalantly, which enraged her.

"Self pity isn't going to do either of us any good – and neither is sitting here!" She was up and gone, heading for the business side of the track with Jim tagging along behind, hands shoved in pockets.

The final practice session was over and lunch was being prepared. As they whisked past the Centaura hospitality suite, the spicy aroma from a huge caldron of spaghetti bolognese wafted into their nostrils, and Marti had to drag Jim away from the scent. At the rear of the garages, numerous transporters, crammed full of spare parts and essentials, were lined up in readiness for any catastrophe, Marti spotted Stephanie. She was carrying a black briefcase and was acting in a highly suspicious manner, darting looks in every direction. With camera poised, Marti snapped the woman gaining access to the back of Javelin's gleaming pantechnicon, taking a further shot as she re-emerged a few moments later, minus the case. Marti then felt a tight grip on her forearm and was dragged behind a small shed. She squealed her nerves in tatters; she couldn't take much more of this! However she was thankfully relieved to see it was Jack, who quickly informed her that he'd got her note from the desk clerk. "Damn!" in all the fuss she had completely forgotten her back-up plan, but Jack was off, hot footing it to the press room where Jim, with a certain degree of trepidation, was collecting an interview with pole man, Westwood, who, though pressed hard for an insight into his contractual intentions, limited his vocabulary to technical data and general 'race speak', allowing yet more scope for speculation which in turn formed the basis of many news reports.

Marti attached herself to Jim as he came from the conference, telling him of Stephanie's activities. Westwood was escorted to Sir James' hospitality suite by a couple of heavies and Marti and Jim followed stealthily, though it was impossible to get near enough to hear what was being said without being seen. Jim had some plan up his sleeve to get to David in an effort to warn him of the illicit scheme in progress and disappeared, leaving Marti to fend for herself. '*Charming*.'

She found a quiet, secluded corner in which to hide and was soon joined by her 'friend'. He was still extremely angry and saddened by the political wrangling which seemed to follow him around the world's circuits. An abundance of natural, untamed energy made him the obvious target for revenge and he was tired of forever being the vindicator. Marti suggested he took some time off, but as he pointed out, this would only serve to satisfy those who were contributing to his demise. The public figure could never allow that to happen and would fight, honourably for justice, to the bitter end. The man within, however had other needs and the incessant conflict was causing indecision and error, something not familiar to 'The Racer'.

Jim returned, highly delighted with himself for securing David's confidence. Marti warned against taking Westwood too seriously but Jim seemed satisfied that all was well. The race was due to commence and with everyone's attentions concentrated on drivers and machines, there was more room to manoeuvre backstage. Up until now, Marti and Jim had managed to avoid detection by anyone other than Jack and David whom they had pursued; they were creeping round the hospitality suites like a couple of escaped mice, when they came face to face with Marion! Surprisingly she was extremely courteous and invited them for drinks. Both journalists were aware of the possibility of being further trapped, but the temptation to decline was overwhelmed by their curiosity.

Accepting Marion's offer they were greeted by the entire female membership of the Fairbrother Family, their male counterparts being otherwise engaged. It was like a college reunion. Even Jim, under his thick skin, felt a touch uncomfortable, being in the simultaneous presence of several women who knew him intimately. But, he could handle it. They were lavishly entertained with champagne and small talk, most of which was conducted by Mamma who introduced Marion – her sister-in-law. Mamma was astutely patronizing when it came to discussing our journalists' career choice and Marti felt the hairs on the back of her neck bristle, every time she mentioned that 'the camera never lies.' Marion was less demonstrative, having had personal experience of photographic techniques. She was an ex-fashion model and her poise and current dress sense suggested that she was top of the range in her heyday. She was curious to investigate Marti's modern equipment, but Marti held on tight to her case and rucksack.

The race was drawing to a conclusion and Marti mentioned they would have to go. Stephanie immediately reacted: "Oh yes! I want to see the finish, don't you, Andrea?" Her sister, who had been totally mute for the past hour, showed little enthusiasm but Stephanie insisted and Andrea trotted along obediently. Marti and Jim made for the finish line. There were only two laps remaining. As they reached the circuit barrier, a red and white dart buckled and twisted as it shot through the Parabolica, hurtled off the track and smashed side on into the wall. It continued its course with a deathly rattle as the metal scratched and gouged at the concrete, before coming to rest in a cloud of dust.

The race was stopped short of its final lap due to debris on the circuit and in order to allow emergency services to reach the stricken driver. He received oxygen whilst still in the cockpit and it was a while before he was stretchered to the on-site medical centre for a thorough check up. The verdict was concussion and severe bruising to the left leg, hip and upper body. Marti felt her chest tighten.

Local hero, Roberto Pasccari took the flag for an appropriately timed first win of the season and the Tifosi went absolutely crazy! A huge red wave surged towards the rostrum, where three elated drivers, backs to the riser, made their stand. Marti found a space on the pit wall from which to take her photographs of the jubilant trio, already spraying each other and the crowd with champagne, whilst Jim fought his way through the bodies to gain a seat at the post-race conference.

Marti could feel someone tugging at her heart strings.

"Hold me!" He was shaking fearfully, struggling for breath. She took his hand and cleared the matted, damp hair from his forehead, caressing its centre soft spot in the process to sooth and calm. But – there was so little time.

Noticing Stephanie in discussion with two uniformed gentlemen, Marti sensed the onset of trouble. Jack was nearby and she thrust her camera into his hands. "Develop it!" she yelled whilst seeking refuge amongst the ordinary members of the general public. The two officers were heading her way. She managed to get out of the pit lane and into the paddock where she skidded to a halt. The rear of Javelin's garage was in utter chaos; their transporter had been completely desecrated and stripped of all its wares. Bewildered by the sudden violation, mechanics wandered in a daze, picking up bits and pieces of abandoned equipment in an attempt to re-establish order.

Their manager was being held under armed arrest whilst several careless officers made a thorough search of the cargo space. An exulted Italian cry went up, shrill to the ears and a guard surfaced with the black case. Immediately the manager was ruthlessly shoved into the back of a waiting police car, its siren screamed to alert the crowds to part as it sped from the circuit.

Marti, no longer able to evade her trackers, was seized from behind; both arms were wrenched up her back and she was pushed to the ground amidst the feet of the growing congregation of sightseers. Her panic-stricken babe cried out. "Don't leave me! I want to come home."

Martha felt like a mother torn mercilessly from her innocent child. One half of her was protecting him, whilst the other half fought furiously for freedom. Her considerable strength had a meagre impression on her two burly abductors and Marti was treated to a similar mode of transportation to that of Javelin's manager.

Her terrifying ordeal, however, had only just begun. On reaching the City Police Station she was strip-searched, intimately and locked in a putrid cell. Marti cried, mortified by the hopelessness of her situation; even her boy had left. She was totally alone and petrified and to make matters worse she couldn't understand a word of what was being shouted at her.

Marti feared it would only be a matter of time before Jim was arrested; or maybe he already had been – it was impossible to know. Then she thought of Jack. Briefly hope returned; he had the film but what if he'd been arrested too? Marti was sick with confusion and the enclosed space was giving her a thumping headache. There was no offer of legal assistance and indeed her demands for advice and contact with the British Embassy had been ignored. She could hear footsteps approaching. A steel bolt scraped across the metal door, a dish slid under the iron bars and the lights went out. Marti's heart raced with fear, she crunched her knuckles together, and her palms were sweating. It was then that she heard his voice. "Try not to worry, I will come for you."

Meanwhile, Jim having managed to avoid police detection had got away from the track with the aid of a mysterious vigilante. His driver was, of course, highly skilled and had full knowledge of the local, geographical landscape and road networks. Jim was driven around the city limits whilst his informant detailed the precise course of events which had occurred, before dropping him off in a side road to the rear of the hotel. Jim's first problem was to find Jack and get into the hotel, without detection. The entire building was swarming with official and unofficial hunters. With a deft approach, he again sought access via service lifts and corridors.

Now Jack, being a wily cockney, already had the developed film in his hands and was poring over the results in his room when Jim knocked the door. Jack, having been sure of Jim's incarceration, was stunned to see him but was willing to pass over the accumulated evidence. Jim did however entrust the safe keeping of the negatives to Jack, who was due to leave for England on the next flight.

"I'll need a taxi." Jim said.

"I'll sort it." Jack picked up his luggage, locked his room and set off to make the appropriate arrangements at the desk when checking out.

Jim returned to the endless passages of the old building, heading for the outside world where after a tense wait behind reeking dustbins he was met by a cabbie. He reached the police station safely and produced the photographs of Stephanie going in and out of the Javelin transporter truck with the case. The gentleman on duty was unconcerned and after a quick glance, reverted his attentions to the porno mag concealed under his duty roster. Infuriated, Jim burst through the swinging gates into the general office space, demanding to speak to someone in authority. He caused quite a buzz and he was, after a scuffle, attended to.

Discussions were difficult and protracted, with neither party having much knowledge of the other's language, but eventually the penny dropped. Marti was brought from her cell and a posse of officers was despatched to the circuit, hotel and airport; 'phone calls were made and at last justice rolled into action.

Stephanie was apprehended as she boarded her father's private jet. She was charged with drug smuggling. Sir James was traced to the south of France. He was picked up a few days later and held in custody, to be charged with a similar offence. Marti and Jim were allowed to return home as was Javelin's manager, having cleared his name and that of his team. With his devious mentors safely tucked away under lock and key, David Westwood was automatically released from the professional and personal contracts which had been hung so heavily around his neck, thus setting him free to continue his business of testing and racing and testing again, in a more congenial atmosphere.

Perhaps now, life for all concerned could return to 'normal.'

CHAPTER 17

September drifted aimlessly, its dawnings moistened by silver mists that cloaked the lush green fields and billowed, effortlessly between the baring boughs of nature's soil securers who, in turn, lay down their coats in multicoloured golden hues, as autumn brought a peaceful death to summer's sultry, heaving breath.

On returning to England, Marti, disenchanted with her profession, resigned from her post at Power Play. The feelings were notably mutual and no remonstration was offered nor questions asked as to her future intentions. Jim, however, was still employed and still in love. A few days after their home-coming, he packed his bags and left for London. Marti and Morris made one last journey to the station. On the platform, Jim held her close.

"Stay in touch," he whispered.

Marti nodded in agreement, and having waved him off, headed for the Knoll.

The days were fast shortening but there was still some sun and Marti watched, in silence as its rays performed a shimmering dance on the waters of the twisting estuary. She traced its curves with one finger, as it flowed in a south-westerly direction towards the sea and beyond to lap the shores of a far off land. Her mind flicked through the printed pages of her summer adventures. Some good, some bad, some brought laughter, others tears. "What do you do when a dream comes true, and it's not quite like you had planned?" She quoted the words out loud.

The grass was dampening as the early evening sun dipped its toes into a liquid horizon. Marti rose from her mossy bed to begin the short trip home; en route, she slowed the wheels several times in order to take in the ancient sites and scenery. At a point where she crossed the M5 motorway she was able to see the Knoll in her rear view mirror whilst in front, in the distance simultaneously, she could see the Tor. She knew all these landmarks well, like the back of her hand, and you might think there was no need for this ritual examination but Marti appreciated the beauty of her own world and it was of great comfort to her to pinpoint each and every geographical monument, just in case it should decide to move one night – or even disappear altogether. This was her space – this was where she belonged.

The task of raking willow leaves from the lawn was never ending at this time of year but, although it was a chore, Marti found it relaxing and simplistically satisfying, even when she knew the garden would be completely covered with them again by morning. All the while, her 'friend' played gently on her mind. Having blown a gasket in setting his story straight, the tension and pressure to perform and conform, which he had bottled up for so long, had been finally released. His dwindling motivation had been replenished with a fresh challenge, albeit one to be treated and pursued with the utmost care and attention. He was now able, if he so wished, to channel his concentrated dedication, and the abundance of skill, knowledge, wealth and notoriety that he possessed into a new dream.

It was a pleasure and privilege to witness his return but, although he seemed content with the path that his professional future was taking, Marti still felt he was unsure of his personal life. He had not quite, yet devised a system of running the two in parallel and although he originally planned to take time out to put this to rights, the circumstances prevailing, meant the chance of self-satisfaction might again have to be shelved.

Monza had provided a suitably fuelled departure from Europe. There were just two remaining events to endure; a four-week gap separated Italy from the penultimate round in Japan. During this period, Marti became the subject of an extraordinarily high level of commitment, bestowed upon her by her 'friend'. In fact he lavished his time on her. He wanted her with him everywhere he went. Many hours were spent at a beach house, a place he seemed most able to be himself. The honey coloured, polished timber floors, on which they danced to the twang of tex-mex guitar riffs and the softly padded, wicker framed loungers, where they lazed to the mellow tones of a whispering saxophone, were comfortable yet practical. A vast window ran the entire length of the property's east wall. From its surrounding balcony, shaded by sultry palms, Marti had watched the sunrise over the ocean a thousand times before. It was from here that they studied the stars and it was here that Marti told him of her belief that each light in our night's sky was the soul of a loved one passed and how sometimes, if that soul wished, or indeed was summoned, it could return to Earth.

Her theory appealed and although many years had passed since he had discussed such elusive matters, he understood the essential meaning. Marti also told him about the book she had written and together, they decided that she should again; try to publish her own work.

On a lighter note, he possessed an impressive array of sports equipment. Both Marti and her 'friend' were equally thrilled by the power of motorised water sports and every game was played at break-neck speed, with a built-in desire to win. He could out-run Marti and such competitive exploits sometimes left her exhausted. On these occasions she would watch him from the white, sandy beach. He liked to show off, and it made her laugh when he dipped in and out of the water on a jet ski, as he throttled the engine up and down its power band. He would stand on the seat, saluting her as he passed on the wake and he seemed to sparkle in the sunshine, as its light reflected in the water droplets that settled on his dark skin and collected in his hair.

However, towards the end of the third week, he became pensive and it was difficult at times even to raise a smile from his soft lips. The fun-loving, chuckling, chatterbox had once more been screwed down. He became solemnly introverted though still desperate, possibly even more desperate, for Martha's company. During these last few days, she couldn't find it in her heart to tell him of her job loss, or indeed, the fact that she would not be attending the race at Suzuka in Japan.

Back home, in sleepy Roebuck, Marti had even gone to the fuss and bother of renting a satellite dish, in order that she might closely follow the progression of practice and qualifying. In the early hours of Sunday 25ᵗʰ October, she settled down in front of her fire's glowing embers to view with some circumspection the ensuing rounds of battle.

The camera depicted every individual car and driver as it sat in its respective position on the grid, each with its own busy mob of faithful attendants. Westwood was up front. An illuminated board registered five minutes and counted down; a siren screamed; the worker ants retreated, clearing the circuit, taking with them their precious technical trappings. As the machinery edged forward to begin the parade lap, Marti felt a sharp, stabbing pain in her chest. A full warm-up lap was completed, tyres were heated by swerves and dodges, now back on the grid, they were held until the last man was in place. The red lights came on – one, two, three. Marti caught her breath in her hands; she could feel the power of the engines rumbling inside her frame. Green! – A huge, pent-up force of energy released itself on the world but Paul Ericson was left behind, stranded on the track. With one arm raised, he could do little else but pray that the skill, awareness and aptitude of his fellow participants would allow his survival. The rest of the field got away safely and Ericson, unharmed, deserted his machine in disgust, leaving it to the mercy of the gathering marshals to dispose of in any manner that they saw fit, whilst he headed for his motor home.

The scheduled race distance was 53 laps and on lap 20 with the leader, Westwood, a full fifteen seconds ahead of the rest, second place man, Veridico, came in for tyres. His team performed a faultless pit stop, providing a full set of new boots in under five seconds, and he was back on track, having only dropped three places. However, two laps later he was back and the sequence was repeated. This time he rejoined in seventh, and stayed there for a while. Marti wondered what the hell he was playing at when he came in a third time and audibly posed the question. He was given yet another set of wheels, the jack man dropped the front end and his pit crew cleared the way for his exit. Unbelievably, he just sat there, dithering over his return to the fray. "Don't think man – drive!" Marti yelled. The loud deliberateness of this outburst startled her, but the tyres turned.

"It feels different!" a timid voice came from within.

"It's not the car! I'll hold you, just drive – it'll be alright." Marti reassured him of her presence with that special kiss and continued to encourage him. "I want to see you on that podium!" she bullied.

After a short, ponderous, interlude he seemed to get down to business and strung together a blistering set of laps, carving through back markers from ninth, eventually to finish third. In the process of this charge, he totally upstaged the newly-crowned World Champion, blowing away David's previous lap record by almost a full second.

On the relatively slow trip back to the paddock, Marti congratulated him on his triumph. "I knew you could do it, once you'd made your mind up."

It was not like him to be indecisive, but he did allow himself a chuckle at this rare shortcoming, before removing his helmet and taking his place on the raised platform in front of a massive crowd of adoring fans. Marti, overcome with tears of joy and flushed with pride, watched him on screen, making mischief with a bottle of champagne. He never failed to get the first shot in here either and after showering Westwood who had secured P1, promptly turned on his team principal, catching him full in the face with a fountain of frothy spray.

Later, around midday – which put the time in Japan somewhere between nine and ten in the evening – the grilling began concerning her absence. Naively, Marti had hoped he would not ask this question, feeling, maybe a little selfishly that her personal circumstances bore no relevance in their relationship and that he merely needed support for the time being. He was enraged, and somewhat hurt by her lack of forthcoming.

"I trust you!" he yelled.. "You should at least give me credit for showing you similar compassion."

Marti felt terribly ashamed by his words. He'd laid out his whole life for her, in words and pictures, gone through the agony of reliving his worst moments. He had shown her – alone, the real man, naked, with all his flaws and imperfections. He'd shared with her his joys, his fears, his beliefs and many – many tears. At this point Marti could feel him slipping away and the thought of losing him again terrified her. Throughout their liaisons, she had tried hard to keep her intimate love for him hidden and simply wished to provide some solace, should the need arise. The reason for her knowledge of such a pending requirement was now clear. Marti knew him, long before he was named let alone famous and ever since he had been resting on the back roads of her mind.

He was sitting on the edge of his seat, head bowed, wringing his hands. Marti heard his faint sobbing and dropped to the floor before him.

"I never meant to hurt you that was the last thing I ever wanted to do." She begged his forgiveness. "Please – you have to believe me, my intentions were good and honest, but I don't walk in your world, I could never expect to, therefore I can't really be with you. The void is too great and the fact of the matter is – that the bridge doesn't reach that far."

Both were crying and Marti let her chin rest between his knees.

"I want you to be there – in Australia." His request was gutting. Marti couldn't possibly make a promise which she was uncertain of keeping.

"I'll try." His dark eyes scowled at her, he expected a greater level of commitment. In the quest to procure his wishes, he made a final plea. "I need you there!"

Marti's heart was aching, fit to burst as his solemn image faded from her sight. "I'll be there!" Momentarily the picture froze. "I'll be there – I promise!"

There were just two weeks in which to find the wherewithal to get herself to Adelaide for the grand finale. In reality she should have been looking for a job, not jetting halfway around the world chasing some crazy dream. But then, another fourteen days wouldn't break the bank – and anyway, the world could do with a few more dreamers. There would be plenty of time to be serious later.

First thing Monday morning Marti telephoned Andy at Power Play, asking for Jim's 'phone number and address. She didn't fancy travelling all that way alone, if she could help it. As it happened, she was pretty much alone, her 'friend' refused to converse during the buildup to the last meeting; and even though Marti could be with him, viewing proceedings, she could not interact with him – she felt she was being tested.

Jimbo was living in a flat in Romford. When Marti 'phoned him, he sounded as if he was either hung-over or on something – it was difficult to tell which, but he made no mention of Andrea, so Marti didn't broach the subject.

"I'm going to Australia!" She announced jovially.

Jim was gobsmacked. "That's great! – I've got my ticket; hang on and I'll give you the details, maybe you can book a seat on the same flight!" He was really excited and Marti could hear the telephone banging against the wall where he'd left it, swinging in the breeze. On his return, Marti jotted down the information and said she would 'phone back with any news. She got directly onto her local travel agents, but the feedback was not encouraging, they were unable to offer her a deal in the same hotel as Jim and she would have liked this. Despondently she called Jim again and told him of the dilemma.

"Don't w...orry." Jim stumbled over his words nervously. "I've spoken to Andy and he's gonna see what he can fix up. I'll ring you in the morning."

That night, Marti attempted to tell her 'friend' of her endeavours. He seemed to be listening but still wouldn't talk to her.

"You're extremely stubborn you know." Marti was put out by his unwillingness to communicate but, as she drifted off to sleep, she felt his familiar warmth at her left-hand side.

Her next problem was what to pack. Marti rifled through her wardrobe, pulling out an assortment of casual clothes – skirt, shorts, jeans (all in denim), t-shirts – the usual stuff which had accompanied her global excursions. At the back of the cupboard she unearthed the red taffeta frock – *We are talking REAL FROCK here.* Would it be tempting fate if she was to slip it into the suitcase?

There was a ring. Marti grabbed the 'phone: "Jim! Hi!"

Andy had done the business and come up with the goods – A seat on the plane, and a room next to Jimbo. Jim would collect her ticket on his way to Heathrow and they arranged to meet in Terminal 3. Marti was on her way.

CHAPTER 18

The Australian Grand Prix is run on the streets and waterfront of Adelaide. On arrival for Friday's qualifying session, Marti, thrilled again to be endowed with a press pass, (purely to enable access to the inner sanctum, of course), sat happily on the pit wall to survey the scenes. Marcus Veridico, besieged by an army of faithful followers, was handing out autographs. He was, as ever, polite to each and every one; and although it must become tiresome by the end of the year, he'd lost none of his charm or charisma. Recognising Marti, he approached confidently, producing paper and pen.

"Would you write your 'phone number down for me?"

Marti smiled, "I don't have a 'phone," she teased.

Marcus was perplexed, having not encountered such a response before. Marti winked. "But I would like to write something for you." His embarrassment saved, she took the pen and wrote:

I wish you all the things in life that make you happiest.
Love and luck
Martha X

She sealed it with a kiss, folded the note in half and tucked it into his left-breast pocket. Immediately Marcus went to retrieve it, saying that he didn't read English well. Marti stopped him as she lowered herself from the railings.

"You may recognise the message, but if you have any difficulties, I'll read it to you at bedtime!"

The corners of his mouth twitched alternately at her flirtatious insinuations. Marti gave him another wink and walked away.

As evening fell, in the confines of her room, Marti's 'friend' paid her a long overdue visit. "I am so glad you could make it!" He was pleased with her efforts and after a few boyish pranks and games, settled in readiness for his obligatory sequence of kisses, before going to sleep. Marti was over the moon to have her cheerful character back and served a double helping mainly because she couldn't resist hearing, one more time, the delightful giggles which emanated as her lips touched his soft spot.

Rain interrupted final qualifying on Saturday and the prospect of a wet race the following day looked increasingly likely. At around ten o'clock that evening, as Marti lay on her bed, reflecting on the day's events and full from a superb meal consumed at Jim's expense, a gentle knock came at her door. "Who is it?" she called.

"Me!" came a tentative, obscure reply.

"Oh good – You'd better come in then," she invited, opening the door.

He was dressed in a baggy blue t-shirt and jeans; there was an absence of shoes and to his chest he clutched a small bundle of coloured, scrap papers, secured with a thick elastic band.

Knowing the man's habit of taking to his bed early before race day, Marti suggested that she thought he would be asleep by now. He was acutely shy.

"I tried to sleep – but I couldn't." A gaping yawn punctuated his sentence and Marti asked what she could do for him. Bemusement crept across his face as he held out the notes. Had she forgotten?

"You said you would read to me!"

"What – now?" she gasped. He was adamant, so Marti made herself comfortable, resting her back against the headboard. He sat next to her, at a distance, picking at the loose, dry skin on the palms of his hands and still yawning.

"You're very tired aren't you?" His eyes flickered as he nodded in agreement,

He moved a little closer and Marti began sifting through her allotted reading material. The coloured scraps of paper were personal letters, each addressed to him.

"I can't read these, babe." She was embarrassed. "These are personal things." But he insisted, picking out one in particular written on flimsy, pale pink copy paper.

"Read about the box, it's a gift, from a friend. It's the most precious thing anyone has ever given me."

Marti had no need to look at the script, she knew the writings well. The gift box was actually a sketch of such an object, carefully and deliberately outlined for strength; inside was everything a person could give; on top of that was everything a person needed but, even with all this, still the box was not full.

At sunrise, whilst preparing to leave, he asked Marti if she would do him the honour of being his guest at the End of Season Dinner Dance. Marti needed time to contemplate her answer. The door half closed and opened again.

"You could wear the red frock!"

Marti felt oddly out of sorts at the circuit, not being involved directly in the workings of the day, although Jimbo seemed to be OK. He was busy chatting up the local birds. It certainly hadn't taken him long to get over his failed romance. Marti found the sight comically inspirational and though feeling devilish, resisted the temptation to butt in and spoil his act.

As she ambled her way between the hospitality tents and on into the paddock, fresh rain was falling and the humidity caused a mist to rise from the tarmac around the pristine motor homes and trucks. Heavily treaded tyres were wheeled on custom built trolleys, too and from the garages; everything looked set for a wet day.

In her meanderings she bumped into Andrea, hand in hand with the German Ace, Mr. Rheutemanne. She didn't seem to want to speak to Marti and hurried away with a baffled 'Rookie' in tow.

Marti bought a can of coke and sat outside a snack bar; it had stopped raining for the time being at least, and she pondered her brief encounters. "It is true that a leopard never changes its spots but, perhaps it's wrong to try and change anyone? If you like them for what they are, why should you want to?" she thought. "They wouldn't be the person you liked in the first place if you changed them." Marti regarded the inner make up of a soul to be its true manifestation and it was this, which created the wonderful sensation she experienced when he walked into a room, and she didn't have to see his face to know he was there. His signals were carried on air waves that vibrated in her heart and set it beating in a perfect, simultaneous rhythm.

The race was to be long and fraught with indecision. They began on slicks but, as they pulled away for the parade lap, rain drops fell on the camera lens. Marti surveyed the sky; dark clouds loomed heavy with the promise of more to come.

The race cars lined up in their respective grid positions and with a thunderous roar, tore into the bleak, distant mist. Rain persisted, growing steadily harder. About eight laps in machines were sliding and pirouetting across the track in all directions. Some began to pit, to take on wet-weather tyres in an effort to gain traction. It was a difficult decision to make and had to be timed to perfection if the race was to be won. To add to complexities, the rain eased off now and then, and some drivers stayed out on slicks in the hope that the surface, aided by a warm breeze, would dry. In the short-term however, this was not to be; the choice between driving on the knife-edge of controllability, utilising every ounce of faith in one's skills and losing time in the pit lane had to be made. This, however, was not the end of the mental torture; by half distance the rain had stopped, water was beginning to disperse, revealing a dry race line. The whole charade was then re-enacted in reverse.

All the coming and going made for a far greater spectacle from a bystander's point of view, but severely tested the wits of drivers and teams and, in some the pressure was evident as wheel nuts and guns jammed in the haste to make efficient pit-stops. It did however, produce a first: the German, Philip Rheutemanne, took the chequered flag and its related number one slot on the podium.

Rain again began to fall as machines drew into parc ferme to undergo post-race scrutineering.

Rheutemanne was obviously thrilled, and overcome with emotion as everybody gathered to congratulate him. Another drew in, parked his car and walked away alone.

Marcus was a three times World Champion and he walked away alone. He crossed the grey paddock area toward Marti who was waiting on the other side of the fence. He recognised her though kept his head bowed. She could see his eyes were reddened and swollen; he'd been crying during the race, hidden by the visor of his helmet and before half distance, he had disconnected the radio link to his pit crew, as if he knew the end was coming. Marti asked quietly if she could take his picture. His chest heaved slowly; he was bashful; his eyes flicked up and down several times, not wanting to give her too long to see them clearly but, with a tiny smile and a nod, he granted her wish.

He was hovering, shifting his weight uneasily from one red booted foot to the other; his hands were playing with his gloves which he'd stuffed inside his helmet. He was trying to speak; the muscles around his mouth tightened but as ever, it was difficult. Marti waited patiently; eventually taking her arm, he led her to the confines of his motor home, where he locked the door.

In silence, Marcus eased himself carefully out of his overalls; his shoulders were rounded and sore from the heavy burden of the drive. He raised his arms above his head, in an effort to stretch the tendons, but their weight was too great and he let them drop limply to his sides. His sweat-soaked fireproof underwear clung to his body and had to be peeled off, like a second skin. The effort required for this act was immense, and Marcus struggled with the task of freeing his hands from the sleeves, before heading for the shower. He re-emerged a few minutes later, with a towel around his waist and another with which to dry his hair. He rubbed his head vigorously, tousling the curly locks, dark and shining, to match the textured coating of his chest and abdomen. Habitually, he tried to flatten the offending quiff that sprouted, just to the left of the centre of his forehead, until; finally, he gave up this futile procedure and took a step toward Marti. She slid back on the bunk where she had been sitting, Marcus leaned over, kneeling before her, he slipped one hand under her skirt, searching her hips, he pulled at the elastic of her knickers and his whole body sank heavily on hers. Running her fingers through his wet hair, Marti swept the strands from his face. Marcus never took his eyes off her as his spine curved, once – twice and as she gripped the back of his neck, he let everything go. Marti stroked his tired torso, the relaxation eased him and it was over an hour before Marcus woke.

Later that evening, in her room, Marti experimented with the red taffeta frock, posing in a full-length mirror; she twirled and flirted with her image. The room was compact and to the rear of the building, there was a small balcony. The warm air drew her out into the night. As she looked down on the street below a black Mercedes pulled up and stopped close to the curb. Its driver got out. Dressed in an elegant black tuxedo with tie not yet fastened, he glanced up at her. Marti fled back into her room. Out of sight she leaned unsteadily against the wall fighting tears. She couldn't go! She wasn't part of his world! – This wasn't the way it was meant to be! – She couldn't go!

Suddenly there was a knock at the door. Marti held her breath and wished that this was not happening.

"Hey! Marti."

She dropped her chin to her chest. It was Jim and she let him in.

"Wow! – You look beautiful – well, apart from the mascara runs. "You going somewhere?"

For once words failed her and no amount of hugs, jibes or cajoling could get her to accompany Jim to the End of Season Gala.

They next met up at breakfast and Jim proceeded to fill her in on the evening's events. Apparently Marcus was late, which didn't delay the scheduled speakers, as the new World Champion, Westwood, was the main act. But Marcus was always in demand and his tardiness was discussed. His guarded explanation was also noted.

As Marti and Jim left the hotel with luggage in tow, she spotted a black Mercedes parked across the street. Part of her wanted to walk towards it, but a taxi drew up in front of them and Jim bundled her in.

The flight home was tedious and Marti spent much of it listening to Jim sleeping. Carefully, she took the marker pen from his hand, which he had earlier been using to highlight the main issues of the weekend in his race notes. She smiled to herself and without disturbing him, wrote her address and 'phone number on the sleeve of his shirt.

Back on the streets of London, Jim invited her to stay. "You can kip at mine!"

Marti smiled in appreciation of his offer of hospitality, but declined and questioned the geographical awkwardness of Romford.

"I know." He laughed. "I wasn't thinking – wanna a coffee?"

Marti agreed and they found a table at a convenient pavement cafe close to Paddington. It was cold and the afternoon air was dampening. Marti put on her coat and Jim continued the conversation.

"The rent's up at Christmas anyway." Marti raised her eyebrows.

Jim grinned. "I've been looking in the Guildford, Woking area."

"Expensive!" Marti nodded.

Jim had lots of other news too. He was in negotiations with Team Centaura's boss in respect of a role they had opening up, involving liaisons with new high tech, communication companies, that were looking to enter the world of formula one.

"Between you and me, I think Marcus may retire," he quipped.

Marti nodded again. "Possibly."

Marti could see Jim was eager for this appointment. She felt it would suit him perfectly, as it would provide an opportunity to use his technical ability and still have the hands-on freedom that he craved. Alas, Marti's train was due and this intervention brought their chat to a close.

On the platform, Jim held her extra tight. "We were good, you know."

"Were?" Marti said. "Call me." She patted his arm whilst boarding and Jim lifted her suitcase onto the footplate, just as the guard approached to secure the doors. The steel wheels squealed and he watched the carriages slowly disappear from view.

"Dear Sirs...."

Martha was dreaming from her office window for the last time. On the street below, another shop front washed in white, displayed the emptiness inside. Only a slogan, scrawled in defiance by youthful fingers across the glass, broke the purity of its past. "Blind Alley!" it exclaimed, and it carried the spirit of a famous name.

Yours faithfully,

———

X

CHAPTER 19

THE FINAL CHAPTER

Early on a Monday morning in August 1993, Marcus Veridico, three times Formula 1 World Motor Racing Champion, successful international businessman and one-time farm boy, locked the door of his smartly appointed Mediterranean style villa. He wore a simple white polo-shirt, dark blue indigo jeans, neatly belted at the hip and Italian loafers. In his right hand he carried a light-weight, black zipper jacket, in the other, a brown, leather briefcase, expensively finished with gilt clasps and lock.

A waiting helicopter whisked him to the airport, where he left the thirty degree heat of Lisbon behind. At 8.30 am British summer time, an unaccustomed and unearthly hour for his waking, particularly in view of the fact that no arresting warrant had been issued for his attendance in England, he landed at London Heathrow.

Unsure of his reasons for being here, Marcus stepped cautiously from the small private jet. He clutched his briefcase, instinctively drawing it across his chest as he entered the terminal. All was quiet. Passively awaiting the delivery of an executive hire-car, Marcus stared through the VIP lounge window. Rain began to fall and he tried to fathom a logical explanation for his actions.

His hands were visibly shaking when he collected the keys to a black Mercedes and he stumbled whilst opening its door. His knees didn't appear to possess sufficient strength to support his body but, once in the driver's seat he ignited the vehicle's mechanics and in appalling, rain-soaked conditions, headed west on the M4.

There were several lengthy, unscheduled, pit-stops along the way which unnecessarily prolonged the agony of his journey, before he reached the Almondsbury Interchange. Here he swung left on a heading due south, he was now travelling a road which he had never before driven; yet oddly, its terrain felt warmly familiar.

Rain lashed at the screen; the speedometer touched 110 miles an hour and the sound of Tex-Mex guitars echoed within the capsule of his sealed cabin. Playing on tape, it repeatedly wound from spool to spool, quivering in places, stretched by overindulgence. Marcus turned up the volume; synchronising its mellow tones, he allowed the lyrics and easy rhythm to soothe and encourage his spirit.

Gradually the speed increased; he was now running on a parallel curve, in perfect symmetry with a shimmering ocean-going channel. The powerful tidal currents of its muddy waters seemed to pull him ever nearer to his destination. The needle on the white, lit instrument panel registered 120 as he breached the county line. Sweeping gracefully from left to right across the carriageway, Marcus barely noticed the uneven tarmac which rumbled his tyres. His vision transfixed; suddenly he could see it, through his own eyes, directly before him – the silhouetted image of a flat-topped knoll beckoned.

Faster still, the engine screamed as Marcus' right foot smoothly pressed the pedal all the way to the floor pan.

A road sign flashed past, warning that tiredness kills. Marcus eased off the pace and the back end slewed as he took the next slip road into a service area. He stopped the car in the second row of parking bays; wrenching the hand brake, he draped himself over the wheel. His breathing was rapid, as if he had run all this way. The station's coffee shop lights gleamed on the wet windscreen and Marcus glanced to his right. He was now directly in line with the flat-topped knoll.

The car was already beginning to cool and Marcus reached for his jacket. He took his briefcase from the foot well, brushing aside numerous, paper cups and placed it on the passenger seat. After fiddling with the combination cogs, he flicked the catches and opened the lid. Inside, were a couple of music tapes which bore no artistic names or titles; another from Avalon; two photographs; several handkerchiefs; a dozen or so sheets of computer information, bearing sketchy notes on data; a bunch of tatty letters, scribbled on copy paper of varying size and colour; a dictionary and a Guide to Homeopathic Medicines. These few items, constituted, in their entirety, the personal effects of a rich and famous man.

Quietly, Marcus studied his possessions. In the beginning, he had difficulty understanding the notes and their significance but, with time he had grown accustomed to their style of language. He shuddered in remembrance of the terrible feeling of anguish, experienced when a friend had thrown his case from the window of a high-rise building and he feared it lost forever. Luckily, Marcus had managed to retrieve it, but at the present time, he was freezing and this condition was disturbing his powers of concentration. Frustrated, he zipped his jacket and pulled up the collar. He was trembling and shut his eyes tight; Marcus didn't want to cry any more and stifled a single sob, but – someone was listening!

Marcus peered in the rear-view mirror; he was ashamed and enraged by the pathetic sight of his emotional state. He sniffed, but not through tears, he sniffed again. The air was filled with the scent of lavender and as he gripped the gear stick, he felt the familiar, gentle, silk-like touch of her fingers as they entwined with his own. Marcus turned the key and the engine hummed with an encouraging rhythm. He engaged first and slowly lifted his left foot. The wheels again rolled forward. Gently he pressed the accelerator, still in pouring rain; Marcus negotiated the narrow lanes until he reached a crossroad. From here it was possible to see the cottage! Marcus felt his cheeks flush with embarrassing innocence at his earlier, pathetic attempts to cajole her affections. Now and only now, did he realise it was an attention that did not need encouragement. The tyres of the Merc. spun on the shiny black asphalt, Marcus could hardly control his excitement and fear as he pulled into the drive. There was a light at the kitchen window which was slightly ajar, unable to close fully with the swelling of age and he was certain that he saw a shadow!

Marcus took up his briefcase and locked the car. He crossed the gravel path to the back porch which was surrounded by potted, lavender bushes. Their grey leaves covered with fresh rainfall, glistened in the light of a full moon. His palms were sweating as he reached for the door handle. It was open, he pushed it with his knee and as Marcus stepped over the threshold, he could taste her sweet perfume. Intuition led him on. He slipped off his jacket, discarding it at the top of the stairs, his loafers where abandoned by the door. Marcus eased himself under the covers, the fresh linen pillow was soft to his touch and the fit was perfection. He could feel her heart beat and allowed his own to coincide with its tempo until only a single rhythm remained.

Here – in the shade of a flat-topped knoll, Marcus Veridico, (warrior of truth), finally discovered the peaceful contentment, which had for so long eluded him in this life. At last, Marcus felt that he was home.

Come softly to me in your dreams
And rest with ease upon my mind.
I'll soothe your pain and tend your wounds,
And listen while you cry.

I'll not judge, nor force restrictions,
Neither will I lie.
There'll be no sense of ridicule,
Nor fear of days gone by.

So stay as long as need be,
For our thoughts cannot be stolen,
And I will always be here,
To take your hand when you have fallen.

God bless,

Love and Luck

x